THE COLLECTED
SHORT STORIES

DERMOT HEALY

THE COLLECTED SHORT STORIES

Edited, with an Introduction,
by Keith Hopper & Neil Murphy

DALKEY ARCHIVE PRESS

LIBRARY OF CONGRESS CATALOGING-IN-PUBLICATION DATA

Healy, Dermot, 1947-2014.
  [Short stories]
  The collected short stories / by Dermot Healy ; edited, with an introduction, by Keith Hopper
& Neil Murphy. -- 1st ed.
    pages cm
  Summary: "Dermot Healy wrote intricate and innovative short stories that, along with works by
Neil Jordan and Desmond Hogan, relaunched the Irish short story tradition. Set in small-town
Ireland and the equally suffocating confines of the Irish expat communities of 1970s London,
Healy's stories show compassion toward the marginalized and the dispossessed. Gathering all of
Healy's stories together for the first time, this collection includes the long prose-drama "Before
the Off" and Healy's final short works, "Along the Lines" and "Images" -- Provided by publisher.
  ISBN 978-1-56478-598-5 (cloth edition : alk. paper)
  I. Murphy, Neil, editor. II. Hopper, Keith, editor. III. Healy, Dermot, 1947-2014. Before the
off. IV. Title.

PR6058.E19 2015
823'.914--dc23

                              2015017348

Partially funded by a grant by the Illinois Arts Council, a state agency
The Collected Stories received financial assistance from the Arts Council of Ireland

Dalkey Archive Press publications are, in part, made possible through the support of the
University of Houston-Victoria and its program in creative writing, publishing, and translation.
www.uhv.edu/asa/

Dalkey Archive Press
Victoria, TX / Dublin / London
www.dalkeyarchive.com

Printed on permanent / durable acid-free paper

The Lost Limb

Feeling for the right word
Leaves me breathless for the many,
As if through a lost limb sewn on
Feeling gradually grew

Through cold young flesh,
Lit some fingers with old identity
And excitement, while the others
Craved possession

Of life withheld,
Hung awkwardly till breathing as one
The first words came like blood
Down distressed veins,

And, with a healing yaw,
New writing began like an exercise
Over and back across an empty yard
Turn, start all over.

—Dermot Healy, "New Irish Writing" page
Irish Press, 22 November 1980

Editors' Introduction: Making it New

The modernist movement began and ended in
Ireland, in full retreat before it had hardly begun,
soon sunk out of light, making hardly a ripple. The
old lies were merely being perpetuated and no great
effort attempted to "make it new." Some exceptions:
Sailing, Sailing Swiftly (1933) by Jack B. Yeats; *Murphy*
(1938) by Samuel Beckett; *The Ginger Man* (1955)
by J.P. Donleavy; *Felo de Se* (1960) (my first story
collection); *Night in Tunisia* (1976) by Neil Jordan;
In Night's City (1982) by Dorothy Nelson; *Banished
Misfortune* (1982) by D. Healy.

—Aidan Higgins, "The Hollow and the Bitter and
the Mirthless in Irish Writing," *Force 10*, no. 13
(2008), ed. Dermot Healy: 25.

Like many of the great Irish writers before him – including
Joyce, Beckett, and Aidan Higgins – Dermot Healy first
announced himself as a writer of intricate and innovative short
stories. Although *Banished Misfortune and Other Stories* was
first published in 1982, many of the stories in Healy's debut
collection had already appeared in a number of newspapers
and journals, including, most importantly, the "New Irish
Writing" page of the *Irish Press*, edited by the redoubtable
David Marcus. Marcus had been appointed literary editor
of the *Irish Press* in 1968, and "New Irish Writing" quickly
became a cultural institution, publishing new short stories
and poems on a weekly basis, and helping to launch the
careers of a whole host of contemporary Irish writers
including Sebastian Barry, Dermot Bolger, John Boyne,
Anne Enright, Hugo Hamilton, Desmond Hogan, Neil
Jordan, Deirdre Madden, Patrick McCabe, Colum McCann,
Mike McCormack, Eoin McNamee, Mary Morrissy, Philip
Ó Ceallaigh, Joseph O'Connor, Lucile Redmond, Ronan

Sheehan, and many others (see Carty, 2015). The initial impact of "New Irish Writing" was consolidated in 1971 with the creation of the annual Hennessy Literary Awards, and by the subsequent publication of several anthologies of stories edited by David Marcus. Marcus also founded Poolbeg Press in 1976, specialising in new short story collections, and this coincided with the establishment of several other independent publishing houses in Ireland, including Wolfhound Press, the O'Brien Press, and the Irish Writers' Co-operative (of which more later). In retrospect, then, the mid-1970s and early 1980s saw something of a renaissance in the venerable but fusty tradition of Irish short story writing, and Dermot Healy (1947–2014) was undoubtedly one of the key figures at the heart of this dynamic resurgence.

Of the four Healy stories published in the *Irish Press*, two of them – "First Snow of the Year" (1973) and "Banished Misfortune" (1975) – won Hennessy Literary Awards, and would eventually bookend the 1982 collection, *Banished Misfortune*; the other two – "The Caretaker" (1972) and "This Side of Summer" (1974) – are reprinted here for the first time. It is not entirely clear why the latter two stories were excluded from *Banished Misfortune*; however, in terms of Healy's rapidly evolving style, they may well have been considered too thematically conventional or formally derivative (although this is far from being the case).

"The Caretaker" (18 November 1972) – which first appeared on the "New Irish Writing" page alongside a poem by one of Healy's early mentors, Seamus Heaney – is told from the perspective of the elderly caretaker of a decaying Big House, which is now up for auction:

> A grey haze had built up on the meadow, and Willie
> could imagine the visitors and potential buyers
> hopping on their toes in the rain and the muck
> when the bidding would start. Men and women
> of all shades of opinion and dress had been to see
> him and the house these last six months. They were

> mostly foreigners or educated people who would be
> driven to despair at the thought of the work to be
> done. [. . .] One Irish couple had stuck in Willie's
> mind – they'd arrived complete with shamrocks
> on St Patrick's Day. Willie had taken to the young
> man immediately. He had a good pair of hands on
> him and an eye for beauty; what's more, a love for
> trees – and that was what the house needed. ("The
> Caretaker," *Irish Press*, 7)

In many ways, "The Caretaker" would not look out of place in
a collection by Seán O'Faoláin or Bernard MacLaverty – well-
crafted, gently humorous, with a wry anthropological eye on
the cultural mores of the time – but it does lack the edginess
of Healy's later work. The "Big House," of course, is a quite
common trope in Anglo-Irish literature, one "infused with
the idea of history as a haunting, and with the notion of a
continuing past of unease and insecurity, often implying guilt
and repression" (R.F. Foster, 95). In the late 1960s and early
1970s, the Big House genre was resurrected by writers such
as Aidan Higgins, J.G. Farrell, John Banville, and Jennifer
Johnson, and "The Caretaker" can certainly be read in this
context (although, as we shall see, houses and homes – empty
and occupied – frequently appear in Healy's work). At the
end of Healy's first published story, the literal handing over of
keys to the young Irish couple is invoked as an obvious (and
somewhat self-reflexive) symbol of cultural continuity and
generational change: "'It's all yours now,' Willie said."

If "The Caretaker" bears the traces of O'Faoláin, then "This
Side of Summer" (27 July 1974) is undoubtedly influenced
by the Joyce of *Dubliners* (1914), both technically and
thematically. The story centres on a young unmarried couple,
Joe and Kate, who move in together to a new flat in the Dublin
suburbs, much to the disapproval of her middle-class friends:

> Had she been more at ease she would have been
> amused at their gravity as they chewed distastefully
> on the garlic bread she had cooked for Joe till it was

nearly black. She would have enjoyed their obvious dislike for Joe and treated their remarks with irony, indifference.

　— He had no teeth either, not a tooth in his head when I met him first, Kate was saying.

　— That must have been interesting for you, the banker's girlfriend intoned with a mischievous smile. ("This Side of Summer," *Irish Press*, 6)

The influence of *Dubliners* is everywhere apparent, from the free indirect style – where the primary narrator's voice gives way to the individual characters' point of view – to the use of the long em-dash for dialogue instead of quotation marks. At the end of the story, the point of view flickers between Kate's chirpy self-awareness and Joe's morose self-absorption, and their shared epiphany is typically Joycean in its abrupt open-endedness:

> Moments were too short. He sat and watched stiff and upright from his chair, the skin drawn tightly across the broken veins in his cheeks. Moments are far too short, he thought, and soon you and I must learn some new industry to bring us again into the world. He laughed a little. She brought in the dark steaming coffee, and never said a word, for it was easy to see that something was troubling him and he was always stubborn when it came to explaining, even frightened. ("This Side of Summer," *Irish Press*, 6)

"First Snow of the Year" (11 August 1973) won a Hennessy Literary Award in 1974, along with stories by Dónall Mac Amhlaigh, John McArdle, and Ronan Sheehan. The award that year was adjudicated by Edna O'Brien and V.S. Pritchett, and in her judge's report O'Brien commended Healy's story for its confident sense of rhythm – "It is told slowly, but has the tension of something about to snap" – while Pritchett found the use of language "very telling in its evocation of winter, rural poverty and passion intensified by loneliness" (*Irish Press*, 28

September 1974). "First Snow of the Year" begins with an elderly postman, Jim Philips, waking up on the first day of his retirement and heading off to the local pub with his young friend Phildy. Beneath the hoary reminiscences and rambling gossip lies a palpable tension, as Phildy is still consumed with bitterness about having lost his girlfriend, Eli-Jane, to his former best friend, Pedey:

> The postman realized that nothing could thaw out the hate in the young man's heart – it was the endless struggle and sin of their small society, the civil war between friend and friend, Phildy's mind was being eaten alive by the loss of a woman to another man, he could not explain or forgive, it was part of the weather of life that relaxes and freezes the pain in the soil. ("First Snow of the Year," *Irish Press*, 7)

That same day, Pedey – accompanied by the now-pregnant Eli-Jane – is burying his mother in a nearby cemetery, and the narrative fluidly cross-cuts between the chatter in the pub, the solemnity of the funeral, and the inevitable encounter between Phildy and Pedey, both tormented by grief and loss. At the end of the story, the old men in the pub debate the merits of different potato dishes, while the younger characters try to negotiate a frightening world of jealousy and desire only partly within their control. As the writer Patrick McCabe recently remarked (in a new collection of essays on Healy's work):

> "First Snow of the Year" possesses not only the same kinetic energy [as Márquez's *One Hundred Years of Solitude*] but the same seamless blend of trance and the quotidian. It was the world I lived in and one that I recognised – but it hadn't been approached like this before. I mean, I never found much of Borges in [Patrick] Kavanagh – but this! If he had read it, Francis Stuart would have perked up like a startled hare – pantheistic, unpatronising, the world's stained glass glimmering inside the eye of a dog. (McCabe, forthcoming)

McCabe is most likely thinking here of a provocative essay by the Irish writer Francis Stuart entitled "The Soft Centre of Irish Writing," first published in the *Irish Times* in 1976 and reprinted in 1977 as an introduction to *Paddy No More* – an anthology of contemporary Irish stories featuring work by several writers associated with the Irish Writers' Co-op, including Neil Jordan, Desmond Hogan, Lucile Redmond, and Dermot Healy. For Stuart (1902–2000), the history of the Irish short story is an ongoing struggle for signifying supremacy between "cosy" realists and "subversive" modernists: between conformists who wish "to preserve communal cultural standards and present the national identity," and dissidents who seek "to preserve the true purpose of art as an instrument for the discovery of alternative concepts and new insights" (Stuart, 5–6). From this perspective, traditional Irish realism – exemplified for Stuart by "soft-centred fiction like Frank O'Connor's 'Guests of the Nation'" – is more easily consumed and assimilated by the dominant culture, and its conventional poetics underpin an inherently conservative politics:

> This writing – knitting would be a better word – is to the expected pattern or formula [. . .]. Familiar sayings and attitudes are echoed with a nudge of humorous intent, the curtains are drawn, the fire poked, and a nice little tale with a whimsical slant is about to be told. No passion, no interior obsession, no real or outrageous comedy as in Flann O'Brien, Joyce or Mr Beckett. (Stuart, 7–8)

Stuart's polemical critique contains a whole series of binary oppositions, which manifest themselves, primarily, in the different attitudes to place. For realists, "Ireland" is insular and nostalgic – deferring "gracefully to the world they and their readers had inherited"; for modernists, it is expansive and forward-thinking – "widening, instead of narrowing, the thought patterns of our society." Consequently, there is a significant difference in the use of language: the idiom of realism is monological and familiar – "naturalistic, descriptive rather than probing, preoccupied with local colour" – whereas the discourse of modernist counterrealism is dialogical and defamiliarizing: "it causes discomfort rather than cosy reassurance in the reader." For Stuart, this formal estrangement of language has Brechtian implications in the way that it self-consciously explores the gap between conventional representations and lived reality:

> National energy, the will, not just to survive but to excel, can only be restored psychically, which is to say within the imagination. In the past societies achieved this through their mythologies or religions. Today, it is [through] the shock of original writing that a community ensures its organic growth. (Stuart, 6–9)

In light of this (post-)modernist or counterrealist call-to-arms, it worth noting that the 1973 version of Healy's "First Snow of the Year" is substantially different in style and structure to the final version published in *Banished Misfortune* almost a decade later – so much so, in fact, that we have included both versions in this present volume (see Appendix I). Readers can make up their own minds about the relative merits of these variant texts, but for the purposes of illustrating the difference between realism and counterrealism, it is worth comparing the opening lines of both. Here is the original opening paragraph from 1973:

> It was Jim Philips' first day of retirement. He realized he was no longer a postman when he awoke, and looked at the stained boards that ran the length of his ceiling. Jim spent the entire morning retrieving his habits as a young man, stayed in bed till late and took his ease about the house, looked up the chimney to check for crows, remembering that time of perpetual youth and céilí music before life had propped him up on a bicycle till the end of his days, a messenger in three townlands. But it was a fine thing, he thought, to outlive your job that you

could die in a time of your own making. He left his
womanless bed with a light heart and laid out his
drinking clothes before the fire, that he might be
warm this day itself in Grady's. ("First Snow of the
Year," *Irish Press*, 7)

And here is the refurbished opening from the 1982 version:

For a few bewildering seconds, Jim Philips, on the
day of his retirement, queried late morning sounds
he had not heard in years. Then his solitary sense of
freedom began. He looked with leisure at the low pink
boards that ran the length of the ceiling, yellowing
at the fireplace, brightening by the window.
Light was hammering on the broken shutter.
Shadows darted across the mildewed embroidery
of dogs and flowers.
He cleared his womanless bed with a light heart,
glad to have outgrown the ache in his smothered
loins, outlived his job that he might die in a time of
his own making. He nimbly laid his drinking clothes
before last night's fire, coaxed first with paraffin, then
whiskey. He hung his postman's uniform in the closet
under the stairs. ("First Snow of the Year," *Banished
Misfortune*, 1)

Although this revamped opening is by no means the most radical
change in the body of the text, it does indicate the aesthetic
shift towards a more imagistic form of late modernism.
Realist description and third-person narration now give way
to phenomenological observation and impressionistic states of
consciousness, mediated through free indirect discourse. Instead
of a straightforwardly linear cause-and-effect plot, the new
version favours juxtaposition and montage, frequently cross-
cutting between multiple and often solipsist points of view,
where memories, desires, and contingent sense impressions
are continually conflated and confused. Throughout the
reconfigured text, jaded idioms and flat expository phrases –
he "laid out his drinking clothes before the fire, that he might
be warm this day itself in Grady's" – are deliberately expunged,

replaced by a series of defamiliarizing images which, as one critic observed, "slam the reader awake" (Redmond, 6). When Jim ventures out of his house after the opening paragraph, for instance, "He saw John and Margaret Cawley, the gypsies, stealing through the yellow gorse with rotten turf. Their children moved from clownish tree to clownish tree out of the wind" ("First Snow of the Year," *Banished Misfortune*, 1). In this more fragmented and disjointed world, characters appear and disappear, and the gypsies play no further part until the very end, when Pedey and Eli-Jane – now called Owen and Helen – babysit for the Cawleys. Instead of the original, drily ironic ending – where the tipsy postman, in a reversal of the usual retirement ritual, gives away his watch – the new version ends on a more symbolist note of melancholy and longing:

> They sat in utter silence. When the children woke, she spoke in gypsy talk to reassure them. He filled the stove with timber and turf, snow dripped from the black canvas. He laid his head on her shoulder and they kissed in a direct trusting manner. Soon John Cawley and Margaret Cawley came over the rocks singing dead verse. ("First Snow of the Year," *Banished Misfortune*, 9)

"Banished Misfortune," the fourth and final story published in the *Irish Press* (5 April 1975), earned Healy a second Hennessy Literary Award in 1976 (the other winners that year were Robin Glendinning, Ray Lynott, Ita Daly, Thomas O'Keefe, and Seán O'Donovan). The 1976 award was judged by Alan Sillitoe and Aidan Higgins, and in his rather cranky judge's report Higgins complained about "the lack of humour in the stories," insisting that their plots were too "predictable" and their diction too "dogged." Higgins reserved his most enthusiastic response for "Banished Misfortune" – "If there is a better account of modern, changing Ireland, I have yet to read it"– and praised it for its "felicity of phrasing, image-making, and magnanimity of view" (*Irish Press*, 16 October 1976).

"Banished Misfortune" centres around a young Northern Irish family, the McFarlands, who journey from the border county of Fermanagh to the west of Ireland on their summer holidays. The story is set in mid-1970s, and although the "Troubles" are only fleetingly alluded to, the brooding force of the conflict thrums away in the background, colouring everyone and everything. By the time McFarland, a traditional musician, and his wife Judy, a schoolteacher, finally get to Galway with their two children, the more relaxed atmosphere in the South gradually allows their repressed fears and desires to rise to the surface: "they had burrowed down so deep in anxiety that happiness was nearly hysterical" (7). After a night of manic and drunken carousing, the primary mimetic narrative ends with Judy and McFarland cautiously re-pledging themselves to a shared future, in a world where the burden of history, and the ordinary trials of everyday living, can so easily grind people down:

> Fear was so addictive, consuming all of a body's time and she wanted so much to share this vigil with him in Fermanagh but what could you give the young if they were barricaded from the present by our lyrical, stifling past? She said nothing, knowing she shared this empty ecstasy with a thousand others who had let their laziness go on too long.
> "I left home too young, that's what bothers me," he spoke again. "There must be a thousand stories and songs about my own place that I hardly know. But when we return, woman, we'll try." ("Banished Misfortune," *Irish Press*, 7)

However, unbeknownst to the couple – and, indeed, to some readers (the point is quietly embedded within the imagistic brickwork of the text) – their home in Fermanagh has been burned down that very night, yet another casualty of the Troubles. (The reason for the arson attack is left unsaid, although Seán Golden, in a perceptive reading of the story, has speculated that theirs is a "mixed marriage," i.e. the marriage of a Catholic and a Protestant, and so the motive is probably sectarian (Golden, 21).) As in "First Snow of the Year," the narrative cross-cuts between multiple viewpoints, but it also flickers backwards and forwards in time and space, and as the critic John Wilson Foster remarked, "The journey through history and geography becomes a form of meditation on Ireland's violent present and broken past" (Foster, 1093). At the end of the story, the diegetic narrative shifts back in time to 1910, when the house was first built by McFarland's ancestor, Saul. In the poignant closing lines, we hear of Saul's hopes and dreams for his family, lovingly built into the design of the house:

> In a foot of land there's a square mile of learning, Saul had said, and he had learned to build from a sense of duty to the beauty of the hilly Erne. [. . .] For in April of 1910, Saul had a bad back but nevertheless he had finished building a church in Donegal town and now with Bimbo Flynn the whistler he set about kissing the air and erecting his own house. And it was a house where the best sessions of music would be held [. . .]. And folks wondered about the ornamented porch that was built out front with the stained-glass windows, and there was talk of a church but when the last stones dried and you could hear the knock-knock of a thrush breaking a snail in his new garden Saul was a proud man. Always before daylight a man thinks of his destiny, as Saul did that last morning talking with the travellers in the half-light of the chestnut hill and he was glad to see that the cream-coloured mare of the gypsies was loath to leave the fine grass now that her time had come. ("Banished Misfortune," *Irish Press*, 7)

When *Banished Misfortune and Other Stories* first appeared in 1982 – co-published by Allison & Busby and the newly-founded Brandon Press – reviewers were generally impressed by the ambitious scope of this relatively slim volume (only 111 pages in total). The stories are largely set in the borderlands of rural Ireland or in the diasporic communities of 1970s London (five of the twelve stories take place in England). Throughout the collection, Healy demonstrates a deep sense of empathy towards the marginalized and the dispossessed, and the language is finely attuned to distressed and beleaguered states of mind, without ever becoming sentimental or clichéd. Unsurprisingly, perhaps, the early reviewers especially admired the more orthodox stories of Irish small-town life, such as "The Curse" or "The Tenant" (the latter won the 1982 Tom-Gallon Trust Award, which is awarded for stories which are "traditional, rather than experimental, in character"). However, some critics were less convinced by more obviously experimental pieces such as "The Island and the Calves" or "Blake's Column," and seemed disconcerted at times by the creamy density of Healy's prose. Peter Hazeldine, for instance, in the *PN Review*, thought that some of stories were "over-compressed, the language dense and intractable," but nonetheless admired Healy for his "willingness to take risks" (87–88). The anonymous critic in the *Kirkus Review* regretted certain "lapses into ineffectual prose-poetry," but otherwise considered it "a varied, occasionally impressive debut, especially when Healy's distinct talent for multi-voiced, overlapping drama surfaces" (n.pag). Similarly, Patricia Craig in the *Times Literary Supplement* suggested that "when he writes plainly, Healy can startle us with the vigour and perceptiveness of his observations", but in general she felt that "intense, wayward and romantic feeling predominates over simple craftsmanship" (642).

In one of the few academic critiques of *Banished Misfortune*, Robert Hogan considered Healy within the historical tradition of Irish short story writing, and compared him to some of his contemporaries from the now-defunct Irish Writers' Co-op, Desmond Hogan and Neil Jordan, whom he collectively dubbed the "Young Bucks":

> The twelve stories in his collection are of various lengths and two manners. "Reprieve" and "Betrayal" are less than two pages long; the remainder range from about five to fifteen pages. "Reprieve" and

> particularly "The Tenant" are told in a conventional
> manner; the remainder, which really set the tone for
> the book, are written with a denser obliquity than
> that of Hogan or Jordan, and may owe something to
> writers like [Aidan] Higgins and [Tom] MacIntyre.
> (Hogan, 201)

In this context, Hogan argued that the attractions of Healy's
free-flowing style "are its freedom, its individuality, and its
suggestion of a sensitive, mysterious, and wildly inexplicable
persona." Against that, Hogan cautioned, "the dangers are
obvious: certain phrases lose their syntactical anchor so
that their position gets puzzling, and their meaning murky;
the public presentation of a narrative gets camouflaged,
and indeed the narrative becomes less prominent than the
narrating" (Hogan, 201–202).

To be sure, Healy's imagistic style and impressionistic
techniques can sometimes make for difficult reading – but
then that's all part of his concerted attempt to "make it new."
As Healy himself noted in an interview in 2011 (speaking
of his final novel, *Long Time, No See*), "I was trying to stay
out of it and let the reader take over and run with it. So I
would often put the meaning of a passage in, then take it out
again" (Healy, 2011). In this respect, Healy's co-creative texts
need to be considered not just in the classical tradition of Irish
short story writing, but in the wider context of experimental
modernism (especially Joyce, Faulkner, Kafka and Borges). As
the writer Timothy O'Grady recently argued:

> They are less stories than rendered sensations of
> consciousness. There is a lack of reference to a set
> of meanings, and no plot. Nor are there hierarchies.
> The sound of a bird or rushing water or the sight
> of the stretched leg of a hare can weigh the same as
> a kicking in a bank of snow or the wail of human
> loneliness. The trick to experiencing *Finnegans Wake*,
> Joyce said, was to read it aloud. I think the trick
> with these stories is to read them twice. Then you
> can take them in as breath. (O'Grady, forthcoming)

For all of its perceived difficulties, *Banished Misfortune and Other Stories* clearly marked the emergence of a new and exciting voice in contemporary Irish literature. Over the next three decades, Healy produced four novels, a memoir, five collections of poetry, thirteen plays, and numerous essays and reviews. Strangely enough, though, and with a few notable exceptions – all of which are included in this present volume – Healy rarely returned to the short story form. However, those few exceptions are also quite exceptional. "Before the Off" (1999) is a remarkable piece of writing, a kind of *Under Milk Wood* for race-goers. The structure and rhythms of this hybrid text lie somewhere between a traditional short story and a radio play, with overlapping dialogue, stage directions, and dramatic scene changes woven into the very fabric of the narrative. Stylistically, "Before the Off" is more reminiscent of Healy's later novels, *Sudden Times* (1999) and *Long Time, No See* (2011), but it also stands out as an innovative and exciting work in its own right (at over 8,000 words it is by far the longest and most layered story in this collection). "Along the Lines" (2012), about an actor having a breakdown, is a much shorter sketch, but it further attests to Healy's great love – and intimate knowledge – of the theatre (his *Collected Plays* will be published in 2016). And in many ways his final story, "Images" (2013), brings us back full circle to the publication of "The Caretaker" and "First Snow of the Year" some forty years earlier. In this haunting and evocative piece, a retired college lecturer spends his time taking photographs of abandoned old cottages, and the central conceit bears witness to Healy's own ecstatic and existential vision of life and art:

> At one old ruin fresh daffodils were shooting up among the debris in the garden.
> Mortality is rife, he said, as he caught an image of the flowers.
> After each photograph was taken he'd study the snap, tip his chin off the back of the hand that held the camera and look closely at the place in question.
> Maybe, he'd say. Maybe. ("Images," 2013)

Although these ventures into the short form became increasingly rare, Healy's affection for the genre never diminished. As the writer Mike McCormack recently remarked:

> He believed that concentrating on the novel pushed out the short story and he spoke of how he missed the genre, the neatness and beauty of it, how it begun here and ended there. But the commitment to the longer form would admit no short excursions, the odd poem now and again yes, but no short stories.
>
> Not to worry. It is a marvellous thing to rediscover those wonderful wild pieces. With their shamanic intensity and electric charge they are more than enough to be getting on with. (McCormack, forthcoming)

It certainly is a marvellous thing. The short stories collected here show the origins and evolution of Dermot Healy's subtle and complex style, and they invite the reader to (re)discover the apprentice work of a modern master.

—Keith Hopper & Neil Murphy
   Oxford and Singapore, February 2015

Works Cited

Anon. "New Irish Writing Awards: Four Authors Honoured." *Irish Press* (28 September 1974): 3.

Anon. "The New Irish Writing Winners." *Irish Press* (16 October 1976): 3.

Anon. "New Irish Writing – Hennessy Literary Awards: Winners through the Decades." *Irish Times* (24 January 2015): web [accessed 30 January 2015].

Anon. Review of Dermot Healy's *Banished Misfortune* (Allison & Busby, 1982). *Kirkus Review* (21 November 1982): web [accessed 30 January 2015].

Anon. The Tom-Gallon Trust Award. *The Society of Authors* website [accessed 30 January 2015].

Carty, Ciaran. "Hennessy New Irish Writing finds a New Home at the *Irish Times*." *Irish Times* (24 January 2015): web [accessed 30 January 2015].

Craig, Patricia. "Forms of Fecklessness" [review of Dermot Healy's *Banished Misfortune* (Allison & Busby, 1982)]. *Times Literary Supplement* (11 June 1982): 642.

Foster, John Wilson. "Dermot Healy" [headnote]. "Irish Fiction 1965–1990." *The Field Day Anthology of Irish Writing*, vol. 3. Ed. Seamus Deane. Derry: Field Day, 1992: 1093.

Foster, R.F. "Lost in the Big House: Anglo-Irishry and the Uses of the Supernatural." *Words Alone: Yeats and his Inheritances*. Oxford and New York: Oxford University Press, 2011: 91–127.

Golden, Seán. "Traditional Irish Music in Contemporary Irish Literature." *MOSAIC* 12.3 (1979): 1–24.

Hazeldine, Peter. "Barricades" [review of Dermot Healy's *Banished Misfortune* and *Fighting with Shadows*]. *PN Review* [Manchester] 13.3 (1986): 87–88.

Healy, Dermot. *Banished Misfortune and Other Stories*. London: Allison & Busby; Dingle, Co. Kerry: Brandon Press, 1982.

Healy, Dermot. "'I try to stay out of it and let the reader take over'" [interview with Sean O'Hagan]. *The Observer* (3 April 2011): web [accessed 30 January 2015].

Higgins, Aidan. "The Hollow and the Bitter and the Mirthless in Irish Writing." *Force 10*, no. 13 (2008), ed. Dermot Healy: 21–27.

Hogan, Robert. "Old Boys, Young Bucks and New Women: The Contemporary Irish Short Story." *The Irish Short Story: A Critical History*. Ed. James Kilroy. Boston: Twayne, 1984: 169–215.

McCabe, Patrick. "Wings 2/6: Memories of Dermot Healy." *Dermot Healy: Writing the Sky – Critical Essays and Observations*. Ed. Neil Murphy & Keith Hopper. Illinois: Dalkey Archive Press, forthcoming 2016.

McCormack, Mike. "Testing, said a voice. Testing, one two three ..." *Dermot Healy: Writing the Sky*. Illinois: Dalkey Archive Press, forthcoming 2016.

O'Grady, Timothy. "Only myself, said Cúnla." *Dermot Healy: Writing the Sky*. Illinois: Dalkey Archive Press, forthcoming 2016.

Redmond, Lucile. "Smokeless Fuel" [review of *Firebird I: Writing Today*, edited by T.J. Binding (Penguin, 1982)]. *Irish Press* (20 May 1982): 6.

Stuart, Francis. "The Soft Centre of Irish Writing" (1976). Repr. *Paddy No More: Modern Irish Short Stories*. Ed. William Vorm. 1977; Dublin: Wolfhound, 1978: 5–9.

A Note on the Texts

This volume is structured in three parts: the first section contains all twelve stories from Dermot Healy's debut collection, *Banished Misfortune and Other Stories* (1982); the second section contains seven occasional stories, which were published intermittently between 1972 and 2013 (these stand-alone pieces, drawn from a diverse range of sources, are gathered together here for the first time); the final section consists of three appendices, which, for reasons outlined below, did not fit neatly into the Occasional Stories section.

Banished Misfortune and Other Stories was originally co-published by Allison & Busby (London and New York) and Brandon Books (Dingle, Co. Kerry) in 1982. The stories in this first edition, though long out-of-print, remain the most authoritative and up-to-date versions available. These extant versions – hereafter referred to as the "base texts" – have been reproduced in their original running order: "First Snow of the Year," "A Family and a Future," "The Island and the Calves," "The Curse," "Blake's Column," "The Girl in the Muslin Dress," "Reprieve," "Kelly," "Betrayal," "Love," "The Tenant," and "Banished Misfortune."

For all of its virtues, the original Allison & Busby / Brandon Press edition, on which the first section of this volume is based, contains a considerable number of typographical errors. The more obvious misspellings and mistakes in punctuation have been silently sub-edited. In general, the punctuation, which varied a little from story to story (especially in the Occasional Stories and Appendices), has been standardised throughout: double quotation marks for dialogue; single quotation marks for quotes within quotes; closing quotation marks after commas and full-stops (any exceptions to these rules have been flagged below). New paragraphs are indented, and section-breaks marking the passing of time get a double line-break (with no indentation). Long em-dashes (—) have only been used when a character breaks off or resumes speaking; otherwise, short en-dashes with spaces – like so – are the preferred format (again, any exceptions to this rule have been indicated below).

Some stories have a slightly more complicated layout: "Blake's Column" and "Kelly," for example, contain a variety of written fragments including letters, reviews, and diary entries. These fragments are usually double-indented, and some (though not all) are italicised, as per the original base texts. All of the stories in the first edition of *Banished Misfortune*, and many of the Occasional Stories, start off with capital letters for the opening words, e.g. "FOR A FEW bewildering seconds ..." ("First Snow of the Year"). For reasons of elegance and consistency, these have all been changed to lower-case.

Occasionally, Healy deliberately flouts the standard rules of punctuation, grammar and syntax for stylistic effect: sometimes he includes commas instead of full-stops and removes distracting quotation marks in order to maintain the flow of overlapping dialogue and thought; he also uses a number of compound words and coinages, and as far as possible these more idiosyncratic features have been retained.

Throughout the volume, English and Hiberno-English spellings are used instead of the American forms. Healy sometimes uses Irish-language words and phrases, but most of these are understandable in their immediate context: a "sheugh" is a furrow, ditch, or trench; "tigíns" are little houses or cottages; "Dún an doras" means "close the door"; a "Fleadh" is a festival of music; a "bodhrán" is a traditional Irish drum; "sean-nós" – literally translated as "old style" – is a type of unaccompanied traditional Irish singing. There is one Irish saying from the original 1982 edition of *Banished Misfortune* which was footnoted with an asterisk – "*Ni bhíonn ac súil amháin ag na nGael anois*" ["The Irish see through only one eye now"] – and this footnote in "Banished Misfortune" remains in place. We have also footnoted "*An síos suas*" ["The down up"] in "Blake's Column."

Some of the stories from *Banished Misfortune* first appeared in the following newspapers, magazines, journals, and anthologies. All of these early versions have been cross-checked against the 1982 base texts, and any significant textual variations have been flagged below:

"First Snow of the Year" ["New Irish Writing" page, ed. David Marcus], *Irish Press* (11 August 1973): 7. This early, more realist version – which won a Hennessy New Irish Writing Literary Award in 1974– is substantially different in style and structure to the 1982 base text. Consequently, for purposes of comparison, we have included the *Irish Press* version in the first appendix to this volume (see note below). This should prove valuable to scholars and critics, but we also hope that it will be of interest to the general reader for the light it sheds on the evolution of Healy's style and voice. A more mature version of "First Snow of the Year" also appeared in *Firebird I: Writing Today*, ed. T.J. Binding (Harmondsworth: Penguin / Allen Lane, 1982): 123–30. This *Firebird* version, which contains some minor differences of punctuation and spelling to the 1982 base text, appeared shortly before the publication of *Banished Misfortune and Other Stories*.

"A Family and a Future," *A Soft Day: A Miscellany of Contemporary Irish Writing*, ed. Peter Fallon and Seán Golden (Indiana and London: University of Notre Dame Press; Dublin: Wolfhound 1980): 177–81. There are some minor differences of punctuation, spelling, and diction between this version and the 1982 base text. One slight difference is worth noting, if only to illustrate a more general principle of composition and revision: in the earlier version, a local lake is named as "Oughter" (presumably Lough Oughter in County Cavan); in the 1982 base text, this has become "Sheelin" (presumably Lough Sheelin, near Healy's birthplace of Finea in County Westmeath). According to Seán Golden (in an email to the editors in January 2015), this change would have been made by Healy himself, possibly in an attempt to shift attention away from the real locale where certain events in the story might actually have occurred. This distancing of people and place is a common stratagem throughout Healy's writings.

"The Island and the Calves," *Cyphers*, no. 7 (Winter 1977–78), ed. Leland Bardwell, Eiléan Ní Chuilleanáin, Pearse Hutchinson, and Macdara Woods: 23–27. This early version is subtitled "Sciamachy 2," and is one of several stories originally grouped together under the working title of "Sciamachy" (see note below). The text in *Cyphers* is exactly the same as the version which appeared in *Paddy No More: Modern Irish Short Stories*, ed. William Vorn (Nantucket, Massachusetts: Longship Press, 1977; Dublin: Wolfhound Press, 1978): 55–61. There are some minor differences of punctuation, spelling, and syntax between these earlier versions and the 1982 base text. In every respect, though, the base text is better edited and more stylistically consistent (it deletes a few unwieldy sentences and qualifying phrases from the earlier text). A radio version of "The Island and the Calves," read by Dermot Healy, was broadcast on RTÉ Radio on 31 November 1979; this broadcast was repeated on 17 November 1980.

"The Girl in the Muslin Dress," *Icarus* no. 67 (Winter 1974) [Trinity College Dublin student magazine], ed. Edward Brazil: 12–17. There are some minor differences of punctuation and spelling between this version and the 1982 base text.

"Betrayal," *Icarus* no. 76 (1980), ed. Gerry McDonnell: 27–28. There are some minor differences of punctuation, spelling, and syntax between this version and the 1982 base text. In all cases though, the base text is more streamlined and stylistically consistent.

"Banished Misfortune" ["New Irish Writing" page, ed. David Marcus], *Irish Press* (5 April 1975): 7. This early version from the *Irish Press* – which won a Hennessy New Irish Writing Literary Award in 1976– is exactly the same as the version which appeared in *Best Irish Short Stories*, ed. David Marcus (London: Elek Books, 1976): 87–102. These versions, in turn, are almost identical to the 1982 base text, except for some minor (but formally significant) differences of punctuation: in the 1982 version, character dialogue is presented in double quotation marks, as it is throughout *Banished Misfortune and Other Stories*, but in the two earlier versions the dialogue employs the more Joycean em-dash (—). (For a good example of this em-dash format at work, see "This Side of Summer" (1974), which appears in the Occasional Stories section.) In his later stories and novels, Healy dispenses with dialogue markings altogether in favour of unmarked, indented line-breaks (cf. "Before the Off," "Along the Lines," and "Images"). For the purposes of this volume, we have stuck with the more traditional – but less formally elegant – use of double quotation marks in "Banished Misfortune," as per the standard 1982 base text.

One other minor variation is worth noting: in the 1982 base text, the titular tune is referred to as "Banish Misfortune"; however, in the earlier versions of the story, this is described as the Banished Misfortune (without any surrounding quotation marks). In terms of the traditional Irish lament that it refers to, either variant is acceptable. Again, though, we have favoured the 1982 base text as the most authoritative version available, so "Banish Misfortune" it remains.

"Banished Misfortune" was later included in the "Irish Fiction 1965–1990" section of *The Field Day Anthology of Irish Writing*, vol. 3, ed. Seamus Deane (Derry: Field Day, 1992): 1093–1100. The Field Day version is identical to the 1982 base text reprinted here.

The Occasional Stories in the second section of this volume first appeared in the following newspapers, magazines, journals, and anthologies:

"The Caretaker" ["New Irish Writing" page, ed. David Marcus], *Irish Press* (18 November 1972): 7. This, the earliest of Healy's published short stories, appeared on the "New Irish Writing" page alongside a Seamus Heaney poem, "Gifts of Rain."

"This Side of Summer" ["New Irish Writing" page, ed. David Marcus], *Irish Press* (27 July 1974): 6. As already mentioned, this story employs the Joycean em-dash (—) to signify dialogue instead of the more traditional use of double quotation marks.

"The Workman," *The Westmeath Examiner* (18 January 1975): 15. Throughout the original newspaper version, an overeager sub-editor has inserted a series of capitalised sub-headings: "SO HAPPY"; "A GOOD JOB"; "DATING"; "PROUD OF HER"; "NEVER SEEN AGAIN." These rather shouty sub-headings are not in keeping with the subtleties of Healy's narrative, and are therefore deleted.

"Jude and his Mother," *Paddy No More: Modern Irish Short Stories*, ed. William Vorn (Nantucket, Massachusetts: Longship Press, 1977; Dublin: Wolfhound Press, 1978): 63–73. This is one of several stories originally grouped together under the working title of "Sciamachy" (see note below).

"Before the Off," in *After the Off* [text by Dermot Healy, with photographs by Bruce Gilden] (Stockport: Dewi Lewis Publishing, 1999), 120pp. This story is in a category all of its own. The original coffee-table format consists of the Healy text, interspersed with a series of black-and-white portraits by the award-winning New York photographer Bruce Gilden (b. 1946). The photographs of race-goers seem to have been taken at an Irish race course (no explanatory preface or contextualising headnote is provided). The original written text is presented in a slightly off-beat format, including a mix of different font sizes and irregularly bolded phrases, and the dialogue is variously aligned – without any governing rhyme or reason – in alternating left-, centre-, or right-justified blocks. For the purposes of this present volume, we have dispensed with this typographical trickery. Instead, all dialogue is now indented; all prose descriptions are flush to the left-hand margin (without any indentation); and section breaks – marking a new scene or the passing of time – get a double-line break. Some of these narrative transitions from dialogue to description are not entirely straightforward, and at times we have had to exercise our own judgement. Above all, though, we have allowed the rhythms of speech to dictate the reconfigured format.

"Along the Lines," *Silver Threads of Hope: Short Stories in Aid of Console*, ed. Sinéad Gleeson (Dublin: New Island, 2012): 137–39.

"Images," *Town and Country: New Irish Short Stories*, ed. Kevin Barry (London: Faber & Faber, 2013): 1–11.

The final section in this volume consists of three appendices. Appendix I contains the original version of "First Snow of the Year," first published in the *Irish Press* (11 August 1973): 7. As previously mentioned, the formal contrast between these radically different versions is quite instructive.

Appendix II contains a story entitled "Legal Times," *Icarus*, no. 75 (1980), ed. Gerry McDonnell: 35–41. (The text in *Icarus* was prefaced by a drawing entitled "D. Healy's story", by Christy McGinn.) "Legal Times" was originally subtitled, in parentheses, as "(An Excerpt from 'Sciamachy' – A Novel in Progress)," and is one of several stories originally grouped together under this working title. This rather fluid "Sciamachy" concept merits further elucidation. In the Headnote to the Wolfhound Press edition of *Paddy No More: Modern Irish Short Stories* (1978), the editor commented:

> At present, [Dermot Healy] is working on two contrasting groups of short stories, "Sciamachy" and "Poverty of Location." [...] ["The Island and the Calves" and "Jude and his Mother"] are from "Sciamachy," a series of interconnected but independent pieces. Sciamachy comes from *Scia*: shadow; and *Machy*: to fight (Greek). Healy sees "Sciamachy" as fighting with shadows, or shadow boxing; also as fighting with shadows of pretensions. (*Paddy No More*, 54)

This original concept of "two contrasting groups of short stories" never materialized, although "Sciamachy" did become the working title – and eventually the subtitle – of Healy's debut novel, *Fighting with Shadows* (London: Allison & Busby, 1984; repr. Illinois: Dalkey Archive Press, 2015, ed. Neil Murphy and Keith Hopper). Thus, at some unspecified point in the late 1970s / early 1980s, "Sciamachy" went from being "a series of interconnected but independent pieces" and became the raw material for an early draft of the novel (to complicate matters further, the novel itself later went through several substantial revisions). A number of excerpts from "Sciamachy" were published in magazines, journals and anthologies; however, most of these pieces are quite clearly fragments from the novel-in-progress and are therefore excluded from this present volume. Of all of these extracts, only "Legal Times" seems sufficiently self-contained – and sufficiently different to the extant novel – to stand as a short story in its own right. (That being said, the story – which is set in the Basque region – does feature characters who will eventually morph into Irish characters in *Fighting in Shadows*: Señor Alarcón will become old Pop Allen; José becomes his grandson Joseph; Manager Francis becomes Manager Tom; García becomes George; and Lawyer Smith is left intact in the final published novel.) In any case, we offer it here as an example of the continual process of revision and refinement that was such an integral part of Healy's vision and craft.

Appendix III contains a memoir-cum-story entitled "The Smell of Roses," first published in the *Irish Times* (6 September 2008) and reprinted in *From the Republic of Conscience: Stories Inspired by the Universal Declaration of Human Rights*, ed. Seán Love (Dublin: Liberties Press, 2009): 45–52. A Headnote to the version in the *Irish Times* states: "In a new story, Dermot Healy responds to Article 3 of the Universal Declaration of Human Rights, as part of a series in association with Amnesty International to mark the 60th anniversary of the declaration." Under Article 3, "Everyone has the right to life, liberty and security of person." There are some minor differences of punctuation and spelling between these two versions, but in all cases we have favoured the 2009 text.

An earlier and quite different version of this story, entitled "City of Hats," first appeared in *Force 10: A Journal of the Northwest*, no. 3 (Autumn 1991), ed. Dermot Healy: 24–27. An Endnote describes it as "An Extract from a travel book in progress called *Christ Wears a Panama Hat*." This travel book never transpired. The early version is more richly detailed but less tightly edited than the 2009 version. In any event, we have chosen to reproduce the 2009 text on the grounds that it is the most recent and up-to-date version available.

The epigraph to this book, "The Lost Limb" by Dermot Healy, first appeared in the *Irish Press* ["New Irish Writing" page, ed. David Marcus] (22 November 1980): 9.

Acknowledgements

This volume of collected stories was conceived and initiated with Dermot Healy's blessing and assistance in July 2013. Dermot had kindly agreed to comment on the final draft typescript and galley proofs; sadly, following his untimely death in June 2014, this was not to be. We do hope that this edition would have met with Dermot's approval, and that its publication will, in some small way, serve as a tribute to his memory. We are very grateful to his family and friends for their encouragement and support in bringing this volume to fruition; any errors in the text are entirely our own.

Immense gratitude and admiration is also offered to Dermot's wife, Helen Gillard Healy, who was deeply involved in this venture from the outset, during early discussions in Singapore and Sligo, and thereafter by phone, email and in person – none of this would have been possible without her help and commitment.

Seán Golden's friendship with Dermot spanned more than four decades, as did his familiarity with the intensely nuanced topography of the work – we have been extremely fortunate to find in Professor Golden a most helpful and gracious guide through the labyrinths of print and myth, at times almost on a daily basis. Brian Leyden has also been an invaluable presence for which we are, and continue to be, extremely grateful. Without the assistance of those who were familiar with Dermot's life and career down through the years, our work would have been, at the very least, far more challenging.

Thanks too are offered to John O'Brien for his visionary Dalkey Archive Press, with sincere gratitude for his continued, steadfast support of this venture, and for his ongoing contribution to literature that matters.

We are very grateful to Dr Michelle Chiang, who offered much-needed support and dedication in preparing the text for publication. Cheryl Julia Lee acted as a very helpful envoy sending valuable missives from the libraries of Dublin, for which sincere thanks. Pan Huiting assisted with an early draft of the typescript, which was most helpful.

Thanks too to Tim O'Grady, Pat McCabe, Bill Swainson, Molly McCloskey, Alannah Hopkin, Aidan Higgins, Mike McCormack, and Annie Proulx, all of whom significantly intersected with Dermot's life and work, and who were all important sounding boards over the past few years.

Dermot's friend and neighbour, the artist Seán McSweeney, kindly provided the landscape painting which adorns the cover of this book ("Blue Shoreline"). We are extremely grateful to Seán for this beautiful image, and to Sheila McSweeney for supplying us with a digital photograph of the painting. Thanks also to Su Salim Murphy for her advice on cover design.

Emma Wilcox, the English subject librarian at the School of Humanities and Social Sciences library, NTU, has, as always, been extremely supportive. Thanks also to Professor Lance Pettitt and everyone in the Centre for Irish Studies at St Mary's University, Twickenham, for their encouragement and advice. We are grateful to Dr Jack Fennell, University of Limerick, for his Irish-language expertise, and to Katie Moriarty-Hopper, Donal McCay, and Paula Tebay for their constructive comments on the work-in-progress.

Many thanks to Allison & Busby, Brandon (now O'Brien) Press, Wolfhound Press, Dewi Lewis Publishing, New Island Books, Faber & Faber, Liberties Press, the *Irish Times*, and the *Westmeath Examiner* for confirming the copyright status of the stories included in this volume.

This work was completed with the assistance of a Singapore MOE, ACRF Tier 1 grant, awarded to the editors in 2014, for which thanks and acknowledgement are registered.

Deepest gratitude, as always, is offered to Niamh Moriarty and Su Salim Murphy, for their constant support and encouragement.

THE COLLECTED
SHORT STORIES

For Winnie, Anne and Maura

Banished Misfortune and Other Stories (1982)

First Snow of the Year

For a few bewildering seconds, Jim Philips, on the day of his retirement, queried late morning sounds he had not heard in years. Then his solitary sense of freedom began. He looked with leisure at the low pink boards that ran the length of the ceiling, yellowing at the fireplace, brightening by the window.

Light was hammering on the broken shutter.

Shadows darted across the mildewed embroidery of dogs and flowers.

He cleared his womanless bed with a light heart, glad to have outgrown the ache in his smothered loins, outlived his job that he might die in a time of his own making. He nimbly laid his drinking clothes before last night's fire, coaxed first with paraffin, then whiskey. He hung his postman's uniform in the closet under the stairs.

He buttoned himself up for the air.

The ground was rock-hard and early frost had frozen the colours about the bog. The valley across which he had been a messenger for thirty years lay stretched out below him in a state of moral predictability. He saw John and Margaret Cawley, the gypsies, stealing through the yellow gorse with rotten turf. Their children moved from clownish tree to clownish tree out of the wind.

He shattered the surface water of the well, and from where Jim stood, the earth was on its side, reflected in every piece of ice, the wind sounding through the gulleys and drains like a concert flute. The bitter cold cleared his scalp and breath as he walked back. Young Phildy was standing under the gable. He felt a kind of fatalism seeing Phildy there, out of the wind looking at the earth, humourless and uncertain. Phildy threw in some frost-flecked sods of turf for the old man and then waited about impatiently till they were ready to go down.

Phildy stood under the gable again, surly-looking, but of

sudden times, nearly by inspiration, his tall frame would relax, his face ruffle with silent laughter.

The bell sounded.

"What are you thinking about?" asked Jim.

"Nothing. There's no change."

"We'll look down from the hill."

Phildy did not answer, but mumbled, with a hint of anger was it, in his voice.

They came to the edge of a small mossy clearing and looked toward the funeral. Jim dropped to his knee. The children of Liz's relations tottered among the appealing shapes of stone and foreign marble, flowers under glass, and when the priest stooped to say the final prayers the mourners turned left and studied Stagg's grave, the hunger-striker who had died in England. Owen Beirne, the son of the dead woman, and his jovial uncles delivered Liz on their shoulders and light as mercury she was lowered down cautiously with leather straps.

The long-jawed undertaker paid out the clay with jerky fingers into the son's palm.

Snow began amid the hand-shaking.

Helen stood with Phildy's child away from the mourners like a stranger. Owen Beirne's woman now, she once was Phildy's. Phildy moved toward her as Jim Philips joined the throng by the grave. Phildy said to himself, "Not to be possessed, not that." Phildy said to himself, "I have no desire ever to lie in her bed again." Helen looked closely at him, the child leaped into his arms. They swung round and round, and when they stopped Phildy said to her, "If you have a baby by that bastard, I'll come and cut it out of your stomach."

The dreadful shapes of the parish surrounded them with guilt and terror. She turned her head.

Phildy moved off with Jim by the History Road, through land killed over, by the Four Altars of stone, past the secluded oak trees that shelter the unfrightened children who died before Christ, a flowerless limbo for the unbaptized in the corner of a field, over the bridge where REMEMBER STAGG was written in coarse white lettering, past the American cars and the hikers sitting smoking in a ditch.

"What did he say?" asked Owen, taking Helen by the hand and then the elbow.

"He said he would kill me," she replied.

"Wait at the house for me," he said.

Phildy and Jim walked into the dim light of O'Grady's public house. "I have been considering what you might call a new theory," said Devine, the second-hand watch-man, his shiny waistcoat and nose covered with snuff, "I have read recently that turf, mind you, if properly compressed could provide a queer cheap and powerful source of power. And I mean well beyond the briquette stage."

"This round is on me," said O'Grady without enthusiasm. "In honour of Jim Philips, postman, recently retired." O'Grady set up an electric kettle on a stout crate and dropped a measure of cloves and sugar into each glass. His wife was throwing darts with the boys in the bar. The light was right for drinking by. Elephants from a circus roared from a nearby town. The radio said: "Walton's, your weekly reminder of the grace and beauties that lie—"

"I'll have a woman above in the house in no time, true as God," spoke Jim.

"Smell that," said Phildy.

Phildy went into the lounge and took a cue off some of the young lads playing there. He missed an easy ball. He broke up the pool game for no good reason. He turned one of the young fellow's arms behind his back. He pulled him to him. "What were you saying?" he asked. The young fellow looked him in the eye. Phildy left two shillings on the table.

He strolled back to the men.

"—when that fellow was a child," continued Jim, "along with his brother I used to push them happily along in a tub down a sheugh off the mountain, and every time I was ready to quit, your man there, Phildy, would pipe up: 'Ah, just once more'. Back up again and start all over. Well, I pushed till night fell and now they've grown and taken all my demesne and I wouldn't say a word against their father."

Their thoughts faded into the interior.

In a field over from there a gambling circle formed around a penny or a bird, a cock crowed by the wheel of a wagon, the sixth bird lost an eye and a wing was slung in a ditch, and the handler picked blood and feathers out of the mouth of the seventh and breathed life back into him, sucked at his beak and rubbed his chin murmuring along the back of the fighter, while the trainer stood away from the fight, another tossing-bag in his hand ready with the oiling tape, the washer and the weights. The men stood with the weight of their feet on their money.

"I saw them go by this morning," O'Grady whispered.

"Did you now," said Jim.

"I did. Dowds did the burying."

"Was it now."

"Dowds it was."

"Driving like a ginnet he was."

"Is that a fact."

"That'll do," said Devine.

Owen Beirne watched the sparse mourners leave through the falling snow. It must have been years since any of them had laid eyes on her, yet the old came here faithfully from their rooms in a vast acreage of wind and cold. Uncle James sneezed and sneezed. Helen, who had nursed his mother up to the day she died, had left dispiritedly, as if she had never once visited misfortune, nor taken old men dispassionately out of their rheumy beds to insert a catheter. Holding their shoddy under-garments. Weeding them of fading hair from armpit and groin. She was terrified for her child and herself. Of other minds speaking with her eyes, her tongue.

His mourning uncles talked of going up the village.

Their families had gone ahead in near ecstasy.

"A man can best fix the orifices of the world," said Devine.

"Helen pressed with her thumbs to see the cat's eye of death," whispered the barman, "powdered and combed Liz to a child."

"Jesus Christ, stop the sound of that man's voice," raised Phildy.

"You're the beast of the mirage, boy," advised Jim.

"Now Phildy, take it easy," said O'Grady.

"Will you stop talking," cried Phildy. His intestines shivered and grew weighty. He saw Owen withdraw from Helen, coursing his penis through her hands. His blood no longer went freely between the isolated and unbalanced part of himself. His white Christian bones grew rigid.

"As bad as 'forty-seven," said Jim when after the first skirmish the void began, and the door opened into the pub to admit Mr O'Dowd, undertaker, grocery-cum-pub owner. He kicked back with his boots as he surveyed the company. Jerky movements fretted around his temple and fingers.

"The worst," he said.

"—ah, but not interrupting you there," said the watchman, as he looked into the distance, studs rattling, "but that 'forty-seven blizzard wasn't so bad in the morning, but by evening it could smother a body. For I lay in my bed that night without an ounce of sleep, thinking myself grown to a statue, and the following morning I lay on and on thinking it was dark, and get up I did, eventually, pushed open the door after a long harangue and lo and behold you, it was bright . . ."

"There is no mystery to the whore," said Phildy.

Owen Beirne sat in an empty pub at the back of a grocery among the tinned beans, Chef bottles of sauce, Saxo packets of salt, where every time someone entered to do their shopping a crisp otherworld bell rang. The soft smell of flour and more bitter odour of rotting vegetables hung in the air. A rich woman delayed over the trade names of certain goods till he hated the living sight of her. A child with his mother's face smiled at him from the woman's pram. The smell of the flour seemed to come from his own living flesh. In that acute silence which the spirit of the dead make their own. And at last his mourning uncles arrived and they talked and talked, the first drink was for sorrow and the second for joy. Owen carried Uncle Festy, a disturbing old villain, to his Ford van.

An explosion in a nearby river rocked the street. The other relations left, speaking with great understanding and humour. His uncles' empty glasses filled the wooden counter. There was nowhere on that counter he could rest his hand with the fingers spread, nor know what should be darkened and what brightened. Thinking of Helen was the last cheerful thing in the world.

"Man to man," Uncle Festy said as he lowered him into the driver's seat. The children were singing in the back. "Remember Frank Stagg," said he. And lastly, "Take your own road, no matter what," said he and his eyes watering.

"And I opened the door and looked out and, lo and behold you, it was bright," the watch-man Devine continued, "so bright that it would dazzle your eyes ... and I stood at the door and I called, and I went up the low hill from the door and I called and called ... the sister within shouting at the greyhound like a woman tormented ... and I thought all my beasts were dead, taken from me during the night ... when, Lord save me, out of the drifts by the galvanize shed they came, one by one, struggling up toward me like the newborn ... and I fed them like a man whose wits had got the better of him ... nudging and poking at my chest ... Lord, wasn't I the happy man when they came up striking out of the snow and took the hay without a word."

"For one bright sovereign sold my life away," a cockfighter was singing. Trucks lumbered into the council yard across the valley. The roads were quick as lightning.

The great juggernauts moved out of the milk factory and turned their dipped lights onto the white plains. Mrs O'Grady, the publican's wife, looked like she might live forever.

"'Throw the clay on top of me,' wailed the sergeant, climbing on top of his dead wife's coffin, and then he turned round and married another."

Stones were hurled across the polythene to keep the peat dry.

And the sea drove shells into the cairn, sounding in Owen's ears as he rode a stolen bike crazily down the hill from the village, swerving in the torrents of snow. The white of the road curved into a single turning tyre. The colours on every side gathered into a frenzied shape, time slowed down to the independent moment. Helen, so delicate a thing, trussed up in the snow beside the grave. The begging trees on the mountain crisp as a child's brain. Owen feared the men looking for him. Those that tormented Helen. And that moment he heard the chisels at work undoing the image of his mother, he flew up the rafters to see. First they shaped those perfect eyes, then gouged them out. Circled and released the breasts with care, and when he looked back they were gone. The cheeks. The back of the head. The builder held his cheek to the small lift of the stomach. Then suddenly butted his head into the interior and the whole figure gave way. When he looked back, the builder was gone. Owen freewheeled on till, at Edmondstown Cross, he went into a ditch with awkward attempts to save himself. As the wheels hit the grass margin deep down, he was carried round and round on his back a few yards up the road.

Phildy, on his way back from O'Grady's, had seen the final impact. He stood silently watching from the far side of the road where everything was normal, not moving, blindfolded. With him stood two other young witnesses, dressed in great gabardines and boots, their hair pommaded beneath woollen caps. A snowdrift in a sheugh had nearly covered Owen, he surrendered gladly to the shock of the fall, lay quiet, swallowed blood from a cut on his lip. He gathered the feeling of pain back into his bones. He raised himself onto his elbows, moaning, onto his knees and stayed there a while till gradually he focused on the dark figures silhouetted against the snow-tipped, serrated evergreens. As he watched, a figure would appear and disappear, stepping forward, stepping backward. Owen called across. "Let it be now, just yourself and myself." The man standing kicked him on the bottom of the spine. "That's for Helen," Phildy said. The others hammered into his face with the violent devotion of the obsessed. Then Phildy pulled the others off Owen and they went up toward Monasteraden their anger anaesthetized by nature for a time.

"Come back and fight, you cunts!" Owen shouted after the retreating ghosts. He gathered himself and roared helplessly, "One at a time," he shouted after them.

"And a few days later," Devine went on, "I took the gun and went down to Lough Gara and I shot some wild ducks, the urchin that I was, 'cause there wasn't a bit of food in the house ... not a bit ... Sure there was no eating in them ... and that mad creature of a spaniel I had rose the poor things, and up they got fighting their cause."

"Yes," said Jim Philips, "and the trams, what with the drifts of 'forty-seven, stopped that day in Brighton."

The undertaker hammered his heels and buttoned his coat up tightly about him. "Two hot whiskeys for the gentlemen," he asked, "and a small brandy for myself."

Owen's feet dragged through the silence like many people walking. While the studs of the watch-man's boots clinked in the yard, and the postman thought of the turf above, it was to fall into Helen's arms Owen desired. He ran this way and that, terrified of the long drop into the bogholes, his senses failed him, and he could make nothing of this white silence where the particles of the mind were dispersed so quietly. He had never known this blind panic before. He stood for a long time trying to get his bearings, but the light was the same everywhere, not the separate light toward which the individual can turn, shining in his own beauty, but dispersed so freely that a great weary record of endless detail began.

"I would not want to be struggling with a woman as to my worth. Not that thing."

"Nor be a woman, mending my ways for others, that little pleasure come of it."

"A new frustration cannot enter the world," said the undertaker resignedly.

"The kali."

"The auld culcannon."

"A skillet full of kali, with the onions and the homemade butter."

"And the boxty."

"The boxty. Ah, man dear."

"And the potato cake."

"Stop! Stop!"

It stopped snowing, the brittle stars came out. Would the dead forgive him if his hands had wandered over Helen's face in the darkness of the mourning house, touching and parting flesh here, and folding his body around her against death? The canoe to the sea. He walked across a new planet, journeying inwards, without thought of his fellows. There were so many clear stars that he found the gravel track on the far side of the bog as in a dream, all beaten up and restored, like the others of his tribe. He ran forward through the shells of snow-filled houses where the elders had lived it all. Through deserted kitchens, middens, bedrooms with nothing to be seen, hearths filled with torn fishing-nets, old potato gardens drilled hard with the frost, turf stiff with snow. He came to Phildy's house, plastered with gravel and ivy, the laughter of the men echoed back from the trees. Sparks flew from the chimney. The abandoned pram on the path filled with berries. He came to his own house. There was no one there. Owen did not search long but followed the horses' path up to the rocks. He crossed the rocks. The stars so low he could have blown them out. Helen was sitting in the gypsy tent babysitting, looking after little Barney and Roger. Her own child asleep between them. The parents were over the road drinking. "Sh," she said. He came in and sat beside her. They sat in utter silence. When the children woke, she spoke in gypsy talk to reassure them. He filled the stove with timber and turf, snow dripped from the black canvas. He laid his head on her shoulder and they kissed in a direct trusting manner. Soon John Cawley and Margaret Cawley came over the rocks singing dead verse.

A Family and a Future

I never saw them go out that way in their cars by night. The new Ford Consuls, perhaps a Morris Minor. Volkswagens were always popular round that recalcitrant time. I can only imagine the secrets the night holds, the vulnerability of the isolated sex-object, the daring curiosity of those frightened, frustrated men and always the rumours of decadent tragedy. Perhaps those frightened, sharp-suited men would be walking up the road throwing nervous glances to the left and right of them. Or more assuredly, I'd say, in the heat of drink and summer they would drive bravely out to that beautiful place, where the Erne breaks sparklingly asunder between the forests, play the horn going past the cottage and collect her at her innocent, prearranged places.

For this is real pornography, to imagine the habits of June rather than describe them with authenticity, those quick flitting affairs where Sheelin thundered. Or the beat of visionary passion across an ancient cemetery overrun with shadows, for illicit lovers have always favoured as their first jousting place the quiet of the grave.

June was three years older than myself. She lived with an ailing though resilient mother, cantankerous, shoddy, quick-witted from dealing aggressively with shy people and successful farmers. June's father had been carried off by a fever from drinking contaminated water. Thus she took on the feeding of the few cattle that remained, carrying buckets of water from a spring well a mile away, dousing her socks, since the nearby well had never been cleared up or limestoned after the poisoning. She looked after the chopping of timber from the multitudinous forest of the Lord, facilitated dispassionately and excitedly the emissions of her neighbourly brethren.

From the locality she extended her doings to the town.

What had been mere sensual caprice became decadent business overnight.

I never then saw her in a pub or encountered her on the way to the Cathedral.

Befitting a hard worker, her body was strong but fat. She was not in the least goodlooking. But, because of the dark lashes, June's brown eyes confirmed that traditional estimation of beauty by the Gaelic bards of the area . . . . You, the highest nut in the place. Tanned from wandering the fields after lost cattle she would wander through the market on fair day, watched by the treacherous eyes of the stall-holders, in ribbons and patched skirt, huge hips akimbo. The Louis heels of her pink shoes worn sideways because of the edge of her walk, dots of mud on the back of her seamed nylons. The street-corner folk would hail her as she passed. She might loiter by the winter Amusements, a little astray among the jargon of lights and fortune-telling, in those days when the giddy voice of Buddy Holly filled the side-streets with "I guess it doesn't matter anymore." But she was always attracted to the rifle range. Cold-blooded curses helped her aim. Her brown eyes squinted down and steadied on the centre of life, on the yellow thin heart of a crow, on the marked cap of a jester.

I was never attracted to her but we always spoke. Like Hallo, and How is the crack, and How is it going.

But I did see her father's polka-dotted tie that held up her worn knickers.

I was sick, about thirteen and on the back of a bike travelling along the edge of the railway lines. Sweeney dropped the bike when he saw June chasing a Red Devon cow across a field, from east to west, and the two of them fell together among the coltsfoot and daffodils, stripped in the frost and she masturbated him and then me, and there was something virulent about his satisfaction, something slow and remorselessly painful about mine.

It was her desire and detachment, my desire of love. And then Sweeney mounted her some time later and she called to him, for a minute, Stop, stop, you're hurting, but he didn't and then she fainted. Her brown face keeled over in the frost, her father's tie round her ankles, and a look of horrified petulance on his face, he stood under a leafless oak, his brown cock unbloodied but fading. He would, I think, have buried her there had she not come to. But what did I say or do in those moments? Nursed her head in my lap, called to her, sung to her? Was I not at that moment as much to blame for her misfortune? But Sweeney returned with water and aspirins from a nearby house, she drank as I coaxed her, her eyes swam and steadied and then she thanked us, once more restored, she set off to capture the beast she had been following. And Sweeney shouted after her, I'm sorry June, and many's the time after they were lovers. For years too I was afflicted by this scene, in my dream I would, too, be about to come, and try to restrain for fear of hurting her, wake painfully in the dark, sperm like acid on my thighs. No, she never went into a pub for she never reached the peak of adult debauchery. Hers will always be the brink, the joyous, disparate moments of adolescence. Till none of the country folk bothered her, till she became the shag, the ride, the jaunt of the town. Eventually the police took a hand and barred her from the precincts, from her nocturnal clambering into parked buses at the depot, doors opened by skilled mechanics, from stretching under an impatient, married man in the waiting-room of the railway station. Thus those cars would be leaving town to pick up June, single or in groups, in the hubbub of careless laughter to spread her juices across the warm leather upholstery.

It was around this time that Benny met her, I think. He had been hired out to a farm in Dundalk for five years previous, and one full lush May he returned for the cancerous death of his last parent. Benny had a red freckled face, wore hunting caps, was a loner. He took her to the pictures, her first normal romance began. She was under great distress, as it was her first time in the cinema and they moved twice till she was immaculately placed one row behind the four-pennies. It was not short-sightedness but enthusiasm. Over his shoulder she stole timorous, enquiring glances at Maureen O'Hara, as the square filled up with wounded soldiers from the Civil War. Benny was to linger on a further three years in Dundalk, but that December he returned again to his deserted house, they cut trees together in the Christmas tree wood and sold them in the snowed-up market place, two shillings apiece, a week before the festival. Pheasants were taken with a shot of blood and feathers from the cloudy skies above Sheelin and presented by him to June's house for the seasonal dinner. Which he attended, the wily gossiping stranger, with a bottle of Jameson and orange.

But that was the first Christmas. The second or third he never came. June had mothered a child. By a solicitor, a priest, by myself, does it matter? That summer too her mother made it to the bath in time to vomit up a three-foot tapeworm. The old lady's skin and bone retreated under the shock. The release of the worm and birth of the child occurred within a week of each other. June grew thin again, her mother fattened. They grew more friendly, dependent upon each other. That year too, during these trying times, when they were burning the gorse and the furze, a fire swept the hill behind the house. And the two sick ladies fought the flames, shouting encouragement to each other, retreated successfully, covered in ash, their blouses scorched, their arms thrown around each other, laughing, and stood together that evening holding up the newly-washed child to look at the smoking field.

Neighbours came and mended their own fences and kept their counsel to themselves.

The drama of that fiery evening was that it led to a reunion between Benny and June and the dry-skinned baby. He came and repaired the scorched sheds, replaced the burnt rafter, renailed the twisted galvanize and played with the child in the cool kitchen, braved the mad, wandering talk of the mother. From the window you could see the water breaking out there like it was hitting watercoloured rocks. Sails skimmed through the trees, boat engines roared, and behind, a less formidable beauty, endowed darkly and modern among the pines, with wooden seats and toilets for viewing the lake, a black modern café with chain motifs on a cleared rise.

Soon the tourists would be arriving. "To paint a dark corner

darker," the old lady said. "Think of who sired him that built
yon." She held the bowl of soup at arm's length, licking her
wrists and fists, grey brown-tinged hair, deep-blue flowered
nightcoat, fluffy shoes, yellow nightdress peeking out at
her strained neck, awkward movements. "The architect, the
gobshite, came in here to explain, all airs and graces. Then he
started a fucking dirge. We told him where to get off."

June was on the grass, on all fours, scrambling away from
the child and Benny smoked by the window.

They married, herself and Benny, the following April. And
the next time I saw them was at a dance at the opening of that
café, where as yet only light drinks were being served, given by
the local GAA. I was mesmerized after a day's drinking, and in
drunken fashion attended to their every need, needing heroes
myself, but at some point I got into an argument and was
set upon by a couple of bastards from the town. They ripped
at my face with fingers like spurs, broken glass tore at my
throat. I heard the band breaking down, heels grated against
my teeth. Lying there babbling and crying on the floor while
the fight went on over my head. June came and hauled me
free and Benny swung out left, right and centre. They caught
Benny's eye a fearful blow and all I can remember is an Indian
doctor in the hospital complaining of having had enough of
attending to drunks in the middle of the night. But a nurse
stitched my scalp back onto my head and my head back onto
my body.

As for Benny, he was taken away to the Eye and Ear
Hospital in Dublin where he was ably attended to and where
I called him. We shared few words, because only fighting
brought out the intimacy in us. My life then for a number
of years was spent in aggravating silly details. Benny returned
to Dundalk to complete a final year and June took on other
lovers, she mothered another child. With his money saved
Benny returned a year later in spring for good. Shrunken
reeds had washed up, carquet, light brown, two ducks flying
together, the dark blowing in. Cars were parked on the

entrance to the café, which was now a magnificent hotel, with C&W stickers on them. The little Pleasure House of the Lord of the Estate had been renewed by the Minister of Lands with new bright pebble-dash, and renamed. Going up a new lane seemed miles, coming back mere yards.

I was out at the Point after an endless day's fishing without a catch, curlews screaming in the background, cormorants fanning themselves in heraldic postures at the top of the castle. Benny and I stood together chatting. But aloof, too, from each other, for things change; sometimes you are only an observer, at other times you are involved intimately in other people's lives, but now as a mere recorder of events and personages, the shock of alienation arrived on me, yet deeper than that the ultimate intimacy of disparate lives.

Benny said that June's house was a well-seasoned, weathered cottage. His own deserted one had grown accustomed to rats; the dead people that had lived in the house, his parents, could often be heard arguing at night by passers-by. He only went up there by daylight to fodder the cattle. The hum of taped music drifted down from the hotel.

"They have everything at their fingertips above," he said pointing. "Take your money, boy, from whatever angle it's coming from."

He pulled out his pipe and knocked it off a stone. A cormorant flew by, its coarse black wings aflutter, beak like silver in the spring sun, that set now without the lake catching its reflection. For it was far west of the pines. Some people neglect their experiences by holding them at arm's length, at verbal distance. Not so Benny, his generosity of spirit was personal, abrupt. Behind us, June's three kids were playing, only one of whom I think resembled him. They were all beautifully turned out, like out of a bandbox, not a hair out of place. The eldest had straight black hair, gypsy-like, and seemed to reflect humorously on things. The youngest had fair curly locks, talked of TV programmes, wide astonished eyes, blue. The four-year-old had undistinguished auburn hair, colourless skin. She stood between us, intent upon the fishing and saying and interrupting all the beautiful encouraging things for life that a child can tell or repel.

The waves were heavy and cold as rock. Feeling was dispersed by the heart, intestines and lungs. Like embryos, sluggishly, drops of water broke away from under the ice and flowed, ice-covered. He, Benny, didn't turn round to look at the cars as I did. He gossiped away, cruel, erratic, interested in the beyond. As if he knew the laundered space of each guilty psyche, and how each family renews itself for the future. For though, over the past few months, myself and Benny may have dispensed with familiarity, except for the cheerful courtesies, all's well. For you see they had his house scourged for years, those amiable frightened men, but now seemingly all's settled. June has given him joy and sustenance, and she maintains an aura of doubtful reserve, and I don't see her any more.

The Island and the Calves

Easter week dragged on in the distant crowded church.

By the houses, too, the spiritual world was ecstatic and sensual. Jim felt he might lose control of each and every moment, deep bass music, The Seven Last Words of Jesus Christ on the Cross by Haydn, till ultimate flight and optimism. He had begun to name with awe each part of the outside world, gaining equilibrium. The early turbulence of wind and rain had deepened the reflections in the now calm lake, a sensual pike rose momentarily across the surface, spills appeared under the drying trees in the water. As if small fry were rising. The Sussex country house was packed with prams and children, wet dolls sat out under the birches, cows nudged at their fodder and drifted down to the unblossomed rhododendrons.

In the deep pool of water, the edges of the purple pines sharpened towards sunset.

Winds channelled through the woods with a low hum. The things that my soul refuses to touch are as my sorrowful meat, was Edward's cry. Down by the lake's edge Jim and Edward were walking. Edward was dressed like a Jew, woollen hat, scapular like a lanceolate that pierced his breast, and eyes so light a blue that the pupil might slip away, melt. And then the brooding irony of devotion. In him the body and soul were one. The actor's idea of the stage and its dimensions were present in his judgement of things. He had just arrived from Gloucester, thence from a further coastline where he and some friends had celebrated the real mass on a deserted beach. The priest was a social worker, the altar girls had tended to him, they craved poverty and the expression of their bodies, how you might never trust a crucifix, the Temple and the Holy Ghost were different but not too different, and Edward's speech concerned otherness and celebration.

They walked on Jim's land.

The figure of the young priest, as a ghost of modernity, walked between them.

By the flush of leaves and waves coming together, apart on the shore.

It would be unfair to show how much they loved each other, that would be to invade them; let their occupations this day speak for them.

Besides the odd human detail. They have, for old time's sake, erected an aerial off a high tree to pick up the Mass in Irish from Radio Éireann, to allow the chants from Jim's home country to permeate the house. A minute's silence here is worth hours somewhere else in a year's time. The preciousness of this turbulence that is not fleeting. Not magic, but possession of something between the rhododendrons and the birch. Young willows flock in the hedges, the catkins have sprung furry with yellow combs. Edward will not listen or look at the trees or the water, all these images, the geranium and the lily have gone within, he has an ambiguous response to man's delight in nature, yet his ecstasy is not shortlived.

Jim burns with the necessity to get things done, a busy self, he perches on the shoulder of his friend looking at the competing world.

The house and the kitchen were wrecked by the chaotic night before, the children stepped over and added to the debris, babies crawled into cupboards, and a neighbour's child was studying the contents of a cardboard waste box. A young girl sat outside eating sand. Beside her, a crisp bag filled to bursting with primroses, thorns, pissmires. So, after their silent walk, the men set to work. That is, Jim washed and scrubbed the kitchen down while Edward talked with hardly credible gestures, or hardly heard what his friend answered, such was his zealous discovery of spiritual energy. He swaggered between the windows and the trees with chopped timber for a fire that was not burning. Popped large lumps of apple tart into his mouth. The radio was switched off during the priest's passionate ritual for the burial of Christ. The timorous martyrdom that crackled through space. In the silence came the sound of oars beating off a boat across the waters. A hare with long girl's thighs and legs stopped short of Jim in the garden.

He appraised the tension trembling in the hare's back, the jump withheld in the sockets of its knees; Jim had interrupted a joyous fling around the wild apple trees.

They looked at each and sauntered off to their various retreats.

Margaret was upstairs sleeping, tired from going to and fro in the world, and from walking up and down in it.

Last night she had screamed, Pain is practical, it's not something you go on and on with. For the men put no trust in their intelligence, expecting only to create well.

Now, today, she had been regretful, knowing how easy it is to inflict the truth on others without considering its possible repercussions on oneself. She listened to the two men downstairs, doubted her heroic capabilities, leaves sparkled on the walls around her. Haydn's music burst through into the final celebration. She was glad that the children had not surrendered to their conciliatory fathers, that she could read on without interruption.

Each morsel of food made her grow lightheaded. Her hair drifted across the pillow, her skin dried.

"Under the boardwalk, down by the sea," Edward was singing in a mock-Oxford accent for the barely interested children.

Now darkness. The much blessed body had been buried under the monolith of ritual, and so Edward brings his Bible in from the car. The coot and the sky-goat blow their horns over the purple lake. Closing the door, the inmates of the house, the trapped butterfly and the sleeping robin under the rafters, all heard the sudden mad screech of the geese rising with a chorus of screams, the lake suddenly fell sideways as they flew off. Emigration had begun. Edward read from the Old Testament, from Job and then from the Song of Songs, from the Natural Law in the Spiritual World, the everlasting kissing and fondling, how sweet the hoofs of the doe. While Jim imagined a priest in sleeveless leather donkey jacket mounting the marble steps, where biblical vegetation was trapped, charcoal dirt on his arms, and then erratic improvisations in the organ loft.

The Song of Songs was Edward's place in time.

For him there was no need of externalizing the presence of God.

That was Edward's totality.

Yet, there remained the music of the ballet, unprecedented for Jim, and without such dancers, the song of the heart. He had followed the movements of the calves for no special reason, other than after wet nights when the wind ranged heavily, he would find them in different places under the hedges. Their farmer provided fodder for their travels. From the general sheet of cold he surmised that the wind one day came from the east. It drove manfully against the wall of the house, repeated itself in dreams, was present in water and in the ruddy veins of the child.

The calves were tucked in against the further ditch of the field. So that, too, was east for them, the nebula. Towards the stones of the Dogs Mountains, under the plural form of myths, they had found refuge. During the night and the following day, rain fell harshly and at noon the wind softened, warmth resurrected, and he surmised from the south the wind came, it softened the eyes, the hair of Margaret, cooled the bushes ... . The calves were now under the ash-and-willow hedge to the left of the unattended Holly Well; hiding from the warm bucketing wind, chopping, straying, pondering, the flaming calf in the lead, all the rest mottled black and white.

Always, one stood while the others rested their chilled hoofs, stared unblinkingly at all who passed.

Now Jim knew the four points of the compass from the wind and the calves, the corners of that elementary field he extended onto the lake to find direction from there. For then there were no books in the house, no radio to guide him. And what was permanent, what stood still, would always point in a different direction to the man or the bird always moving, recognizing and turning, lifted on a current of air. He moved the field mentally out onto the water, between those lines of white surf, sallied forth with those early calves onto the rushing waves from north, south, east and west.

And even though this was an emotional, fundamental fashion of discovery, yet when the wind died down (no west wind ever blew) and passion departed, when passion departed and reason returned to the branches of a tree separating the heavens and the earth, when he stood bewildered by the strange simplicity of the sorrowful day that follows the joyous day, when man's heart might take that agile journey towards always discovering anew, still the points of that compass held firm.

The edges ran sharply out onto the murky headlands, over beautiful, distressed places, tapered off on mountain peaks and toppled palings on hawk and pine heads, beyond what he could not get to the other side of, remaining here, always imagining.

Now for Edward, he places the field on this island, though in a further lake. It took this sunshine, calm waters and relentless perception. He boated out to the island, drew a map of it, the monastery walls, the nest of the heron was east when his plan was finally completed. In a line east from the house on this particular day you had the red calf, the birch, the aerial, the hawk, the heron. Fossils he collected for charms, as in older times; the knowledge of structure went undisturbed. The purple of the waves stained their arms. History became the studying of disappearing softness, for hardness always remained, the most accessible material of man.

Here on the island he experienced the distance between the island and the field, the pleasure of nesting in the warmest part, like the calves. Where all the brilliant stones have been sketched upon by the bones of fish, shells of molluscs, cups of coral, the brains of kings and labourers. This island, morning receiver of gifts, plants and water, up where dawn's light had slipped from its chilled moorings and drifts among the tall heads of the spruces, where the herons are babbing, and where the deer once slept with its nose on its tail, closer to the Word, and no closer for all that energy spent.

The children screamed to be allowed on board, maddened by Jim oaring so constantly, seeking relief between home and the island, his pockets weighed down by stones, his hearing half-gone from the warfare of startled birds.

His house that day took on more and more the appearance of an abandoned novel, the children and he and Margaret could no longer sustain any kind of order. For at last he had authenticated the outside world, and each part was now sustained by itself and no longer needed a deity or an interpreter for a tiring audience. Into this house, then, as Margaret came down the stairs for a light supper, and the geese beat their way off in the appointed direction, Edward trustingly brought his Bible, sought solace, and then, unprompted and sonorously, began his reading of the Song of Songs.

The Curse

The canal comes from where I live, fast as horses, taking along the twisted leaves from the strange plants in the tropical garden that settled there after the last war. She goes under the church and takes the spire along a quarter of a mile. Next, is crushed by the walls of the mill that go up a hundred feet, so that she is brick-coloured and hampered by false rapids. The rats slide down the wheel and sometimes the army boys in their stiff boots pick them off with pellet guns.

Keenan's is on the bridge above.

And here we are like tadpoles in the water, but hardy and fine.

We are proud of the shape of ourselves, especially when one of us swims quick below in the shadow of the mill, darting through the other's legs like the perch that come up the canal in quiet schools, catapulting from deep hole to deep hole, weaving without moving.

But we keep to the shallow pool, where we can climb up onto the mossy wet walls and dangle our legs like white roots in the water.

The sun moves past like a big yellow cork, bobbing above and brightening the green beds. Each side of her is stiff and cold. The two boys go under to collect things, and stay down there bubbling away, to look up, as they beat backward with their soles at the flowing sky, as if the world had never happened. And when the girls arrive at three we will all drift under water, holding our breath, in a circle that drifts and shifts, till we surface with aching lungs, shooting up like people on springs.

Nobody comes here but ourselves.

Then suddenly, we are sitting on the wall, the new Triumph Herald, the first in the district that we have studied above in Kildare town, comes over the bridge, turns with a scream of wheels and crawls down the open path with its engine off. It is being steered by Pat Whelan, a big likeable gauger, who comes from the Ring, same as my father. He is general dogsbody for Ted Webster-Smith, the horse-racing man who sits, wrapped in his tweeds in the passenger seat, smoking with the confidence of a man of the world.

They are just in off the Curragh.

Webster-Smith is the son of General Tom, who was buried along with his famous stallion, Tain Rue, but Ted only goes through the rudiments of horse-training. They sit in the car, with its flashing fins and wings, a moment talking, they look over at us, and we watch the two men wondering.

Next, they get out and we can hear them laughing behind the car, urging each other on. With Ted in bright togs and Whelan in his big drawers, they start running down to the canal.

Pat Whelan's belly bounces. "Is she warm?" he shouts over. We nod. The two men are so white that none of us wants to look at them. It seems that this is the first time they have ever had their clothes off, that their paunches have seen the light of day. Both have whiskey-red faces. They have no muscles. "How are you chaps?" Webster-Smith calls across, nearly as if he knew he was invading our territory. Then, at a signal, Webster-Smith leaps off the pavement stones into the canal at the deep part, and Pat Whelan, blessing himself, jumps in at the shallows.

They both hit the water like baby elephants, with great splashes and roars. The water level rises.

Pat Whelan gets out to jump in again.

He doesn't seem to mind that his drawers have fallen a little, so that his hairy arse is showing and when he turns around we can see his mickey, all shrivelled up with the water, like something made out of putty and not finished.

But undaunted, he hauls up his drawers and leaps in again with a painful belly flop.

Webster-Smith comes up on his back, spouting from the

mouth and beating each side of him with his arms. He comes to his feet. "Not bad for an old fellow? Can you do that?" he calls across. We shake our heads. He repeats the performance, swallowing more water than he ought to, and when he again comes to his feet, we can see that his pot belly and thin chest are lined with red weals. He winks at us in a boyish fashion and goes under holding his nose, and next we can see Pat Whelan struggling where Webster-Smith has got a hold of him. The two men fight and cheer and pull at each other, all as show for us, till they fall and go under. Next, Webster-Smith appears up-stream with Pat Whelan's drawers held aloft in his hand.

Then, poor Pat surfaces, blinded for air and spluttering, just as the girls come down the path, running with their towels. They want to know how long those big idiots are going to be here. We shrug. All Pat can do is squat in the water. Webster-Smith hauls himself out, goes to the car, "It's all yours, ladies," he says, passing, and begins drying his legs and shoulders with a towel big as a bedspread. His shoulders are thin and bent forward. He is laughing all the time at poor Pat who everybody knows is always trying to put on airs. And though it's true that Webster-Smith, despite his fortune, has never kept a decent horse, and because it's also true that my family tell me I will never grow a screed taller than I am, I turn to the boys and say, "Watch this," get up and cross to the car, which I admire as much as I can, running my finger over the wings, the bonnet, then, now . . . .

"Would you have a job out at the stables?" I ask.

"Are you like the rest," he says, "mad to be a jockey?"

"Yes, Mr Webster-Smith."

"And have you ever been up on a horse?" he asks.

He slops aftershave onto his chin and under his arms.

"Many times," I says.

Back behind us Whelan is growing hysterical as the girls approach the water.

"I'll give you a job," he decides, "if you'll do something for me."

"What's that?" I ask.

The girls skim the water like swallows.

"OK, Patrick," Webster-Smith shouts down, "I'm coming," and he saunters over and puts Whelan through further anguish by leaving his drawers on the bank out of reach, till the poor gauger, flushed and bad-tempered and naked as the day God made him, flounders up onto the shore and pulls on his wet drawers looking around to see if anyone would spite him. But the girls all look away and slip down-stream through the now quiet canal. Webster-Smith gives me two shillings, and with the extent of his laughing coughs up mucus against the back wheel of the car.

"Clear off," Whelan shouts at me, "and don't be annoying Mr Webster-Smith."

"I'm working for Mr Webster-Smith now," I says.

The two men look at each other a moment, then puzzled by the state of affairs Whelan goes behind the car to put on his clothes. Ted pulls a comb through his hair, looks into the rear-view mirror and makes a parting sharp as a knife-edge. He draws on his brown leather boots. "Right," he says, "give me a mo till I work something out."

I go down and pick up my clothes and the crowd follow and gather around, looking from the pair above to me and back again. "Where are you going?" Sally asks, looking over my shoulder. "I haven't a clue," I says, "but the next time you see me it'll be on the back of Sir Ivor booting for home." "Aye, aye, aye," the lads say, shifting uneasily in their loose togs. "Wait and see," I says. The boys beat the moss off their purple knees and elbows, trying to come to grips with my self-importance. "Well," says Sally, "wherever you are going, Mr Knowall, you had better be around for me at nine." "We'll see," I says.

The two men are waiting for me in the car.

I climb over into the back of the Triumph which is known to every pub in the district but still important for all that. The seat is filled with crops and other riding gear, and so big it is impossible to sit still, as we swing up and around the bridge, the radio, like a miracle, bursting forth with the turn of the ignition, and I know I am in a different world when so much can happen at the same moment in time. I put my hands each side of me for balance, except for one last wave at the gang below, still looking after us.

Pat Whelan tries to pretend to know everything by telling Webster-Smith of my name and age and background, and the fact that my father knows more about gardening than he does about horses. But Webster-Smith takes no interest.

We stop outside the Grenville Arms Hotel.

"Now, Charlie," he says to me, flicking back the wet hair out of his eyes, "go in those glass doors, through to the lounge, and past that into the residents' lounge. Get your bearings. You'll see a bloody little bitch behind the bar called Molly Burns, who keeps the travellers in drink till the small hours, but insults us locals. Do you know her?"

"I see her about town," I says.

"That's the one," confirms Whelan.

"Well, she has insulted me and my friend here," continues Webster-Smith, "and I want you to go up to her and say, 'You rotting cunting bitch', then clear off out of there." He studies me. "Have you got that?"

"Yes," says I, "and when do I get to ride the ponies?"

"We'll see," he says, "how you get on with this job first."

Webster-Smith gets out and tips his seat forward.

The minute I'm out of the car they accelerate across the road, turn and speed to Murphy's bar. I go up the steps cautiously, knowing their eyes are on me, and on in through the glass swing doors. Another world where I must pretend to be about some business. Along the soft carpet, feeling my wet feet slip along in my sandals. I step, remembering I have left my towel in the Triumph. On again. The knob of the door into the lounge turns around and around in my hand but won't open, till I have the common sense to push it on in. The Dean from the Deanery is sitting right inside taking his afternoon coffee with one of his aged parishioners. His strange eyes seem to bore into mine. "I'm looking for my father," I blurt out. He loses interest in me, and shakes his head sadly toward the lady. I am swallowed up by the airless music and the dim lighting, till I see a small corridor leading on into a further, smaller lounge in which there is no one. The place smells. Empty bottles and stained glasses on all the tables. I peer under the drop-leaf of the counter and see Molly Burns on her hands and knees, pushing a scrubbing brush over and back across the raw boards. I bend and stand behind her a few seconds, trying to get wind for the rhyme that is going over and over in my mind, thinking to myself, my chance has come. She seems to feel my presence behind her, and tugging at the mat under her knees, she comes off her haunches and turns, so that her glasses loosen. "You rottin' cuntin' bitch," I whisper and run without looking behind me. "Come back," I hear her shout. "What did you say?" And I flee past the pictures of famous horses, past the Dean, through the glass doors and out onto the street, over the road, till, breathless, I pin myself against Murphy's wall.

The men step down from the bench in the snug where they have been watching.

"You did what I asked?" asks Webster-Smith, steering me into the open bar.

"I did," I says.

Pat Whelan laughs and laughs till the tears run down his cheeks.

"And what," asks Webster-Smith, "did the dear lady say to that?"

"Nothing."

"Well, you are a good chap, Charlie."

"And when do I get to ride the horses?"

"We'll have to see," he says.

I stand there waiting while the joke is passed down the bar to the local gamblers who are listening to the radio. They laugh, as is expected of them, and shuffle their feet, and look bemused as Whelan slops his drink and repeats over and over what I told Molly Burns, "You dirty rottin' cunt," he says, "that will put manners on her, by Christ." I wait.

I can taste there in the air the sweet smell of weakness and failure. "Can I come out tomorrow?" I ask Webster-Smith. "No, not tomorrow," he says, looking ahead of him. "Thursday?" I ask. "No, not Thursday either," he answers, half to himself, but without impatience or embarrassment. "Don't be annoying Mr Webster-Smith," says Pat Whelan in a sharp whisper so that the others, in their long gabardines, cannot hear.

The locals are going back to the racing pages, over the runners and riders where my name should one day be, and sometimes they call on Webster-Smith for his opinion, but only out of courtesy, then they disagree among each other all over again, as if driven into exaggeration by their inferiority.

I go as far as the door, thinking maybe Webster-Smith will take pity on me if I stand there long enough.

But purified by their sobering jump in the canal the pair go on drinking as if they didn't notice me.

At last, I turn one foot into the hall, open the outside door, and shout backward to all there, "You dirty fat English gets," and clear off up the street diagonally, thinking, if it comes to it, I can run forever. I hide in Farley's bakery and see Whelan appear. He makes no attempt to follow me, but takes a stroll up and down outside the pub with a troubled look on his face, as if the life he has been leading has whittled away all his energy. Then he goes back in again. Minutes later the two men emerge, wait for Dunne's haulage to pass, then cross the street to the hotel to see the effects of my curse.

The Dean walks out, parts with his parishioner and salutes Webster-Smith, who speaks down to the little man for a few moments. The Dean takes stock of the evening sky, then turns toward St Brigid's. On his way he buys a half-pound of mushrooms, going up on his toes to check the scales. I decide that there is no use crying over the number of doors closed to me in that town from then on, so I accompany him, pretending, for today at least, to be other than I am, and much more besides, while he, thinking he knows me, talks of superior breeds in the sprinting world.

Blake's Column

I

A TIN OF SARDINES

Mr Humphries's Selected Essays, *which will certainly recommend him on Judgment Day to the Creator, may not succeed so well in our more petty habitation. I think he has settled for the well-turned phrase, rather than exert the imagination, so that what once ran cleanly through the ocean has been parboiled, salted, oiled and tinned, still it bears a very fine Christian label.*

We have need of such lies to sustain us through our drab inferiority . . .

. . . Coming from Granard, loaves in a parcel, Ben hanging from the rafter, How do you know what you are coming home to or from, we are broken and have no words for this. This is forever. *An síos suas.** The greatest gift I have is the gift of forgetfulness, she whispers, On from Granard by train is best, he explains, for here, because the damn bus may never arrive . . .

Mr Blake got up from his small table. It was seven in the morning and he was again caught between different destinies. Cattle were straddling the ditch in an attempt to find shelter from the sleet. Hills went off into the mist, and when they saw him, the young calves came up the frozen garden and licked the window panes, snorting at him inside.

When he bent forward they reared back in fear. He should not have moved like that, so quickly.

How suddenly all these beings had thrust themselves into his consciousness and as suddenly withdrawn, because, maybe,

* "The down up."

of his lack of sympathy. What might stay in opposition and never find a home. *Weaxan*/grow. Mr Blake stood a long time there looking out, his two hands stuck in his jacket pockets, finishing with a flourish what he had not yet begun.

II

The bicycle shop was a vast open space with forms and benches and a drip from the roof that ran down the oily bricks.

On the bench under the old leaded windows, Mr Blake, the well-known columnist, fell into a fit of coughing.

This ended a long and joyous reverie considering the faults of a certain play of his and questioning the reasons why people had praised it when it first appeared, 14 August 1972. Like all others of his creed he was superficially hardened toward unhelpful criticism, but especially anxious over praise which he had not earned. The bicycle-man came over to see was he OK, but backed away from the combination of Vicks and garlic.

The bout of coughing sent jarred images of Mr Blake's contemporaries before his eyes, and for a moment he was defenceless . . .

"I'm all right," he sniffed, "a certain cunt of an actor just went the wrong way."

"That so," said the bicycle-man, returning to the *Evening Herald*.

If he was to persist with this line of questioning, Mr Blake's wits told him, he might render himself insane. Worse still, he hated the language in which this barrage of guilt presented itself. I must get out of this, he thought, this internal humiliation—

"Goodnight, Henry."

"Goodnight."

He wiped his eyes and mouth and wheeled his bike up the village, loath to go home. But fortunately he spied two cars of well-known solicitors parked by the village pub. He entered unobtrusively and ordered an orange. The three men were sitting among the peasant furniture, well inebriated, and dressed to the nines. He saluted them, but beyond the usual formalities, he could tell they did not want his company. He persisted. "Slumming?" he asked. Two of the men smiled, the other continued talking, except for the odd backward look of the eye. "Look," said the talker, Jack Small, turning on a further interruption, "We are having a private conversation, all right?" Mr Blake knew domestic trouble when he saw it, so he plucked the folds of his trousers into his socks, rode home the country road, lungs and heart free from alcohol and cigarettes, and in compliance with the dictates of his column (you might say, he thought) began that night a series of features on certain figures in the trade union world, beginning with *real* notes collected on the factory floor, then to the *unreal*, speeches from the politicians and the like, on to the *ambivalent*, meaning the employers, and finally, the *fatalists*, the union leaders.

He tried to cease from interpretation when he wrote, seeking as far as he could to create, but for the moment creation had become abuse against those he considered self-seeking, including trade-union officials, junior and senior, who over the years had given him important information. And knowing, as he wrote these rebukes to people who had trusted him, that he was cutting all ties with security, Mr Blake assured himself, Yes, sir, this is only the beginning, for even if he were left with only gossip to glean from, then he could move toward an ever more formidable betrayal.

III

CHAPTER 15

The fields were sodden with melting snow and the gutters full. All morning there was the unceasing slap of water on the streets of the town. He walked through the brilliant morning carrying a sack on his back. In it was the body of his child. He thought this was the case, to let him grow cold on his back. His father-in-law watched him through a slit in the curtain pass by.

A great deal of the tension had died in him and now he could feel every cold inch of his body. Some knew of his recent distress and others didn't, but only towards evening did someone say, "Ah mister, mister, why don't you go back to the house?"

"I think I'll stay down a while longer," he said. "I'll not go up the hill yet."

How your face froze! How the lines gathered! A fight in Bridge Street. In summer, here, a thunderstorm. To start again at the morning, he walked in the road from the lakes, and did the usual things of the single walker. Xmas lights glittered in every window, unsafe lights in the early morning. As he came in Farnham Road, soft pellets of rain sharpened his brow. The sack he covered with his coat and his face froze.

"You're out early," Mr Jenkins, the solicitor, said. He was walking his Great Dane and was clothed in a heavy green Aran jumper and wellingtons.

"I was thinking just now of that dog," the man replied.

They walked together along the railway track, whistling to the dog and thinking their separate thoughts. In the town, bottles were sprayed across the streets from the night before. What he looked forward to was spontaneity, even for the carcass he carried on his back. The people had worn it thin, the spontaneous love.

"This morning," said Mr Jenkins and his fingers shaking, "this morning, rummaging around the old house among my mother's things, I opened a bag and found . . . "

Birds flitted about the old Abbey in which Owen Roe rested, his poisoned intestine blistering the coffin.

The moon was a disc slanted and thrown off into the distance.

Now, last night and the night before, what great things did I dream? Sharpest dream of all to see the child wounded in the neck by an arrow. His hands tugging at the arrow. And the man's wife saying, We will always be leaving by different doors and he answering, OK, that's OK, I wouldn't change it for the world . . .

" . . . palm leaves if you don't mind."

The rain barrels were drumming throughout the town.

But to begin again at the morning when he had awoken as the waves beat a slow retreat from his door. This lack of affection between us must cease, she said, for we mean everything to each other since everything is so vague and unfamiliar. This absurd lack of affection. He lifted his son onto his back. He kicked back the wet grass across the fields. He strolled into town.

IV

Dublin

Dear John,

I feel that whatever your intentions, the form of muckraking you are now at in the dailies seems to be saying, Look! Look! How good I am! Soon no one will care what you have to say. I am terrified of meeting any of our old friends. You know I will always respect you and I do not mean to be cruel.

I expect you do at least eat well. Ben has grown big as a house and plays chess with his friends.

I think you began as a dreamer but developed other conceits. Why don't you begin again in strange surroundings. That place is no good for you.

With winter here, the dress trade has gone slack, but Mother is nothing but encouragement. Maybe you should return to the city, for we both know what isolation can inflict on a body. Wishing you well, oh yes, I was attacked and robbed of my handbag on the way home in Donnybrook, of all places, the other night. I am without the gold chain, as for the money it means nothing. The police were less efficient than the lads, one of whom said, It's all right Mrs, threw me against a signpost and whipped the bag. I was screaming and screaming, but no one came. But I am all right now.

Love Sheila.

PS My drama teacher says I have the right voice for the wrong century. Yesterday I read "The Overcoat" by Gogol. I miss the country but Mother says we can't go down till summer. See you then.

Ben.

V

With Sheila's house coat around him, Mr Blake was full pelt at it with the bellows. Smoke poured through the kitchen. He cursed and swore. Then at last he did what he should have done in the first place, opened the flues and collected the soot. Steam poured from the wet ash, but the fire grew and smoke poured out the open door, over the frosty roofs of the dreary outhouses.

Then he returned to his writing.

John Blake was a small, feverish man with red, seedy cheeks. Sheila and Ben had left him a year and a half ago. Because. Because. He now lived in the cottage alone, taking his morning walk at cock-crow, with the collar of his coat up to his ears and taking in all he heard. They had moved into the cottage three years ago after a lifetime in the city, but he had been born near here. At seven, years ago, spent six months on his back in the local sanatorium. Gone to school over the road. Next, the diocesan boarding school, and after that, two years in an insurance office where the underwriter in the motor section cut all his letters by half until he learned to convey only what was important.

By night he now ploughed into the private journal that

took up his whole life. The journal had once been his master. Now that he was alone, it was his companion.

And through it he tried to fight off the mindlessness of fourteen years in a newspaper office.

The wind roared from the south-east.

He dropped his column off at a post office run by three orphaned daughters.

From Wednesday to Friday he stopped over in Dublin at an old associate's flat. The rest of the week he spent here, in The Valley, an old cottage rebuilt with broad-flanched chimneys, floors of patio slates cemented into stone, walls of rusty brickwork with hangings from Colombia, the windows austere and tight against the wind, but because some of the rooms were only half finished, he lived in the kitchen and slept bundled up in blue rugs in the child's room above, next to the immersion heater.

In summer, sweet pea climbed across the iron trellis of the porch. And come spring, the daffodils returned in tight clumps, then bunches of Herb Robert that remained till autumn.

Like all those who live in the country, but whose minds are elsewhere, he never exercised his intelligence among the country folk but adopted a distant role, accepting their folkish advices and repetitive narratives, but today of all days he stopped the Pools collector as they went up the lane together and said, "Take our Minister, for instance."

"Yes," said Brennan.

"Minister of the Environment, born in Corlurgan, yes?"

"True for you."

"This is what happened. He told me himself. As a whippersnapper, himself and the boys knew old Ferguson, yes, who had no indoor toilet and each day slipped down to the ditch to shit into the drain. He had a reliable branch there he used to hang out of. Well, your Minister went down there, nicked the stick with his penknife. The boys hid and waited. Old Ferguson came and let his trousers down, swung out over his deposit and down he went. I ask you."

"Boys will be boys," answered Brennan.

"You're not concerned that this man is responsible for the welfare of the country?" asked Blake.

"Makes no difference."

So Blake was forced into further coloured reproofs that got nowhere. "I must be about my calls. Good day, John," said Brennan, who tipped off up a garden path, his briefcase hanging loosely from his left hand. "See you tomorrow," Blake shouted after him. Brennan put his thumb up without turning round.

VI

AN ATTACK ON VIRGINITY

I have made my laborious way through Mr Arthur Beymont's book recently, a man who relishes the socialist cause with an innocence tantamount to virginity. It seems to me a lot of horse shit, or excuse me, apocryphal ravings, to believe that socialism has yet to come. It is already here, and we must get on with what we have. A writer like this could not sustain his confidence for the length of his breakfast, never mind a book, but our socialist press will continue to present us with feeble English thinkers, rather than pay a good translator to give us the masters.

The other books of the month bring no surprises, unless you think of living as a life sentence, which most of the Irish do. Mr Eugene Williams will go on and on about the bric-à-brac of childhood, not a day's sickness, inverting Gogol's style who knew a stranger when he saw one. And Mr Sampson, please do not think otherwise, you are a yes-man, no matter the number of negatives you employ. Brendan Little continues to whine with the authentic cries of a drowning cat, albeit it with more style. And Mr Butane, if you persist in telling us of your dear Aunt Helen from Sligo, I will personally take a pistol to the principality of Monaco and shoot you.

In the other fields, politics for instance, O'Neill has us back where we started, thinking Union with Britain is a superior breed of union than Union with Ireland, for a people who are wanted by neither, except by him and for his own reasons. As he deals with women in his private life, so he deals with politics, gets into bed with all of them to prove his devotion to his wife. And as for the editors of this paper, who think Union with the Republic is the be all and end all, it seems the twentieth century has passed them by. Because the Irish have no idealism, they chose Republicanism, yet this fight started out over work and wages, not nationhood. A life in Insurance terms is worth what? £40,000 (with inflation)? With these sums we could be laying the foundation stones of small factories. Each life has a monetary value, but not in Unionism, Protestant or Catholic, so, would the gentleman who pays me for my piece please refrain from his ecstatic mumblings (I hear talk of his inserting a photograph of himself alongside), so that the cartoonists might have peace of mind. I might add that I think I am suffering from a failure of nerve. But I intend to write more of that in the future.

VII

Mr Blake was out feeding the finches in the crackling snow and sunlight when Mrs Robinson from the cocktail circuit directed her car down the lane. This was indeed a surprise. Knowing his tantrums, she parked nose-up against the gate and let herself into the house. By the repeated acceleration when the car stopped he knew it was she trying to wrestle her way out of the car with the ignition still on.

He piled the fat with the crumbs, sucked his frozen fingers and looked through the window to see what she was at.

Mrs Robinson was peering at the page in his typewriter.

He scooted round to the front of the house, took two deep breaths, and leaped into the kitchen.

Mrs Robinson was sitting in his armchair by the range, the kettle in her hand.

"Ah, it's you," she said, smiling.

"It is me," he replied.

She put the kettle on the open range, patted her lap and drew out a cheap cigarette. "I have news for you," she continued. "You and I have guests this evening."

"At your place?" he asked.

"Nowhere else, to be sure," as always calling on the uncalled-for certitude. "You'll come?"

"I will, if I'm allowed to get a bit of work done around here."

"Of course, dear." She tapped her cigarette into one of the cooking rings. "And your wife?"

"Mrs Robinson," he said evenly.

"Yes, John."

"Why do you continually ask after my wife? My wife has left me."

"We live in hope, John."

She stayed a half-hour, enjoying the heat and casting aspersions on the filth around her by adding to it. He went about his business, trucking in with wood and turf, then aired his feet before the fire. My God, she thought. His toes looked like they had been soaped in mud, then crookedly bent forward as if they might crawl off in shame. This was a pleasure Blake enjoyed.

"I have brought you a present," said Mrs Robinson.

"Aha?"

She took out a muslin bag of curried seal meat, which the two of them tugged and chewed with their milkless tea. It was delicious. Not bad at all. Excellent. Then Blake unearthed a jar of mussels. Oh vinegar. It suffices. Through the window the calves, half-hidden by the fossilized prints of their tongues on the glass, looked in and wandered off uncertainly, this being the first day of snow they had seen. A chain-saw buzzed nearby, leaving a gap in the sky and when the scream of the blade died, the bell of the saw continued on.

"Well then, can you . . . ?"

So, Mr Blake stepped over the snow and, watched by Mrs Robinson, he drove the car into his yard and turned it, so that it faced back up the lane. Pulling on her gloves, she drove in first over and out of sight, disappearing with a loud bark of her horn as she hit the main road. Tractors pulled into the ditches to let her by and her small Morris was followed by all the dogs of the townland.

VIII

CHAPTER 17

I break into a run after all the others. Though my soul won't catch them. Not during the long jealous hours of daylight or the short fretful minutes of the night. There is an enemy sleeping with me. Like me in every movement. But I brighten and rise to walk over the splink in the fog curled round the few hazy lights of the man Brennan who lives haphazardly on his own and makes fortunes for others that he might increase his own by a ha'pennyworth, and behind him another, and behind him another with his suffering sister, their lights all on in the early morning, the sister's brother crossing the one field they all share in the fog, caught between going and coming by the bare pattern at his feet, carrying timber and cardboard, stopping for the traffic of morning sounds, knocking on his neighbour's council door till he drops his head for the answer within, and out it comes, exaggerated by the early muffled light and the horn of the sun, "Yes, yes, just a minute, Henry," a chair disturbed and a cigarette dropped into the ashes of the holly and cherry trees, the two men finish the bottle of port and watch me swim past through the wet bushes toward your kitchen where none have yet been to bed, I'm relieved to see you, but then I know you are not up alone, "Here he is," he says, "It's in his cup," the fortune-teller tells the company gathered, "That fellow there, for him it's here at the bottom, he is cursed with the sickle and the sword, aye," James the fortune-teller, delighted with the extent of my innocence, laughs across my head, "He has many enemies, aye, and they are telling lies on him." Everywhere in the room and beyond is the sweet chorus of the patriarchal instruments. James steps toward the muddy, unimportant hay, like me in every movement. "Will I sleep with him sometime?" you ask, "Whenever you wish," I answer, and outside the three men and the single sister are crossing and recrossing their field, heating up their prefabricated tigíns with debris from the ditches, sallies and shavings, their voices warm as thrushes' eggs, carrying bread and milk, light timber and cardboard, reading out the Garda summons over the last jet of gas and burdened with hunger that slights them, "Are youse off to school?" James the fortune-teller shouts from his perch in the lofty barn after the dead postmistress's daughters as they saunter into town. Then the sister comes to scold the men and rifle their pockets for the evening meal.

IX

It was a bad day for Mr Blake. Nothing went right from the beginning. The electric pump had frozen. He could no longer write because nothing came and he stopped above in the child's small bed, freezing and hungry. All his colossal arguments had deserted him, and he longed to hear someone down in the yard.

In the afternoon he heard the cry of the beagles coming from the direction of the lake. He ran down in his dressing-gown in time to see the fox dart across his frozen garden, minutes later followed by the dogs. The men came up, undid the two gates and streamed through without a by-your-leave.

From the other window he saw the fox flying along the hill toward the village. Then, Mr Blake dressed and, fighting a desire to hide above in the bed again, he ate a breakfast of cold porridge and honey, heated up a pot of rainwater over the gas and bathed his piles. He was squatting like that, over the saucepan, in the centre of the kitchen floor when his brother-in-law came to collect him. It was an embarrassing moment when he saw the uncomprehending face at the window.

He let his brother-in-law in.

"No, not that," Mr Blake shook his head, "But I am afflicted by haemorrhoids."

"Well," said James, his brother-in-law, "it was not a pretty sight."

"Not mad yet."

"Catch you."

They walked up onto the road and waited for the taxi from Smith's. While they waited his brother-in-law read his hand, rubbing his thumb over and back across the wrinkled palm. But before he could hear his fortune, Smith came over the brow in his Datsun. They drove first to Percy's where John-Pat was collected, onto Bridie's for Hughy, then to PJ's who was waiting at the door, back up across the tortuous hills in the crowded car while Smith kept up a harangue against the cost of doctors and prescriptions. They pulled into a side road to avoid a funeral coming from the other direction. Then reaching the town they all went their various ways, to meet again by the monument at eleven, where Smith would fume and rage as the clock wound toward midnight, and the countrymen would not appear having found after-hours drinking in the lax hostelries of the area, and when they did come, piled high with parcels of bread and tea and butter, Smith would speak ne'er a word to anyone, but pull away from each dropping point with an angry acceleration, "And if you did not speak up," the brother-in-law had it, "he would fly past your fucking door." Then finally dropping off Blake, who was always last and soberer than the rest, Smith would whine,

"Now, Boss, you see what I have to deal with, day in, day out," as he held each pound note up to the light. And arriving back after his day on the town, Blake would look over his journal and feel appalled, powerless to justify his existence, till he obliterated all his weaknesses and censured the living past.

X

I detect in myself someone who would own up to another's crime so my own might be considered and my fame increased accordingly. No hint of flesh or hair could persuade me that I existed at twenty, nor companion at forty give evidence of my worth. Nor could I defend myself from reality, when, as some part of me chooses to consider the exciting and deepening possibilities of my life ahead, there for one terrifying moment remains only my life before. And from these unwilled insights, emerges myself, unwilled, judged, unreasonable, and from this flow the lives of other people.

XI

The bus ride to Dublin was a cold, cheerless affair. He changed at the outskirts to a 54. The familiar city instilled a certain hopefulness that was always followed by sentimentality as the bus chose to pass the house where Sheila and Ben lived, out of their element, trying to deal with meaningless exchanges. He searched the street for a sign of any of his family. No one. The hedge newly shorn and the clay turned up and dug for spring. A green bag of Irish peat at the left side of the door unopened. A Chinese lantern hanging over the pale blinds of the living room. The bus got by the roadworks and wheeled on into the midday traffic and Mr Blake looked ahead, oblivious to the "request" programme pounding through the radio speakers, but listened, instead, for the bus operator's gargled voice interrupting the station with organizational trivia, like a voice

at sea keeping contact with lost souls, and he was glad when
their driver was called on to answer and give his position,
twice, because of bad reception. And he was delighted, too,
to find that his stern brogues and heavy coat were of more
durable quality than those worn by his superiors at the
newspaper office. The editor appeared at his desk, complete
with crumbs on his lips from an overwrought lunch. Mr Blake
argued the toss with him, and leaving, tried as best he could
to avoid the new journalistic successes, female and male, who
sat perched by their typewriters, sounding like daft parrots, as
they whittled away at their self-infatuation, till they too might
end up like him, rearranging the editor's words in his ears . . . .
"The best thing for you, John, might be to open a small
business," he smiles, "a restaurant."

"Aye," answers Blake, knowing his place.

"There is money in it," he continues, "mark my words.
Then you can poison them all at will." He throws back the
sheets. "I can't use these."

Blake puts them back in his briefcase.

"Don't take it personal."

"My cheque?"

"At the desk as usual."

To the library. But Blake could not settle there for long.
He phoned Sheila, but received no reply, then got through
to Freeman who told him that his bed was there as usual. He
bought his herbs and spices, his dried fruit and wholemeal.
Fled from corner to corner in the rain and met Freeman at
last, just when his patience could no longer sustain him across
known thoroughfares, pretending to a course of action, he
adrift from his moorings, at the corner of Eccles Street. There
was much to talk about. Freeman had no illusions and was of
happy, warped nature.

"You've set the cat among the pigeons, Johnny, my boy,"
he said, "but it's only literary stuff. You don't fool me."

"I didn't think for a moment that I would."

"Are you still off dainties and on a herring?"

"I'll manage a pint."

Again he phoned Sheila, and when she replied, he had nothing to say for himself except to ask after Ben, who came on and described with accurate and bloody details a fall from a tree. She, too, offered him a room, and his sleep that night centred around a review he had written earlier in the week of a book of essays by Humphries, an egotistical man, who had befriended him in earlier days. His review, he hoped, had been noncommittal. Those who did not want to hurt the writer in question had returned the review. But now, in his dream, he saw that the writer was dead, laid out in his tweeds, his red hair bleached by the light, his thin feminine hands each side of him, dark eyes looking around, a hint of alcohol on his lower lip. His left eyelash stirred like a bird, balancing. Humphries was dead but kept looking around. Mr Blake, much younger here than his years, took him by the hand and led the distressed writer a few turns round the room. Humphries moaned and moaned.

He jumped at sudden noises, was obviously distressed and clearly dead.

Mr Blake awoke in the dead room, a pale blue light was flickering on Ben's woollen scarf that hung over the single item of furniture, a King Edward chair.

He woke full of love to find that Sheila and Ben were sleeping in the room just across from him. He was filled with excitement and longing that after a while passed. He thought of himself and Humphries, and of his many friends who were like that, feeling they were leading a dead man around the room, a turn or two, before he would lie down and die. Of them all he loved this writer best. He got up and dressed himself, turned up the collar of his coat and made for the bus without disturbing any in the house, because he should not have come there in the first place. The calves, he told himself would have broken through into his garden. Blake made many excuses to himself. He and two others were the solitary passengers, and on his way home he bewailed writers undone by fawners, who in their need sought religious or spiritual advantage, ravaging the emotions of their families, rather than deal with what their uncomplicated senses told them.

He prayed that he would not in time give in to extreme disorders, that the task he had set himself might prove fruitful.

In such hope Mr Blake spent his days.

The Girl in the Muslin Dress

Moody Alex was singing "Under Milk Wood" to an old Welsh air she had learned from her grandfather.

Aimless lighting hung unhealthily from the glazed street corners, signs swung a little, the wind was strong enough. And I felt more tired now than ever before and could have sworn the rain, as it hopped off the bonnets of the cars, was speaking of something that happened in October. And then the alleys, crowding with the ghosts of gossiping women, talked of the secret life in England and lifted their skirts for all the world to see till, tiring of the orchestra, I pulled the hood of my duffle coat down tight, shutting out all the insistent voices, muffling the sounds of my steps.

Alex, walking way out in front with her sharp, strained assault, disappeared.

In panic, I lengthened my stride to a near run till I had her in sight again. You could hear the rumble of late and early trains thundering across the tops of the houses and my shoes were letting in both back and front, not at all the ding-dong business walking is for other fortunate gentlemen of the metropolis. Only for a certain softness of the head I might have discarded the shoes and gone barefoot, paddling along on my misshapen feet to Victoria and Pimlico, even further. But some loyal, affected passion deterred me from abandoning them in a strange parish. Standing in a doorway to light a cigarette, my life a matter of distances and disguises, I felt the racking, nimble drug suddenly move in the blood.

Around us the city was coming up for air.

Whole streets moved into focus, filled with washed-out colours and, looking up, I childishly felt the helter-skelter of the rain on my face and saw the dark clouds separate slowly under the coarse morning light. Above the shops, the skyscrapers, with certain hazy lights left on overnight, shoulder to shoulder stepped it down the sky. And I was badly thinking of lying in the thousand strange beds of Alex, old English lavender, hyacinths before rain, till in the moonless night exhaustion and relief might finally coax both of us away, worlds apart.

Up ahead from me she stopped and disappeared into the doorway of a chemist's shop. I approached her expectantly but always looking hard ahead as if I hadn't seen this change in strategy. She had sat down against the door and was flicking the wet hair out of her eyes. I came and stopped and looked at her a while and went in and sat down beside her. "I know it's coming," she said.

It was a whole little world in that doorway. Her body was cold and wet, even the wind could not smuggle some colour into her bloodless cheeks. "I was beginning to lose you back there," I whispered. "It goes on and on," she said and we gave way our tempers for that kind salvation, touched hands a bit while the rain beat down on those blue-grey tiles just short of our outstretched feet.

A draught blew straight out from under the door and we had to shift tiredly about trying to avoid it but found our places, hunched up together, eventually.

Sleep, girl, sleep. I nursed Alex in my arms. It was coming up to six o'clock a church-bell said, repeating itself above the pious saplings and humid stones. She cursed under her breath. I don't know who, someone out there where dreaming happens, perhaps myself. The days pass.

"Look," said Alex. A timid-looking man in jamboree had come round the corner of the street opposite, carrying a large box against his chest which he set down against the closed gates of an underground station. This intoning man, dressed out in a squat yellow cape with a beret pulled down over his ears, disappeared round the corner and returned a long time later with another large box and a smaller one. Music could be heard like a serinette for the lifeless city and everywhere the rain was falling flat out from a great height down the grey sky, thousands of well-wishers, till they sputtered out on the broad swerve of the roadway. The reverent shook the bitter rain from his head and set the two large boxes together in a daft fashion, shoving the smaller one underneath. From inside his dripping coat he took a sheet of polythene which he quickly folded over the lids to protect them against the rain. He seemed satisfied enough and secured the ends of the polythene with some stones which he always carried for that purpose. Then he gathered himself up against the jagged gateway, shoved his hands deep into his pockets and, grimacing a bit, peered up and down the street, kicking back with his left foot.

He hummed a number of ancient concert-hall tunes. Meanwhile a dapper black man went by on a bicycle, wearing an Indian hat and a white coat down past his ankles. He was swerving from side to side and laughing ridiculously to himself in a plaintive, nearly familiar, manner. Like the ribald winos under a tree in summer. The man at the station shook his head sadly and turned and rattled the gates, taking a dekko this way and that down the length of the deserted station. Once, he seemed to make his mind up about something and went over and urinated in a corner, shaking his leg afterwards like a spare limb. A blue van came quickly down the street, throwing up arcs of rainwater on each side like the swish of the Spanish dancer's dress. It parked outside the station for some ten minutes, the engine running, the wipers working like mad and feet moved over and back below the level of the van. Then, by hap, a railwayman, dressed in peaked cap and stiff dark mackintosh drawn to the chin, smoked carefully over the puddles and joined the others out of sight.

When at last the van drew away after the democracies of the early morning, the boxes had been transformed by a multicoloured collection of newspapers and demotic magazines which the man viewed from all angles, the sky-washed polythene pulled across them, the brazen headlines sheltered in iron frames. The gates were open and voices echoed out from the windy station. The newspaper-man sat within on the smaller box, his legs crossed as he smoked, tapping out

in mid-air a fair representation of a circle with his raised toe.
Alex and I struggled up out of the doorway, hitching up our
wet clothes and shivering, and then we crossed the road by the
subway, the wind getting up so heavy down there that we held
each other distastefully till we resurfaced a few feet from the
newspaper-man, outside Hanger Lane.

"Christ, it's Sunday."

"I don't know, mate. I don't know why I'm here or what's
coming over this country. The birds can explain. It used to be
a picnic once upon a time but it's been downhill all the way
since the war. Put them out of their misery, I say."

The pink night was dying out. Rendezvous would be made
here later. We tiptoed past the ticket-collector's office. He was
inside, engrossed in lighting up an evil-smelling oil fire with
his back turned to wave the wand. In the slightly drunk office,
a faded soap calendar from 1939. Among the posters on the
walls for sorrow, a distant picture of Alex would soon appear,
an advertisement for a shorthand and typing firm in which she
wears a wig after the operation when those intuitive lights dulled.
Pass by. We made it down to the open-air platform unseen
while up at the entrance the newspaper-man, after watching
the manoeuvre, the mint from her dresses, gave us the thumbs-
up sign long after we had gone from view. The two of us sat
huddled up on a bench, the sky full of metal beams and wet
glass where the riffraff, the sweet-papers and coupons ducked
their heads and scattered, sailing right out of sight above the
delving trees. When the first train came up the line for reveille
and stopped like the end of the world, the pair of us collapsed
into an empty, scrubbed apartment, drunk from tiredness,
savouring the soft feel and warmth of the cushioned seats.

"I can feel it coming on," said Alex. "I'm afraid."

"I'll get you home," I said.

And Alex slept again though she might dart awake and look
around as we hurtled to a stop in the various stations where
Sally with the tortured legs and wearing the muslin dress had
flown to work each morning in the kindly Indian engine-

driver's cab, holding on for dear life in the musky, electric
tunnels till that man had got switched to a different line.

It was a dull grey morning when we emerged in Pimlico.
We passed the wrestling school and the creamy house of the
mediums. And sometimes we could hear the parable of the
Flying Oats blow up the gliding streets from the round world
of the flyovers, the pigeons picking themselves up with grave
dignity from a roof of verdigris on a cinema. The streets themselves were empty and grey, all except for a few lone Queen
hustlers who made their way giddily along the pavements,
their make-up withered, ashen faced, looking round behind
them now and then. "Penny for your thoughts," said these
friends slipping by. And I did a nice 1920's shuffle with the
aged boots in reply, a rendering the father had taught me on
the kitchen floor. "My, my," they said, skipping away. Alex and
I walking together now. We had begun talking in a slow,
effortless manner, mixing up all kinds of words, faint-hearted,
Alex's eyes so tired now, burned down to a hollow darkness.

She hesitated at the steps of a tall staid Victorian building.
Come on. But she was watching slowly, moving back. The
dull nightlight had been left on and behind the wavering glass
panels of the glass door it seemed that all the walls and, even
further back, the domed ceiling, were covered with flowers.
The cheerful, fragrant inside of a flower shop. We climbed the
steps and looked in, glancing round with wonder. Hundreds
of rich flowers, long green stalks going this way and that, a
crevice of weeds, roses and tulips, strange wonders crowded
the walls. And now they were murals which must have taken
years upon years to paint. Jabbering excitedly, we suddenly
backed away in fright as a huge round face appeared behind
the glass, a Leviathan of a man looked out at us with curiosity,
speaking away. He smiled with some kind of recognition,
then these enormous hands turned the key in the lock, the
door opened, the drug stalled.

"You like the painting?" he said in a choked, foreign accent,
his hands demonstrating the ease of paint brushes.

"Yes. Yes."

He shook those paint-stained hands of his again and, touching Alex's hair with a finger, knocked away a bead of rain.

"Tsh. Tsh. Come from the rain."

We followed him in gratefully. The place smelled fresh and warm, it could have been a hospital yet there was no hint of the claustrophobic or disinfectant aura of those houses of rest from the streets. He took great satisfaction in pointing out all the flowers lying this way and that in the breeze, tucking a wing away here, a petal there. "Kan ... Kan ... Ka ... Ka," he said with a hand describing his seaman's breast, swaying his arm like Queequeg poised to take the long fall with the harpoon, "I am Kanka." "What?" asked Alex fretfully, "what did you say?" "Name," he said with the same mattoid antics as before, "name is Kanka." "Oh," said Alex and we laughed and she understood this strange, radiant giant and her eyes lit up and she told him our names and he nodded his huge head firmly at each syllable and said both names with a gentle assurance, copying her Welsh pronunciation with an easy accuracy, his head cocked to one side as if he was listening to something far off.

Above our heads could be heard the children's voices and tiny feet padding over and back.

"The little one's awake. Come below. I have tea."

"Well, it's . . . ."

"Come."

Alex, fearing for her sanity, dug her nails into the back of my hand. Then she nodded.

We followed his great bulk down the herbal galaxy. He could scarcely fit between the bannister and the wall but hopped along nimbly enough, carrying his great weight with apparent ease. His child-cotton shirt round the armpits and down the small of his back was drenched with sweat and with his every movement, muscles turning to fat rippled the length of his body. On the ground floor, as we walked along a soft-coloured corridor, he stopped beside a plastic curtain hung from a short railing. "I show you what Kanka loves." He pulled back the curtain and there was a fresh, glowing shower room, complete with drape-like towels, back brushes and lilac soap. He sort of skipped into the shower and pivoting dextrously on his toes and heels, showed us how he scrubbed himself, giving off a pretence of girlish satisfaction at the feel of unseen water, his eyes shut, one little finger flicking imaginary soap out of his ear.

"Three, four times each night," he beamed, his breath tasting of pastilles.

He opened another door and we were met with a tremendous blast of heat and light, two immense oil furnaces ran the length of the room. He opened one of the furnace doors and gestured within to the frantic, sanguine balls of fire and he showed the thermometers and the brass fittings with an air of importance, brushing the pan pipes with his sleeve to bring up a shine. "My work." He sat into an enormous, swaying armchair filled with all kinds of soft, colourful cushions and talked while he drank from mugs he had placed on fine-woven Turkish mats. From a slender box underneath the table where the empty, bleached bones of a fish lay, he extracted a large envelope from which he in turn extracted an old mnemonic poster with loving care, which he carefully spread across the table. He wiped down the upturned corners, turning his head sideways and, with his fingers, imitating the falling of tears. On the poster was a picture of furnace-man Kanka, dressed in a loin-cloth with four leopard-skinned ladies on his shoulders in the shape of a pyramid.

A nurse led in a pale-faced, smiling child in pyjamas, who sat up on his knee.

"Since the war, yes, I spent thirty-one years here with the children, night after night. England has been kind to me. Before, I travel the world with the circus."

"Look," said Kanka secretively to the child and drew up his sleeve and flexed his muscle, a small foreign Christ in an oleograph behind his head, the bend of his arm a small bed for the child who nipped him on the stomach. Kanka closed his eyes, talking, turning in the flap of the canvas tent, the mad ponies from Ankara steaming after the run, the heavy lion-smell from the cages, the women who drank with him swinging out of danger, the Moroccan dwarf who sat on his knee like this tousled child and smoked kif, puffing away like a steamer, talking of Meknes and Fes and the cooling sherbet and a thousand others, nearly out of reach of his placid mind.

"The war, you see. Every night I am warm and wash." He shook his hand behind his back, imitating the action of the brush in the shower and . . .

"You must go now," he said, bitterly. "It's like lies, lies, lies."

Alex nervously jumped to her feet.

He and the child, aloft on his shoulder, left us to the back door where we climbed clumsily among the cold church-goers.

Leaving the lightsome hospital behind, Alex put her head on my shoulder and, crossing Denbigh Street, we could see the twin chimneys of Battersea power station belching their thick black smoke, the shadows scudding along the swollen Thames. So tired now, for we had not slept for days, livid in shirts and dresses. And Alex's legs had begun to give in, she seemed to somersault across the puddles with this last effort for a stranger's home. My legs felt lightweight. Still, we made it to the notorious house and climbed the stairs that seemed to lead off to the top of the sky. A key had been left for us. And I dropped it many a time, she watching with a glazed, distant look till I pulled the blinds down and sank into a man's wasted bed and suddenly the blessed sickness came on Alex, she bit into my arm, screaming into the old laundered bed, close friends knocked on the hastily-built walls.

Then, when the fit passed, she made me promise never to let her go because she knew that was what I wanted to hear. Now, back in normality, no dreams come, the future separates us.

Reprieve

They took a taxi out of Birmingham to their modest lodgings. She sat so silent, it seemed her mind had slipped from her. Peter paid the driver handsomely. Then he argued with her in the room. "There is still time to go back on this," he repeated. She held her silence. She undressed and got carefully into bed. He kept talking away, fretting, worrying her. At this last moment he had ceased being the most generous man in the world.

Yesterday she had had the final consultation with the doctor. "It seems," he said, "that you have your mind made up." Sheila said: "I have." "I see no reason then for any delay," he replied. She had got up and crossed to the door, counting every step, trying to appear a confident, mature strong woman. She must, she had thought, show him. At the door she fainted. She blamed the heat in the room. She said: "Don't take this for weakness or anything like that." The doctor nodded.

Tonight, this man here, her confidant and financial adviser and lover, was having his moral fidgetings. At long last it came, what had been building up in her all night. From the first anxious strain at her heart muscles, from all the days moving between the cottage and the town, now it would happen. The tears burst out, oh just burst out of her eyes, streamed away from her. They came from her loins and wrists, happy life-giving tears and, God, it took the agony out of the room. He tried holding her, thinking his advice had won her. She let him. Then, as the crying subsided, she said, "Look what you're doing! Your boots, ruining the white bedspread!" That his untidiness should strike her just then was unbelievable. To have cared for a strange bedspread in a strange house where she would only spend two nights! But why should he lie there, turning his boots into the bedspread, talking so manfully of choices and life and marriage?

Morning, he dropped her off at the hospital. She was the youngest in the ward. Most were married women of about forty who didn't want any more children. A doctor came and gave her a spectacular shot in the arm. He said, "This will relax you!" There were an awful lot of women being pushed to and fro, and she among them, in wheelchairs. You waited about in wheelchairs for your turn. They chatted there in the corridor, high as sparrows on the morphine.

At last, it was after a day, she was pushed in on a trolley to an amazing place she had never been before. There was the great light-orchestration of the operating theatre, and the doctors in their green outfits moving about talking quietly.

"I want to tell you something, doctor," she said. "You're awful nice, but that injection you gave me. It was very good. But, you see I'm mad awake!" She laughed and laughed. "What has you so happy?" he asked, filling a new syringe, so thin and fine against the round tubular lighting. Of course, all she looked at was his eyes to see if he was a man or a boy. She couldn't tell him, but the flesh between her elbows and shoulders flushed with giddiness and happiness. They pulled back her single white covering, "I hope," she said, as he again lightly tipped the pinprick into the crook of her arm, "that this one works."

Kelly

When he awoke Diane softened the wax in his ear with a kiss. He dressed in the wardrobe, with the door open and the mirror closed. The child was humming softly to himself like a violin searching for a mood. Later, Darcy edged away from everyone to write his diary.

> *March 3rd*
> *I have lived with faith yet never found its expiation. If I have discovered anything it is that life is bare and vital, embroidered by language and laughter, and still so quick that no image can satisfy or symbol call up all the longings. I am at least free of associations. Names have fallen away. The village people have become like shadows, like stains years old. Stains not of blood, for those are the city people walking the streets, alive and caricatured, but the village shadows are old friends, like decaying domestic matter.*
> *It is said that in the shadows hearts beat like the cheers of children greeting someone emerging from an underground station, the sudden stinging of sunlight and sky . . . .*
> *Enough.*
> *Enough.*

The previous year had been composed of two sounds for Darcy, lake-sound and city-sound, and as time passed the shadows merged but did not strengthen into something articulate and real. The birth of the baby had come with its attendant joys, but was forgotten with the same mediocrity with which his own birth was shelved, allowed slip into his subconscious to snap at him in conventional dreams, as if that reality counted for little. Alternatives and distinctions he found hard to make. His diaries, he felt, were full of a weak-minded subservience to emotional decay. Yet the blurred outlines of life provided a form of happiness. Off Shaftesbury Avenue, one night a week, he spent at the roulette tables playing the same number, red five. Friday and Saturday, Diane and himself and the child travelled to the races. He loved the sight of a two-year-old running into form and the fall of the chips on the green velvet tables. The roulette wheel became smaller as he won. His bets at the races were small, even if they disturbed the rations in his pocket, they hardly exacted any tribute from his soul. By day Darcy slept in the parks, bought newspapers which he read deeply, setting up for himself the panorama of the world with what perspectives he could conjure, but as he limited himself to reviews and features even his reading became a boring ritual, second-hand. Speeding on Sundays till his jaw locked, he never questioned the matter any further but lay back listening to his two sounds as they developed into shreds. Litter of all kinds filled the streets he walked in at night. In the vegetable markets the drunks sat by their steaming fires, eating bananas and tomatoes and the frosted leaves of cabbages till they curled up for the night by their dead fires, bottles upright or fallen beside them.

That night he waited at an Italian café off Wardour Street for the quarter-full bottles of lager the waiters left out with the rubbish. A glass could only take three-quarters. Here, on the hour, a stiff political drunk used to go. A coloured girl inside the café sniggered when she saw the two men. They sat on a step outside a Chinese supermarket and shared the bottles.

"This is your street?" Darcy asked.

"Yes. You could ask the police," the Pole told him.

They drank some more. The drunk poured his lager through his handkerchief into a paper cup.

"Perhaps I'm drinking your stuff?"

"In this country it does not matter," the older man nodded and together they squatted under the brightly-lit windows filled with white frozen fish and rice alcohol. Darcy knew that the Pole talked politics because he had heard him denouncing the crew that slept at Bishopsgate and when a Scotsman had threatened him, the Pole had wrenched a burning ember from the fire and whirled it. The argument had gone on all night with the rest shouting obscenities out of their sleep, though the two antagonists had seemingly parted without injury at dawn. Darcy asked the Pole about the night in question, but the man never answered. They broke cigarettes and rolled them in Trafalgar Square where they watched a film crew taking down their lights above the fountain. They shared names, Darcy being pronounced with a long "s" sound that the prayer people use in church for the whispered name of the recurring Jesus. The Pole shortened his name to Kelly. Kelly on this occasion was the dominant, cheerful personality. And Darcy felt a kinship based on a sense of turning from the righteous to the disendowed. Gaining enthusiasm he tried to bring up the older man's philosophy of socialism, but the Pole maintained, "It's firm promise we want, not utopia laced with vodka. Being a pauper does not make me a socialist, you know."

"I did not mean that."

"Do not use me as a ploy for criticism. Perhaps your individual ignorance will blind you."

But Kelly knew the merits of London, he named buildings and their owners with malice and confidence, as if the world were the size of a two-penny piece. His English was perfect except when he was aroused and then the verbs were half-checked by a foreign emotion. Darcy explained about the two sounds that troubled him and Kelly took his time until the whole matter was explained and then he, too, said he remembered fields and suchlike, but it was a long time ago. The industry, the material of the world, mattered as much to him now.

"I was a railway man and then a teacher. Even still I listen for whistles in my sleep, feel comfortable when a train passes. I like the railway yards, building sites, the sounds of a building growing, everything that I find half-buried in the ground that a man made, that he made to make something else."

"Do you mean archaeology?"

"No. No, I do not mean archaeology."

And then he asked Darcy for exact pictures of his heart's place, and nodded and nodded and questioned again.

After changing their minds many times they reached Kelly's house in a derelict row near Battersea. Her jaw was swollen out like a red head of lettuce and her upper teeth hung down threatening to pierce the awful, permanent swelling. She was drinking tea by the window when they entered. The Pole took off his coats and shirts immediately. He hung his socks out on the window ledge. Pigeons walked on a ledge opposite with their chests puffed out. They were seven stories up in a grey-bricked smoky morning and the tea was strong that the Yorkshire woman made. Lucy was her name. Despite her condition, her internal sympathies had not stopped – they had deepened. More tea was made. She spread the table again after cleaning up every crumb. Every few minutes another cigarette. Endless journeys into her bag. Time was compassionate yet irrational, what with the everyday complexity of news she used to read. All of four or five popular papers. Darcy had often seen her speaking to the Pole in the Labour Exchange in Victoria, carrying her six Woolworths' bags of odds and ends that she sorted out and arranged as she waited for her money. The officials treated her with humanity perhaps because she was an easy case to identify, checking her bags constantly for nuances, for relief. Kelly made soup from leeks and onions he had collected in the market, adding chunks of potatoes and carrots. Lucy cut bread and then read out the sporting pages of the *Evening News,* naming each horse that was running with a quiet, humorous wonder.

"Dark Sky, Wephen, Venus of Streatham," she said.

"No two horses, dears, with the one name," she said.

They slept on two sofas while she slept in a double bed the Pole had taken from downstairs when they'd broken in. Everything had been hauled upstairs, paintings, plants, old shirts, a breakfast cooker, Sunday magazines. The local social workers had come around to help them. Lucy laughed when they were mentioned, saying how sometimes they came up here and smoked dope and once Kelly had unwittingly left them in fits of laughter when he described the night he had been knocked over by a car, left for dead and come to soaked by a cloud-burst.

"The radical intelligentsia drive such cars," Kelly muttered at the end of her story.

They talked about Darcy's family from their various beds. "I'd like to have had a child," Lucy said, becoming serious, as if she had just realized it for the first time. But later Darcy was to discover that this was her way, each act of faith, of belief, even of memory, had to be relived time and time again, each gesture reaffirmed.

As they bedded down the metropolis was coming alive. The guilty were innocent again. "It's the creation of the artefact rather than its use enthrals me," whispered Kelly, "the will of the people to act in a certain direction." There was silence while Kelly collected his thoughts. "But sometimes socialism gained in theory through the competitiveness of its masters, rather than out of concern for humanity." He nodded, turned and slept. And the two sounds came back to Darcy. He wrote in the silence.

> *March 4th*
> *For the first time I understand that real tragedy is the sudden vision of unceasing humanity, unceasing nature. It could even be personal. It could even be optimistic. This man Kelly is very funny. An emaciated walk and a dry smile. Half the time he spends making up proverbs. If I remember properly, he said earlier: "The making of things is not a function of the things themselves but of the people who make them". He does not like the Irish. "One does not seek one's likenesses," he says. He says, "Where the working class is divided, where one half is nationalistic and religiously different from the other, then those that fight on either side are predominantly fascist. The Irish will not grow up. They*

want to be loved or feared, yet they will surrender their country eventually into the hands of the bourgeoisie." He makes it sound very easy and fatalistic and as if politics were to be taken seriously. Politics are shit. Don't I know.

The Pole slept with his eyes open and often the other man thought Kelly was looking at him even in his dreams and his stomach turned with fear at the paleness, lifelessness of the sleeping expatriate and before morning had passed he crept over on his hands and knees, first closed one lid, waited a while then shut the other, and after he crept back and fell asleep he was unaware that the older man's mouth had fallen open.

Darcy was crossing St James's Park the following afternoon to see his young wife. He was making sure that they would not argue, knowing that confrontations usually resolve in new patterns of uneasy co-existence. In a way, he knew his plight did not matter. The day was warm and everyone was relaxed. But inside him his mind hungered for politics, like all guilty emigrants. *How hastily drawn the mind is,* he wrote down below his piece of the night before, *How sober its sketches.* What he shared with his wife was a quiet desperation that no fantasy could sustain. He walked past Anne's Court, down Victoria Street, up Rochester Row past the military and police barracks, across Tachbrook Street Market and all the time he was thinking, repeating, stopping. It was getting darker and little lights caught the white-coated girls and straw-hatted men under the small stalls. Corsetry, wools, haberdashery. Seedless sultanas and green grapes. Shellfish and scampi. Delph sets, light blue and green with castles and small churches painted on them. Viennese whirls, chocolate delights and cherry delights. Tripe. Past the Duchess of Clarence.

Spanish voices mixed with English.

The cats of Pimlico were abroad among the vegetables and a kitten he had befriended once he saw slip, hold on to her step, as she walked a roof ledge four stories up. It seemed a shame that he could so easily identify with a kitten when there were a thousand human ghosts in whose limbs he could climb dangerously, look from their eyes, feel their hunger.

"Welcome home stranger," said Diane. She left him and the child together while she went shopping. The boy was dreaming a bit, letting little murmurs that she said resembled the "sky-goat", after the sounds of a snipe's wing. And it was just that sound, a sudden flurry from the side of a marsh, a bird-scuffle. She had that knack of naming those faraway sounds, not romantically, but exactly, finding their complement among their lives and it was her clear eye sometimes he envied. He stole from her secret place under the carpet a pound, and lifted up the child who had nearly begun to cry. They hung together in the room.

"Dadedadedada," he sang to his son.

"A measure of figs and barley," he sang.

The child looked up and frowned, he nearly had a personality his father could recognize. He pulled at his clothes and at his ear. Was what the child saw something of warmth, something of decay, a face that he might never focus on, that might never emerge from the half-light. The man saw the distance between himself and the child. The child like his wife was learning to live with a hypocrite, he thought, and then they moved together again and the boy murmured ah . . . aho . . . ahoahao-ahaooahhahoooooahahahahahahao . . . ah. He whirled his fists in the air and smiled. And frowned. The room was impeccable. Darcy lay on the bed with his son on his chest and felt for a few moments the warmth of lying in his own place. Diane had a new plant marked thistledown on the chest of drawers. The place had been like a discarded planet when they had moved in but now she was gaining confidence, they had cleared a bathroom, broke into a drawing room. When he stayed too much at home he shared his inertia, but while he stopped away things got done, the child grew.

When he kissed the child, he kissed his wife. The dishonesty lay on his side because he harboured thwarted

ambitions. Arguments abounded, as if too long had been
spent in interpretation without the satisfaction of creation. Or
it might have been because he loved both equally, that himself
and Diane transferred all their nervous energy through the
child, Lester.

Lester was a vehicle for their fear.

But the child, when he smiled, refuted all this.

"I can imagine a time," said Diane when she returned,
"when the two of you will be enemies of mine."

His son had fallen asleep across his chest and Darcy lifted
him, his head hanging lifeless, into the Victorian cot. "He is like
a postage stamp there among his blankets," Diane remarked.
Tiny pebbles of milk dotted the child's lips and Darcy wiped
them away before heading down into the street, intense with
afternoon sound, as if structure and movement had locked in
an anti-climax.

He read what he'd written down of Kelly's words.
"Everything at work in the factory complies with some known
law of the outside world, and was in existence previously
in Nature and in harmony with it. This, socialism would
preserve."

The Pole was on his hunkers in the Dole. He was rocking
gently on his soles. Darcy saw him through the window. They
did not greet each other. It was as if the Pole did not recognize
him. The queue reached out into the street, a mixture of actors
and actresses, the drunks and the poor. An hour passed before
he reached the inside of the office. Late spring rain began to
fall and the perplexed sleepers on the pavement and doorsteps
awoke and stumbled off into the park next to Scotland Yard
to find cover beneath the trees. Kelly was claiming that the
Exchange was stealing money from him. "Yes, you," he shouted
across the counter, his fists tight against his thighs. "You steal
my money, you bastard." The official withdrew with a smile.
Darcy cashed his giro in the post office and won an easy twenty
pounds in the bookies. He walked at the crowds, loving the
sense of flow, the endless human silence. Again. The Pole was

arguing with two policemen outside Scotland Yard. He could even have been asking them to arrest the official in the Dole. A young policeman was taking the argument seriously, much to the chagrin of his older companion. The young policeman shook his arms trying to restrain the argument of the stiff, small foreigner, who would walk off, return, and start all over, till the policeman turned eventually to a baffled American who was looking for directions.

Kelly strode angrily off into the rain.

Darcy followed at a safe distance behind him through the park. Kelly interrogated passers-by over simple things, leaving the complex alone. Kelly mad knew much more than Kelly sane. Darcy prepared what he would say to him when they met, but at each approach he faltered. What he meant to say became a ridiculous rhyme in his mind. Eventually, in the Mall, they met and the Pole was genuinely happy. They embraced a long time. They drank Valpolicella in the park. Throughout the summer. Sometimes the cold wet bit into their hands. Till eventually, gardeners, with their arses in the air weeded and rooted in the flowerbeds, while tractors circled, following the piles of leaves that were fed into cages drawn behind.

"What did I think?" Kelly was saying. "It's so. We had a great empire and were ready for dictatorship but other countries were quicker. Our revolution happened elsewhere, among our enemies. Our sense of Nationalism never happened so that Internationalism might follow."

"Then Ireland has a chance?"

"No. No chance at all."

Still, their friendship was sealed. And so began the process of learning for Darcy, a mixture of ambiguity and anger, the loss of guilt, a trimming of personal ambition. They moved about the city throughout the following months, picking up a day's work washing or serving in cafés on the Serpentine or hotels in Knightsbridge, sometimes arguing, sometimes drinking in silence. When Franco died they read the Spanish poets, when the rains came they sat up in the bandstand in St

James's Park conducting an imaginary choir, they buttressed the ends of sidewalks with a gang from Mayo, served food at a wedding in Brixton, and by the end of the winter Angola had risen, Rhodesia was beginning to tremble and Solzhenitsyn had visited England, complete with the laurels of Western policy. The workers' marches had begun earnestly in England and Russia had again taken its historical place as the threat in Europe, and looking back a hundred years on, as we look back a hundred years to slums and hunger, the historian will see how the slums have moved to the Third World out of harm's way, how hunger and recrimination increaseth. And at the mention of Stalin Kelly would break out into his own language with a merciless tirade. And in Northern Ireland people died under the same circumstances.

The pattern was complete.

And in November Darcy burnt his hand at a fireworks display.

December 2nd
Myself and Kelly got work today cleaning a number of Odeon cinemas. It means we will see four different films in a fortnight. With the money we will eat well at Christmas.

Sometimes Diane and the child accompanied the two men on their trips, as did Lucy. When the two women met for the first time it had proved frightening. It was the night himself and the Pole got drunk in Piccadilly and had arrived back to his wife's squat in the small hours, dragging Lucy reluctantly along. His wife was asleep when they arrived. They tiptoed about the room. Kelly kissed the child repeatedly, amazed by the sudden surprised looks, Lester blinking in the sudden light at night, the hand thrown, the legs askew, watching the stranger till the end with the contemplation of a child. When Diane awoke and saw the Yorkshire woman sipping Guinness at the bottom of her bed, she buried her head beneath the blankets. When she had properly woken, they were reconciled and Kelly gave a long and garbled speech. And after Lucy had fallen asleep, Kelly stood a long time in the moonlight looking down on the ruins each side of them, talking quietly to himself, as if he underestimated Darcy, and then he lay down while they turned over their good luck in their minds.

But over the months Darcy succeeded in owing a lot of money. And though everyone disapproved, still he gambled at roulette and racing, and his debts grew larger. It was something crept up on him. His notes and diaries remained untouched and now his dreams were of winning, of breaking even, of leaving gambling aside. But each morning his nerves resolved and the game began again in earnest. Diane cooked extraordinary meals each evening and they prepared to go down in style, Kelly, Lucy and themselves. Each took turns to feed the child. And each imagined fearful diseases they could catch from each other and everyone feared for the child because he suspected no one, but thrived among the crowds in the kitchen.

Through time the lakes and fields that once existed were forgotten, the park, a peremptory pause between buildings, as Darcy moved from tension into conflict.

It took only meeting a distraught Kelly in the park to defuse Darcy's enthusiasm. The older man's nose was running, but he had an answer, "Everyone thinks they see my weak side opposed to my strong side, against my will, in fact it is with my will, my whole being spurs me on."

The last day they spent in the park the air was hard and sharp, the water covered by a white cloud of seagulls and among them the green head of a duck, the black compact body of a waterhen. The unlit lights over the bridge hung down in the fading daylight like blue leaves. Yet in the sombre unreal air Darcy was full of a tremendous enthusiasm, his heart sang. Now that he had nothing he had allayed his sins, the poor were his family. At first he had only dimly understood, but now the old selfish haunts of his psyche had been exorcized and his despair was no longer self-perpetuating. Darcy's need to understand and the need to contribute may have been what depressed Kelly, but Darcy continued, "Of course I have doubts." He saw that this new political consciousness gave a certain security, especially in London, that could not be tested. He was begging Kelly for praise. For theirs was a type of intimacy not easily entered into, a sarcasm that severed Darcy from his old personal wounds yet frightened the vanity of his individual soul. But his old comrade was drunk. "I'm not quite the happier emerging communal spirit today," he said. Darcy was aware of the drumming of veins across the back of his comrade's hands. Over the past few weeks Kelly's drinking had increased, he had been growing impatient and this afternoon's walk was shorter and tenser than ever before.

It was as if they suspected each other of insincerity, as if their companionship had been merely neutral and intellectual.

For the first time Darcy found himself alone and his mind was blank.

"We could travel," Diane said. "It's time for travelling."

"We have no money. The child's too young."

"What's wrong with you is you're bored. When people are bored they are destructive. You could go off by yourself."

But the thought of travelling alone frightened him.

The following day the Pole disappeared and nothing was heard of him for a fortnight. Darcy searched the streets by night and the Yorkshire woman joined him one fearsome winter's night when the heavens had burst. The rain dampened and opened one of her bags so that all those treasured papers spilled in a line behind them, as if to say that things would never be the same again. A couple of weeks later he received a note from Kelly.

> *Dear fellow Catholic,*
> *I am recuperating here. The drama of the people is every-*
> *where. Each day I think of the turning of matter into*
> *an element and its history is like a great poem. We are like*
> *earth, water, air, fire. My body is not so quick so I shall take*

my time here. It is warm and comfortable and my brother's
pills keep me amused. Give my love to Diane and Lester.
      Yours, J. Kowaleski

PS You probably expected me to be in a madhouse – that
would suit your romanticism.

Darcy immediately crossed London to the suburbs where
Kelly's brother kept a transport café. He bought a coffee and
sat down among the lorry drivers and security men. They
talked horses.

After his third coffee he asked for Kelly. The woman directed
him to a hospital that lay up the road from the café, set in
its own elaborate grounds. It was not grey like city hospitals,
but newly painted with yellow and green and surrounded by
intricate shrubbery and cane plants and gravel paths that led
hither and thither across the lawns. His enthusiasm forbade
him to think, for would they not embrace each other as of old.
In the foyer he imagined he heard the cry of the "sky-goat."
A nurse explained that Mr Kowaleski was a day patient and
was out walking. Minutes later Kelly was led into the clinical-
smelling waiting-room and they embraced. They walked out
onto a broad glass-covered terrace where patients in pyjamas
and nightgowns were talking and looking down the lawns,
complaining softly to each other with terrible intimacy.

The heat in the enclosure was intense, although outside it
had already begun to snow.

"Look," said his comrade, "I am lucky. And behind that
hill there is a library and down that path a pond."

But Darcy was shocked by the mad lifeless gleam in
the Pole's eyes. It reminded him of the night his eyes had
remained open while he slept, like cracks that opened to
nowhere. Death was closer here than on a battlefield, yet
Kelly cajoled and talked and joked. When he coughed at his
own mirth he turned away. Through the hospital seemed to
flow all the treason, all the tragedy that man could encompass.

"This is my friend Darcy," he said, imitating his Irish accent and the patients shook hands with him. "To the nurses here I am a healthy man so you must say nothing," he whispered as they left for the café. "I like to laugh and talk with them and give no cause for fear." They drank two glasses of wine with his brother, who never spoke but looked continually at the ground as Kelly joked with him, and later Darcy left for town, drinking all the way, and arrived home, dead drunk.

> *April 5th*
> *Kelly is not mad, he is just invulnerable. His apparent sickness has left me with a long way to go. The distance frightens me. I am aware how I clung to him when he wanted me to let go. It was to guard myself. Now I am aware of this disorder, I can become an equal and a friend. Next I must free Diane. The absence of a god makes my heart lighter.*

When the next note arrived from Kelly a few days later he put off the moment of reading it till he arrived under the great wall of scaffolding that cramped St James's Park underground station. Warmth came up from under the footpath. He was sad knowing purity was impossible. And was purity important anyway? Was purity not a lack of knowledge or non-acceptance of change and growth? What was important was the encountering of demands greater than one's limitations. A sense of purpose. But what saddened him most was the personal defence mechanism that destroyed a relationship so newly born.

Above him the traditional Greek music of building went on. First a hammer sounded, an engine roared and these were answered by a gong inside the building, a crane swung by in silence, huge buckets opened with a crash into a dumper, pigeons flew by in silence, a yell, taut wires screamed and hauled a load of concrete overhead while he sat watching, gazing, and painters inside were painting the walls a deep office-grey, while the great sheets of cellophane that covered the building tossed in the wind, flapping like a soul trapped by temporary materials.

At last he opened the letter.

> *Dear fellow Catholic,*
> *This Christmas five years ago my neighbours were gunned down in the shipyards of Gdynia. I pray for them now. What I hate most is how the young live off the old, it drains me of strength. How they make images and likenesses of themselves. Watch now for the blackbirds in the park for this is their time of year. We are timeless. In Poznan in 1956 the workers hung the militia men from the lamp-posts, lynched them, or in Gdynia flung them into the sea. It will happen all over again. All the things I have told you can be found in our literature. I have no drink for three days. I am sick but not dying and perhaps will see you again on my return. Give my love to Lester and Diane.*
> *Yours, J. Kowaleski*
>
> *PS I dream continually of women.*

Betrayal

This man and woman, he in his late thirties and she in her early twenties were lying behind a tuft of thistles and weeds, a small raised place, alongside the river. They lay away from the village towards the lake. Waterhens moved quickly from them as they kissed and went out of sight by the reeds, and then appeared again, moments later, swimming easily without haste. The man was coughing and the woman was kissing his chest. When he turned on his back there was sky, so abnormally huge and filled with colossal movement of blue and white that no vertical could last there but must burn itself out before a straight line could ever be righted. She, and then he, changing position, looked into the earth. Hoofprint and daisy. She accepted the burning thistles at her back. He looked around once in fear of being seen.

This man and woman were driving aimlessly along until they came to a village. He took her around. She was perfectly natural and quiet among the people. In the house of the postmistress she talked little which attracted attention. He wondered, as the son of the house spoke with nostalgia of the past, how much he loved her. For surely he must love her? He had no need to invent anything to protract their time together, the truth became like the act of imagination, reaching right out of their lives, till only what mattered was separated. What they bridged flowed freely beneath them – it was great for him to be with such a person. He took her down a river he knew. First to show her the separation of the two lakes under the eighteenth-century bridge. On one side brown trout were kept from coarse fish on the other. Now the dangerous dam was outdated, yet still held the two powerful waters from each other. The second lake had since been cleared for trout, but in the deep waters the coarse fish still persisted. Trout now danced on both sides. The couple kept walking out to the mouth. Not a long journey, sufficient to point out all that happened as a child, cows eating swimmers' clothes and the coldness of river water. They lay away from the village that they might not be seen. Ducks fled them. A pike ran out of the new, deep, muddy water by the reeds.

This man and woman talked of their worries. Then they stopped talking because of the indulgence and the emptiness. They were not drawn to this place. The act of walking together, bit by bit, brought them closer to a small slight place in time. A fearful human place. Their situation, outside of these few moments together, appeared impossible. She slipped into mud hastening in the wrong path after him, just like a trusting young girl. The entire river was filled with the smell of new-mown hay; no trees sheltered the path and approaching the mouth a dry cold wind blew in over desolate bad land. They lay in the ugliest place. They felt each other not with abandon or passion or discovery, but slowly, fearfully, treasuring. Neither did they make love, for the inner tissues of her vagina would cling coldly to his weak penetration. Nor could they satisfy their need of being swept away, from the dam and the separation, to the mouth and the open sky. But they kissed and held each other gratefully, and returned singly, though they would have loved to hold hands throughout this village, along the banks, amidst the people.

This man and woman were bound and exposed to others. The man was coughing and the woman kissed his chest. He kissed her childless breasts. They looked down to the blonde lip of the vagina, the thin red lip of the penis. Desire passed through their hands, each to the other. Yet nothing happened and nothing drove them away. He was impatient and she was eager. She was waiting on him in a traditional manner, till he might break with his responsibilities, as he before in a previous but continuous life, with a different woman, had broken with other social decrees. Hurrying, she said he would stop as he was. And he thought he would leave, but going meant leaving everyone, even her.

He satisfied himself this way, and would not be betrayed.

Love

Her house was a half-hour's walk away, time when anything might happen, up one of the many steep hills at that side of the city.

As he climbed, forgetting places the minute he passed them, he arrived at one house with bright lights on in the living room. Books were piled on pine shelves from ceiling to floor and a newly varnished table sat in the middle of the room. The room was empty. Whoever they were, they didn't care except for cleanliness. But a few streets away someone was playing a record loud enough for him or her to own their own house. That was marvellous too. To be able to cross your own floor without fear of tomorrow. The houses were modern, each piled lower than the next, with little lawns, and sometimes two cars in the driveway, parked hurriedly, and odd times a motorcycle, the front wheel swung sideways and the pillion gleaming with dew.

Also in many of the rooms people were reading upside down.

The rooms had that look, the blinds drawn half-way and the light low enough to be beside the bed, the atmosphere concentrated as the reader pored over the pages and his shadow drifted across the ceiling like something constant, so that he might be living anywhere in the world, looking back on himself from above.

He stood in the gateway opposite the house and looked up at her window.

Soon, he sat up on the pier, enjoying the sensation of leaving the pull of the earth behind, and he began to coax her out of bed, into her clothes, through the thin bedroom door, down the stairs quietly.

He looked at the door, willing it to open.

The door did not open.

But the old house swayed on its foundations like a single man drunk in a crowd of men desiring a woman. It swayed like that a long time and would not settle.

Next, he stood on the pier, gently balanced there, as if he might reach the same level as herself.

He thought of her, warm and comfortable among the dry sheets, looking at the ceiling, waiting on her house to grow still. Just now she would be slipping out of the heavy cotton nightdress that came to her ankles. Searching in the dark for a clean pair of knickers. Pulling them over her warm cheeks so that they nestled around her groin like a soft loving hand. The skin stretched between her shoulder blades. Next, she pulled the knitted dress over her head and tugged it down about her back, swivelling her hips till it fitted. The boots and the white socks. Looks behind her, taking along her brother's oilskin coat and, maybe, a flower-patterned toilet bag. Across the landing, her father stirs in his sleep on the sitting-room couch. She approaches the door on tiptoe. Jimmy waited anxiously.

But the door did not open.

The street remained quiet. Nothing moved. He walked up and down.

The night swelled up like something about to burst and as day descended he confused the contours of the window and the door, then the house became the same as the others in its terrace as the sun branded the new day on the loose curtains.

Finally he ran down the hill at half-five, past the solitary workers climbing from the poorer areas below in their donkey jackets, with innocent, bad-tempered faces. The cleaning ladies letting themselves into the insurance offices turned to look out through the glass doors before they began their work, as if obliged to go over the paths that took them there. But their leader, who was deaf and dumb, had already begun; she lashed out at the first step, while her laughing conversation with herself echoed all the way up to the seventh floor, returning like a tribal memory. He caught his breath outside his home and went in, sure of his terrible crime, and yet he went on counting until he had reached a figure that would redeem him. The bed was so cold that it seemed like a deserted ship in which monkeys travelled, but lying there he did not feel misery or loneliness, but planned ahead for the next time, telling himself that tomorrow night she must come.

Frank kept shouting from the street below, "Come on, mate, get up," his hand pressed to the horn. The boy sat into the Transit and said nothing as the remorseless drive through the caged roadways began. "Are we in love?" Frank asked, laughing. "Leave it out," said Jimmy. "Nothing I like better than driving straight at the bastards," said Frank. Once they started working Jimmy was not too bad, for his enthusiasms multiplied without his knowing, but after a dinner of chops and mushrooms in the transport café, he stretched out his legs so that they were filled with warm tired blood and he fell asleep with a grown-up sigh in the green, wooden chair. "Bloody hell," he heard Frank saying, "are you off again?" "I'm not sleeping," said Jimmy, irritated, without opening his eyes, "I was just thinking, like." "Oh yeh," replied Frank, who then, finding something suspicious in the eyes of a lorry driver at the next table, forgot all about Jimmy, turned aside and sang along with a record he hardly knew.

Somehow or another Jimmy got through the day.

But they had problems, Frank and his apprentice.

For while the timber was prised along the levels of the old walls, the spirit level continually called for more adjustment and as they hauled the hardboard onto the roof, they left behind them a trail of asbestos slates that must be mended. He kept Jimmy at it so that they could finish early, and gave him the easy jobs, like stacking the unused wallboard under the rainproof sheets in the valley of the club house where he could look over the tennis courts, cricket fields and bowling greens to Highgate Hill, and each time he looked he turned to Frank and the two would stop working.

"It's weird, isn't it?" Jimmy would ask.

"What's that?"

"I'll go up there and she mightn't come the next time either."

"I hope for your sake she does," then Frank dropped the lead soundlessly onto the path, looked at it and said: "A man is always exaggerating what he don't know."

They resumed work and Frank skated along the ledge, his hammer hopping off his thigh and his hands searching, like a stall lady's, in his leather apron for the proper pins.

Strange thoughts on the edge of sleep entered Jimmy's head as he waited in his room. Sometimes he found himself speaking across to Frank in his dead father's language. Though Frank was twice his age, in this fantasy they were equals in age and experience, so Jimmy had no fear of telling the truth and Frank, for his part, was devoting a lot of time to listening to Jimmy, who was telling him a way out of certain difficulties, same as they might be seeking to seal a joint or to find the best way to let the tension in their planks carry a dead weight of material away and beyond what appeared possible.

In this talk a great deal of responsibility rested easily on Jimmy's shoulders, and when he realized himself again, he would have dearly loved to talk, talk yards, for Frank was reluctant to leave go of him.

Eventually though he put on his corduroys and a T-shirt that didn't fit him.

He fondled the pay packet in his pocket, saying, I have control again.

This time he took his torch and, because of the message instilled in him by the imaginary conversation with Frank, he stopped outside his mother's door. She was snoring in a faraway lonely fashion, troubled by the hot night, sounding as if she had fallen asleep too suddenly to retain any of her memories. Her door gave way to his touch, and he looked carefully in to see that the single sheet had slipped off with her continuous turning. Her breasts and groin were like those of another, younger woman who took her place when night fell.

He withdrew quietly, like an intruder, put the torch in his knapsack and slipped out into the street. Tonight the streets were more alive, the Indian shops smelt of cardamom and the supermarkets of hosed-down floors and every so often he met groups of three or four people ghosting along, very sure of themselves, as if there was great safety in numbers.

"Rassholes," he whispered to himself.

At the bottom of the hill, he passed a house where a party was still on.

Here the woodwork was aged and slanted and the house itself seemed to tilt towards the road because of the hundreds of plants on the off-angle sills. He waited to see would anything happen, but the room where the repetitive music was playing was in darkness, except for the thin glow of joints, and in the room above the party a woman passed over and back with a baby at her shoulder, and he waited until the woman had found relief for the child, losing himself for the first few minutes of another's distress, then he went up the wandering footpath, under the little bridges, through the tunnels, up the rows of steps till behind him the lights went around the face of the city, lighting up what was immediately beneath their steaming lamps.

He looked back to see how far he had come and it wasn't far.

He looked especially along the houses each side of him, but this part of the hill was dark.

It was only the old and retired lived here.

You could tell by the broken gates and the absence of cars, and by the care given to the vegetables growing in neat lines, onions and cabbages, where elsewhere there were easy lawns. By the windows, heavily protected with curtains, the gnomes nestled in the overgrown shrubbery. And sometimes a face appeared at a window that may or may not have been there, cringing at the stupidity of the mysteries left from the universe they started with, just a second ago.

The moon was held by a firm hand over the village. He looked up with a catch in his throat. The white curtains were pulled in her room, but next door, in her brother's room, the light was on. This was it, Jimmy said to himself. She is waiting on him to go to sleep. He sat on the wall opposite laughing to himself. I've made it, he said, shaking his head. He never took his eyes off her brother's window. He could tell by the sense of the room that people were up there walking around, but now he wished tiredness on them, it was half-four in the morning. The light went out. Then the front door was opening. He jumped over the wall, stretched out on the grass and waited, the pulse beating in his wrist like a cyclist's foot. Someone shouted goodnight, then footsteps crossed over to where he was. He hugged the wall. The steps continued alongside where he lay and went down the hill. He looked up. The house was in darkness. Now, he thought.

He gave three sharp bursts of the torch.

Waited.

Searched the windows and the door. Again. Nothing. He shone the torch into his face for a full five minutes, throwing all caution to the wind, expecting at any minute some strange hand to descend on his shoulder. He switched the torch on full and turned his face upwards to her window, so that his features became distorted and appeared like those of an old man, who, starting with his eyes, was slowly becoming transparent. When he switched off the torch he could see nothing for ages, but heard only his own voice reciting numbers in a nightmarish fashion.

The street was spinning away from him.

He rubbed his eyes in panic, but when his normal sight returned, her house was as it had always been and now, earlier than last night, becoming part of the terrace again. The morning traffic started to thunder into the city limits and stray voices shouted from room to room their indifference to the watcher in the street below.

For the first time he dreaded failure.

That he might take the easy way out. Let all these objects pile up to infinity so that he might have no power over them.

He saw nor heard anything on the descent. The street off the Holloway Road was scattered with debris from the night before. The skips full of rubbish and the leavings of parties. Not without caution he entered the house, then darted under the stairs when he heard someone moving above. His mother was talking to his sister. "Where is he?" she was saying. "What?" asked his sister in a sleepy voice. "He's not in his bed, I tell you." Jimmy pulled off his clothes and bundled them out of sight. He tousled his hair, and with a perpetual yawn went up the stairs in his vest and Y-fronts.

His mother was returning from his sister's room when she saw him. "Oh," she said and pulling her housecoat about her disappeared in the recesses of her bedroom, as if nothing had happened.

Jimmy slipped down and brought up his clothes.

And lay a long time looking at himself above, while in their various beds his family found more comfortable positions, sighed and tried to forget about everything. Jimmy tried to drown out the selfish complaints of his sister's boyfriend, who had been woken in the rumpus and wanted to know what was happening. His complaints called up an image of something becoming less than it should be. He did not dislike the man for himself but for the burden he brought to bear on his sister, and Jimmy blamed her for the weakness in not waiting to take someone who would have given her the pleasure she craved. But soon their voices stopped, their complaints became echoes and the boy had the tired morning to himself. That was strange, too, how short the distance to her unfriendly house was becoming. It was nearly as if it were next door, only a wall separating them, if you came down to it. He turned to the wall, his two fists hugging his rib cage and steeled his mind from other things till he could see her cross to the window, you must be doing that now, just now, Oh my Lord, push the curtains aside and search the street for him, yet not see him though he was there, Here, over here, he whispers, then she goes up onto her toes so that the nightdress rises a fraction, looks off to her left, he runs into her line of vision but she looks through him again, then suddenly his mother interrupted from next door, "Go down and pay the girls, James, man dear. Right?" And then, anticipating her dead husband's reply, she continued in a soft sympathetic manner, "Ah, but they are worth it, James, they are worth it," and, greatly pleased that he was back again, she lifted him up like an infant into her arms.

Jimmy woke with a heavy headache from hunger and a sense of having slept through many crises. The house was empty. They were at the sale-of-work in the church opposite looking for bargains. The TV was on. The pot of stew simmered away, its grey fat having come to the surface with bubbles of paprika and parsley. He peeled the bag of sweet blue potatoes and left them ready in a bowl of water. Ate some Weetabix and treacle. Looked around the hot, shimmering garden.

He could concentrate on nothing and his heart kept pounding away so that it wasn't easy.

Madge's boyfriend came in.

"You were all in good voice last night, as usual," he lisped.

"I'm sorry," replied Jimmy, speaking for them all, "I can't help it."

"Yeh, we are living in a hen house."

Jimmy sat there hoping Stan would not start on about women, but still he could not bear to leave the kitchen, afraid that what he had might be suddenly taken from him. Stan liked to talk to Jimmy about sex, because the boy would grow perplexed and inferior. He thought he would soon break down the boy's reserve. He wanted to kill that look of fear in the boy's eye, stamp out that stupidity by talking of all the obscenities he could conjure up. But what really drove him to these excesses was Jimmy's untroubled affinity with the women of the house, and the pleasure the boy took in their company, meaning, Stan reckoned, that the boy was dependent, would never know women and maybe grow to hate them.

"Look at them motorcycles go," said Stan.

Then, Madge and her mother came in carrying two pairs of Tesco bags. Madge had got two scarves, a tartan skirt, some old-fashioned bead necklaces and four striped pillow slips. "What do you think, Jimmy?" she asked, holding the skirt to her waist. "It's good," said Jimmy.

"Get out of the light," complained Stan.

"Will you like me in this?" she asked Stan.

"I'd like you," he laughed, "no matter what you were in."

After dinner, Uncle George arrived.

His hair was brilliantined and he was in his finest blue serge. He had that enthusiastic Saturday-night air about him which everybody in the house knew so well, and two library books for his sister-in-law which he slapped on the table, tapped them with his finger and quickly told the story of each, though none could follow him. Stan showed him the new freezer. Uncle George said he had found a place where you could buy meat for bargain prices in Kentish Town, then, "Peggy," he said, before he could be further drawn, "I'll need the lad tonight, the cursed guards are becoming a menace," and before she could reply, he went on about the outrageous cost of the boat back to Ireland, and his remonstrations against public bodies carried such weight that his intrusion into his sister-in-law's private life was forgotten, so that she nodded absentmindedly and lay back on the cushions of the settee, the way Jimmy loved her to lie, stretched out in a comfortable position from which to view her family, till Uncle George slapped his thighs and kneaded his hands, saying, "We'd best be off," and Madge and Stan saw them to the door in order to see whether the car would start, and for their pleasure Jimmy opened the door to let his gross uncle enter, slammed it shut and walked around the car with a soldier's bearing, then drove off with his right hand raised in a posh farewell.

On the trip to the Feathers, as always, Uncle George found it necessary to turn from his entertaining self into a responsible crank, belittling his sister-in-law for staying behind closed doors. "It can't be good for her, you know," as if going up to the Feathers with him would somehow extend her life, but turning into the car park, his uncle relaxed from this meaningless tirade, gave Jimmy a wholesome nudge, and said, "Ah, never mind me."

And then, "I'll look after you after." He took the long way round.

When Uncle George was inside drinking, Jimmy sat in the car listening to the radio.

Sometimes on a night they might drive to five pubs, picking up more passengers as they went on, for Uncle George only braved company because he could not drink alone, and the drunken men in the back would praise Jimmy's driving and George's reasoning, a pair who could so well spite the law of the land, and they talked of the barmen as if they were close relations, fathers and mothers to them, the best or the worst in the world, and other brave talk while the nights shortened and their sons grew.

"What more could I ask," Uncle George would happily maintain, "than to have my own chauffeur?"

In the Feathers they were playing tunes that Jimmy could not remember.

Outside, somebody stepped it out, enunciating in clear Italian cockney his story from the Bible. "In my house, yes sir, there are many mansions," then the speaker strode along in an easy but determined manner, telling what the Lord says, and encountered without stopping those coming in the opposite direction, his clean boots striking the pavement in a kind of joy, he swung across the street, looking up at the shop fronts to see where he was and went on.

"Right, lad, the Indians," said Uncle George at closing time. He was tilting towards Mecca and accompanied by a blonde woman of about forty, with washy brown skin, whose ailment in her back was now forgotten.

Uncle George stuffed a fiver in Jimmy's lap and kissed him full on the lips. Jimmy drove to the Holloway Road and stopped at the café where the pair bought Ceylon hot mutton curries and cold lagers to take away. Then he drove them to the block of council flats where his uncle had a bachelor flat on the fifth floor.

"It's a roof over my head," Uncle George explained.

"Won't it do you?" she joked.

They did not move for a few moments but sat in silence, looking out each side of them.

"Make sure," his uncle said, banging on the roof of the car, "that you bring her back tomorrow, matey, in one piece."

"Shut it, Georgie," said the woman. She searched in her bag as if its oddments never ceased to surprise her. Then, finding nothing else, she pressed a Mass card for her dead brother into Jimmy's hand. The black, tiny photograph smelt of old perfume. "He was the spit of me," she whispered, as if to find some reason for what she had done. Some people were like that, Jimmy knew. He reversed the car, turned and shot by his uncle who, with a bewildered grin shouted, "Tomorrow," then let go with a long whistle between his finger, thumb and lip that echoed across the concrete playground, then the two stood side by side under the dilapidated floors waiting on the urine-smelling lift to descend.

Madge and Stan were lying on the living-room carpet watching the end of the late night film. The sight of them together looked so false that a feeling of nervous sickness attacked Jimmy's stomach and he sought to escape, with that desperate knowledge that all ways led back here, among relationships he had no place in.

Stan got up and putting his arm around the boy, he led him into the hall.

"Here," he said, taking Jimmy's hand, "go on, further down. Now that's what's keeping your sister happy."

"That's what you think," answered Jimmy.

"It embarrasses you, doesn't it?"

Jimmy looked away.

Madge nodded to him cheerfully out of the coloured daze around her and said goodnight. He stood a few minutes trying to get the story of the film, his heart parched with terror, then went upstairs. His mother came into his room, tidied away his clothes, perched his boots by the unused fireplace and then, sitting on the edge of the bed, she watched him.

"Did he make a show of himself?" she asked.

"No," he answered.

"Was your Uncle George off with another woman?"

"No, Mama."

"You sure, boy?"

"Yes."

"Yes," she complained softly, shaking out a shirt and folding it over twice, "I don't want the whole world knowing while I remain ignorant."

"No."

Jimmy could see the distorted jealousy, combined with worry, on her face.

"There was no one," he lied, "I promise you."

"Join them," she said to herself, "they're on both sides." Then standing with her back to him in the doorway, holding the knob in one hand and tracing the side wall with the other, she spoke without turning around, "Who is that downstairs?"

"Madge and Stan, that's all."

"Oh, yes, Madge and Stan," she repeated with terrible tenderness, then closed the door quietly behind her.

The warm kitchen floor was alive with beetles when he walked across it barefooted to steal a drink from the fridge. He took a can of Goya Nectar from the shelf where it sat beside the transparent red snappers, and drank till it flooded his ears. The birdcage was covered by the green curtain and he thought of the cockatiel inside standing up asleep, her head, with its stiff yellow feathers and red bruises, under her tossed wing, like his mother upstairs. He let the car roll, started it in second and drifted down. And because he was alone, he became disorientated, so what should have come to him naturally had to be planned and foreseen.

By seeing the end of the journey before he had begun, all his excitement was lessened, as if he had passed a certain stage in his life that dissipated all that had gone before. The Renault groaned as it climbed the hill to Highgate. He grew terrified of the noise and had to stop, bringing the driving seat forward so that he might have better control of the pedals.

Then the car refused to start.

So, finally, he started in reverse, drove smoothly by her house, turned in the village and stopped high over the city, facing the car back down the hill.

Her house was again in darkness, but there was a veiled light at the bottom of the front door. He did not look up at her window, nearly as if he had forgotten her. Instead he undid the gate and went up the gravel path. The front door was ajar, and from a room further on in the hallway he could hear everyday voices. They were talking about sport and animals. But it was the smell from within the house that made him stop there on the straw mat. He breathed it in, over and over, and looked up the narrow stairs to where her room was, tasting the strangeness and the flickering of shadows along the landing. He thought of her above and what she would think of him were he to enter now and noiselessly ascend from step to step. But he did not move, for whatever happened she must come down of her own free will. He stood there. Then stepped out again and without hesitation pulled the door to behind him. He closed the gate. He looked up at her room. And the more he looked up, the more he became aware of the light in the room, but now he did not know whether it was from outside coming in, or inside coming out. He sat into the car.

And in the silence, like a river about to overflow its banks, he began counting again, so that each number might somehow raise a buttress against the flood that raged about his senses, threatening, with its lusts and jealousies and self-pityings, to sweep him before it across useless places, and he spoke the numbers out loud so that if anyone came they would pass by, knowing he was counting the shapes that fevers leave behind on walls and ceilings, on cars and houses, where shadows no longer reflect the lines of real objects but discard them for the imagined and the unknown, and so he began to unburden himself by mouthing the numbers at the image he held of himself, that it might disappear and, returning with a merry intelligence, admit to the existence of a world other than he had known, where the loved one would always be free of the lover.

So down there on the left, leaving identity aside, is eight thousand, no hundreds and fifteen, somewhere, there above, eight thousand, no hundreds and sixteen, eight thousand, no hundreds and seventeen, eight thousand, no hundreds and eighteen, eight thousand, no hundreds and nineteen. The man above, eight thousand, no hundreds and twenty. The seagull below, eight thousand, no hundreds and twenty-one. Eight thousand, no hundreds and twenty-two, eight thousand, no hundreds and twenty-three, eight thousand, no hundreds and twenty-four, he rested his head on the steering wheel, hey what are you doing there, man, and now we have another voice, goodnight, eight thousand, no hundreds and twenty-five, and then, what came to his mind next he knew to be wrong and he searched in panic each side of the number in his head for the right one, up and down the scale of all he could remember or see, but once lost, it went adrift and could not be found.

He could not recognize the place where he was.

So, he must start all over.

There was no light in her room. She had not come out the door.

He panicked, began counting, and this time, so that he

might not forget where he was, he started on all the animate things he could see, those that could be identified and those that could not, so that his counting might have some reason, but he refused the number of times he thought he saw her appear by the window or the door, for that was foolishness, some numbers were not for counting, and he no longer mouthed the figures in rhyme but at irregular intervals, leaving out sometimes whole centuries; and when he arrived back at random among the tens of thousands, and when he knew everything to be seen in Highgate, from the magnolia spots on plane leaves to the terracotta slates on a stranger's house, the insipid blur of a horse descending behind the elephants, the massive drones of the bull elephants that could have come from a boat on the distant Thames, he allowed the figures to slip away into his consciousness where the counting could continue unabated but without his constant care, and finally, he consigned the crack of light, where her door had stood ajar and he had entered, to his mind, the last sane item and bearing the highest number he had yet reached, then as that last chance receded into forgetfulness, he stopped counting so abruptly that everything lost its shape for a long time to come.

Madge was sitting at the bottom of the stairs when he returned, her head gripped tightly in her hands as if she had suffered some unbearable fright. When she saw him she tried to hide, grow smaller, if that was possible, so he sidestepped her, not wanting to breach her loneliness. "Ah, well, see you later, then," she called, and reassured by his presence, with her arms crossed, she hopped up the high steps after him.

The Tenant

It was one of those cold Sunday mornings when dismissed Christians came home swiftly from Mass and only packs of good-natured dogs roamed the streets, jumping out on unsuspecting cars.

The heady smell of dinner drifted out through the shutters of the old colonial hotel. The drapes were drawn across an excess of windows that looked down on bleak shopfronts and indifferent private houses. Because of the lack of stimulus from without, the Swanns had filled the foyer and lounge of the hotel with hoards of comfortable retreats and the walls with pictures of streams, rivers and wild life.

The single-roomed bus station was perched down by the real polluted river. The clerk left the *Sunday Independent* cartoons aside when the 12:30 arrived from Dublin, and he and the saloon taxi drivers gathered around the front of the bus.

Here, in a cold February of the 1960s Mr Franklin stepped down, skirted the offers of the taxi drivers and, changing his two cases from hand to hand every few yards, headed towards the hotel.

In the suburbs, Mr Johnson, lately returned from England, lived with his wife and two sons. He had built the two-storey house himself, plastering the porch with seashells, but gave outside contracts for the plumbing and electricity because he did not want to invite any enmity from those trades. For the first six months after the house was completed he had worked as a petrol pump attendant then moved on to a nice quiet number as a day porter at Swann's Hotel. Everyone believed that Johnson had a fortune put away, but whatever the truth of that rumour, it was conceded that he seemed to have few ambitions left.

On this particular Sunday morning, Johnson was hoovering out the breakfast room before dinner, when he was called to attend a guest who had booked into No. 4.

He first saw Mr Franklin standing soberly in the doorway of the hotel, his hand holding back the lace curtain so that he could see into the street. Each side of him stood two leather cases without stickers or labels, packed with just sufficient worldly goods to suggest no hint of bulk or untidiness. The bottoms of the trousers showing under his coat were pressed and narrow, which was a sign of the times.

"Good morning," said the porter.

"How do you do," remarked Mr Franklin, turning abruptly.

They climbed the heavily carpeted stairs in silence, past the brass gong, and went down the dark corridor where loose boards swayed under their feet like old familiar springs. Mr Johnson swung open the doors of the wardrobe and pulled out all the drawers of the chest. He looked into the wastepaper bin. "Dinner, one to two, tea, half-five to seven, breakfast half-seven to nine," he said, about to pull the door behind him. Mr Franklin seemed to have something more on his mind as he looked around the bedroom.

"Yes?" asked the porter.

"Do you have hot water throughout the day?"

Mr Johnson walked over and turned on the high brass tap in a little sink under the window.

They both watched the water run until the steam arose. The porter nodded, left the room to get on with his cleaning, while the guest knelt by his bed in front of one of his cases and stared impassively at the heavily-patterned wallpaper. Then he took a wad of notes from his inside pocket and counted them with the skill of a cardplayer, his thumb reaching for a watered sponge that wasn't there.

He did not count them again.

He looked out the window at the small miserable town, the fighting jackdaws on the sagging slates with their burden of moss, the flat roof above Woolworths' with pools of water on its dark-green felt. The porter below was emptying rubbish into a colossal bin that stood two hands higher than him. His every movement echoed in the red-bricked alleyway. A rattle of buckets followed the clash of the lid. The twin sounds of the latch lifting and descending.

Mr Franklin opened his cases and began putting away his shirts. He hung his two spotless suits in the old camphor-smelling wardrobe and, perched lightly on the bed in his carpet slippers, began eating a thin ham sandwich, one hand cupped under his chin for the crumbs.

That evening Micko Johnson remarked to his wife, "The new cashier booked in today."

"What is he like?" she asked, turning over a page.

"A strange bird," he mused, "but don't get me wrong, well-mannered."

"Keep in there," she rebuked him.

Next morning, Mr Franklin began work at the Bank of Ireland in Main Street, behind a mahogany counter where the hand-painted floor mosaics stopped and the linoleum began. The work was no more difficult than he had known before. The principles were leaner than those in Dublin, and the complexities few. A coal fire blazed in a yellow-tiled fireplace which was kept going by a small uniformed porter who responded sullenly to orders and kept his own judgements of how things should be run. The manager had an open, liverish face and the movements of an undisciplined army major gone to seed. The world of finance in the small town had made him accept less than the notions he had started with. Interest rates did not change, inflation was unthinkable and the steel vaults were not affected by war or the price of gold, but by the price of livestock and land which rose without indecent haste.

The times were colourless and benign.

The last cashier had been transferred because of a scandal, but, as yet, Mr Franklin was only a temporary replacement,

since the transfer had occurred in a hurry lest the tone of the
bank should have been affected.

There was no time for Mr Franklin to find his way around.
He had to start work immediately.

The first customers avoided him. They searched for help
elsewhere, and when they were referred back to the new
cashier, they still addressed their transactions over his shoulder
to more familiar faces. But he continued to smile and speak in
a low democratic voice, so that soon he was accepted as a timid
soul, without airs or graces, certain not to grow impatient over
complicated figures; and his advice, when he was eventually
asked for it, was precise and all-embracing.

That afternoon he approached Swann's for his lunch with
an exhilarated step, breathing in the new town like a drug
that would always be better than the rest. The townsfolk
watched him with anticipation, seeking to find in him the
dissipations of his predecessor. At best it was expected of him
that he should have irregular habits and the eccentricities
of the educated. But his gait was purposeful and only the
frequent pinch of his fingers told remotely of an inner life.
Nor over lunch did he display any self-consciousness that sees
incorrectly the before and after of things; instead he treated
each overcooked course with special interest, as if he were
being treated to such pleasantries for the first time, and this
won the waitress's heart, who told the cook, who told the day
porter, of the new cashier's impeccable civility.

"He's a saint," repeated the waitress as she spread a mushed
dollop of tinned apple into a bowl of stiff semolina, then in
her black frock and white apron, altered at home by herself,
she sped to his table, where he waited, handkerchief across his
lap and his hands resting positively on the table.

"Thank you," he nodded.

The Bank of Ireland was a stiff, colonial building, contempo-
raneous with Swann's Hotel itself, belonging to the day when
they both overlooked the mud-wall cabins of the town. The

barred lower windows were pointed, and the lower frames filled with stained glass. The brass knocker and the letter box were polished excessively by the bank porter because that job enabled him to talk to passers-by. The stone walls were kept an impeccable grey. The manager and his wife lived in the large rooms on the second floor, and here the manager's wife often looked out suspiciously at the precocious life below. In her earlier days she had cut herself off from the social life of the town, but now, intrigued by the persona and bearing of her husband's new recruit, she sent word that he was to be invited up to tea. The other clerks shook their heads wisely.

Mr Franklin told Mr Johnson that the hotel staff need not set a place for him that evening as he was dining out with the manager, Mr Moran.

The porter, having heard the rumours of Mrs Moran's self-enforced isolation, and her probable distress at the activities of the previous cashier, was taken aback.

"That's certainly a boon," said the porter, holding his chin low and a cigarette cupped to his thigh.

Mr Franklin smiled briskly.

The third floor of the bank held old tills from the turn of the century and large unframed photographs of the opening of the bank. Watching the ceremony were animals roped to the carts, with their drivers looking the other way at an approaching band. Files bound with ribbons were stacked from ceiling to floor, and they were flanked by piles of old blue coin bags filled with outdated cheques, large as magazines. There were children's toys and a collection of soldiers who marched in perfect order behind handmade tanks in a cracked glass case. Two outdated safes, containing some still important material, stood in the old unused servants' rooms, with the maker's name cast in circular fashion around stiff handles that had to be cranked like village pumps before they swung open.

"Here," said Mr Moran, reaching in, "is the memoranda of our first deposit."

Mr Franklin held the frayed piece of parchment up to the

light. "They have amalgamation plans afoot for us above, I believe," whispered the manager. "I hear talk of it," replied Mr Franklin delicately. He admired with a nod of his thin skull the faded handwriting, each small figure sketched with the reverence given to millions, and the symbols for sterling like musical notations giving what came after the appearance of poetry, and above all the name of the parent bank, their present employer who might any day merge with the enemy, drawn with hieroglyphic intensity, and then each side, the brown scales of justice.

"An important document," agreed Mr Franklin. "They took things serious then."

"They had their priorities right," the manager said, "and treated everyone with the same courtesy."

"Of course," Mr Franklin summed up, "we were dealing with less customers then."

"That's why," affirmed the manager, "my predecessors could afford to throw nothing away."

They descended the dimly lit stairs, one behind the other, their grey heads bent slightly forward as they searched for the next hidden step.

The ceiling of the living-room, burdened down with brightly painted plaster fruits, loomed like a frantic reflection of life elsewhere. "Yes," Mrs Moran explained, "It was the governor's town house." The floor was carpeted in thick autumn gold. At the northern end, armchairs and settee sat by the fireplace, by the door cane tables and chairs.

The manager's wife had already prepared a chicken salad which Mr Franklin found unsettling for that time of the year.

"It is a wretched town in which to buy decent lettuce," Mrs Moran said over tea.

It did not escape her notice that Mr Franklin was avoiding his lettuce. "The lettuce here," she continued, trying to bluff him with her small ink-spotted eyes, "is forever dried up and inhabited by slugs too countless to mention." Mr Franklin lifted up his knife and fork and, with a lashing of salad cream, again attached the limp leaves. "The lettuce leaf direct from the garden is God's bounty," she ended the discourse which had been directed unflinchingly at the cashier's bowed head, which rose intermittently, only to refuse further allocations. "The Government leaves us no choice," remarked the Manager, "but to concede to the foreign Industrialist what should be going to our own people. The blackguards abscond with the grants and leave unworkable second-hand machinery behind them." His wife, with a small cough, gave thanks. Mr Franklin made no sign that he thought little of the small store she set by her cooking, or that he understood the nervousness that kept her aloof from her fellow man, for he could read all these malfunctions in the eyes of her silent husband, who afterwards layered his bread with strawberry jam in lieu of dessert, an act Mr Franklin found impossible to follow, despite goodwill, acquiescence or his decayed sweet tooth.

"I can envisage that chap," said Mr Moran when Franklin was gone, "becoming a permanent fixture below."

"I could make nothing of him," his wife untruthfully replied. Mr Franklin, wrapped in his overcoat, sat reading in his hotel room from the collected works of John Ruskin. Before going to bed he went downstairs to warm his thin shins before the lounge fire. A group of men finishing their drinks were sitting in a circle around the glowing grate while their secretary summed up their party's affairs. But Johnson the porter was behind the small bar. "Did it go well?" asked Johnson in a sly intimate fashion, as if he and the cashier from that first morning had entered into some undignified partnership. "It was an interesting evening," replied Mr Franklin. "I bet you could put them boys straight," said the porter, indicating the group by the fire while he spun a glass in his hands. Mr Franklin savoured the responsibility his job gave him by offering the porter a modest smile. "The man before you did not leave things any easier," said Johnson, raising his eyebrows in a further show of uncalled for sympathy. Mr Franklin said nothing. "Hold the fort, then," said the porter, "because I know what you are after."

Nervously, Mr Franklin stood by the bar while the porter slipped away into the kitchen. Mr Franklin, ashamed of his carpet slippers and white exposed ankles, felt an eternity go by. The porter returned with a piping hot enamel hotwater bottle.

"I know," said Mr Johnson, in his slight English accent, "How to look after my guests."

So began a nightly ritual that continued throughout the rest of the spring months. Whatever step Mr Franklin took he was sure to run into the porter who seemed to work inordinate hours at the hotel. While Mr Franklin himself, trying to hide a deep well of impatience that troubled his very being, worked late hours by his desk, bringing troublesome accounts up to date and sorting out new business without resort to the old class distinctions. For it would be unthinkable for the manager or the old clerks to see their bank as merely a shop that sold money. They still treated workers with the customary disdain, leading them into the inner sanctuary that had about it the stiff, unwelcoming air of a confessional. They had power over the people because they knew their secrets, and the sinners would emerge from these meetings, rebuffed and withdrawn. It was a practice Mr Franklin disapproved of, for the lower-class Catholic trade with the bank was on the increase because of the new flurry of public relations, and this new business needed careful handling. And the new public image also meant the increased employment of women and the big question was, would they wear their own clothes or a uniform? It was hard to believe that money would now be channelled through non-masculine hands. And after the women, to the utter bewilderment of the older clerks, would come the computers.

And after that would follow all the chaos of the common world.

The male parental care of previous banking generations was at risk, the whole family of banking men being exposed to lesser lights, in a time when asylums were sacred and promiscuity shared outside the home, and it was the talk of strikes that drove Mr Moran further into his shell, so that Mr Franklin was now not only permanent but indispensable, and it would be on his bachelor's shoulders and prematurely grey head the burden of approaching modernity would sit, meaning that he must like women and like machines that were programmed to undermine his domain by calculation and grievances beyond telling.

"You are one of ours," the little wizened bank porter told Mr Franklin one day. He tipped his skull with a knowing finger. "I can tell."

The cashier's evenings were spent either reading or working. There was plenty of time for frivolity in the years ahead, and like the manager and his wife, he rarely graced the streets of the town with his presence. He was fitted out for a new suit in McKenna's which was much to his liking, with the most perfect waistcoat he ever had, and lapels thin as knives. In old sheds down the market yard at night he could hear from his room the youth of the town dancing to the Beatles, and on market days mountainy farmers slouched on the chairs of Swann's eyeing him for weaknesses, then in the late evening the lonely Indian doctors sat around the piano, drinking cold gins and tonic, while a local drunk pounded the keys, and bought round after round for them because they were different. Flour lorries vied with Esso tankers on the narrow streets, so that all traffic came to a stop, till the lorries mounted the footpaths driving the pedestrians before them.

"I'll tell you what," exclaimed Mr Johnson with exaggerated courtesy one bright summer's evening as he chased along the hotel corridor with a broom, "why don't you move in with us?"

Mr Franklin spun the key in the loose lock of his bedroom door.

"Sleep on it," continued the porter. "My wife can cook good as the best of them and you'll find us half the price of the hotel."

"I'm quite happy here," answered Mr Franklin at a loss.

"Just bear it in mind, all right?" the porter said unwavering. "You of all people should know the right and wrong of these things."

Later that week, Mr Franklin took a walk out in the country, identifying modes of pleasure that might sustain him as his nature homed in on the need for domestic security, and Mr Johnson's house was pointed out to him by a road sweeper. "You can't miss it," said the road sweeper, dipping his hand in a stiff wave, "It's neither one thing or another." The house, bare of trees and shrubbery, seemed to have newly emerged from the sea with a coating of barnacles. The cockles were of the type that coat heavy lamps. The garden was pitted with cement and building materials, and the cut into the hill was still not healed, except for pockets of light grass and clumps of builders' poppies.

Muddy water ran across the road from shores not properly realigned and little sandalled footprints that ran down the path must have been left by the porter's youngest son before the cement had set.

The house looked somehow innocent, in a word, bravely decent.

On the day he moved there Mrs Johnson explained to Mr Franklin that only families that returned from England had the gumption to take the stranger in.

"The rest," she explained, "think it's beneath them."

She was a small balding woman, who trotted rather than walked, and spoke, like her husband, ahead of herself, as if all introductory conversation was unseemly. Her quiet withdrawn son looked as if he, too, had been on this earth before and stored up unaccountable vengeances from his previous stay, though now, with his steps forever firmly planted on the path, it seemed he was treating this present existence with seriousness.

The eldest lad, Mrs Johnson acknowledged, was bright but full of stops and starts. They were climbing the stairs. They were touring the rooms. "His father got him into McArdle's," she beat Mr Franklin's pillow, "because there was no way of continuing his schooling here without the Irish language, and there he'll stay till he can better himself."

The first thing Mr Franklin noticed in his newly-painted room was that he could dispense with his overcoat and that he would not be awoken by jackdaws. The radiators, set into roughly plastered holes, sent out a constant traffic of nauseating heat. Against the blinded window a second-hand desk with roller and pens had been placed, where, the porter explained, Mr Franklin could go over his figures. A statue of the Virgin Mary stood in a recess with a hideous viper baring its fangs under her white rounded feet, that stood on what? Perhaps a half-globe of an uncoloured, unfinished world. And the great joy was the walk, benign in good weather, exhilarating when the wind got up, from the house into the town when Mr Franklin would receive a variety of greetings from all and sundry, who among themselves, were astonished by such exact timekeeping.

The bank by now had begun to tackle the forthcoming formidable task of decimalization.

Thinking in tens rather than twelves was driving the elder clerks to desperation and they feared the chaos ahead of them in a couple of years, as another man might fear to be thrown out of his home. The new order would restrict advancement, amalgamation limit superiority. But having no other stability in the world except his work, Mr Franklin relished the architectural cleanness of the metrical system, the satisfaction of teasing out patterns that brought new areas of the mind into play. He kept the decimalization tables always by him and his only sentiment was that he saw very early on that, like the half-crown, the old silver sixpence would have to go.

Soon Mr Franklin's reserve, and sometimes curt replies were his solitude in his room to be interrupted, became unsettling for Mrs Johnson. She heard stories of bank clerks who were bedwetters and some who were thieves, so each day after his departure she checked the cashier's bed and desk, but everything was above board, except for a certain briefcase that was always kept locked, which seemed more disloyal than dishonest. Mr Franklin noticed, but took no umbrage at her searching, for he had long ago accepted the necessity of others rechecking your credentials and your figures, and in case she might be fretting over the briefcase, from then on he left it open on the bed. This demoralized Mrs Johnson. And sometimes, when he sat with her in the downstairs room to smile blandly at the Dave Allen show, she could hardly contain herself.

It became necessary for her to wait till her tenant had retired to his room before she could talk at ease to her husband.

"He's neat, he's tidy," she said one evening, "but there is something evil about that man."

"What are you saying?" asked Johnson.

"I don't," she muttered, "like to be left alone in the house with him."

"Well then," said Johnson, "you'll not be too happy to know that I transferred our account to him today."

"That's the last straw," she said, unable to bear the thought of an individual knowing the secrets of her purse, without once acknowledging his debt.

Mr Johnson gave up his night shift at the bar, financially leaving them where they were before they had taken Franklin in. His wife's meals, which had improved immensely on the arrival of the cashier, were now served up in a desultory fashion, the soup was thin and buttons of undissolved Bisto floated in the now frequent stews. The porter began repeating after meals and endured excruciating bouts of indigestion, and his only consolation was that the cashier must have been going through the same suffering as himself. Franklin, for his part, had further complicated things by taking a liking to the eldest son, Ronnie, who would sometimes accompany the cashier into his place of work, and then pass his father somewhat arrogantly as he swept the footpath outside Swann's. In the house Ronnie waited on the cashier hand and foot and sought his advice where before he would have gone to his father. Thus the parents had to curtail and expurgate criticism of their unwitting tenant in front of the son for fear he might carry it back.

So, at last, their only privacy in the new house was in the bed with its electric blanket, where their first intimacies had begun.

"Your Mister Benjamin," said Mrs Johnson ironically after one especially exasperating evening, "will have to go."

But in his room Mr Franklin was enjoying all these evenings, while his eviction was plotted across the landing, an unwarranted feeling of satisfaction and peace. Ronnie would pick books off his shelf and bring them back filled with cigarette coupons as markers. Aerial photography was Mr Franklin's joy, because he held that what is seen from above mitigates all that's seen from below and gives us a grasp of what the future might hold, when the common traveller would have recourse to wheels only for landing. And how our forefathers, because of their sympathies for the skies, built forts that looked upwards, as well as across, dangerous and uncharted territories.

A night in September came when the bank's annual do was being held in the White Horse. Mr Franklin went, accompanied by the Morans. So the Johnson family had the house to themselves except for Ronnie who was off dancing at the Wonderland Ballroom. While the clerks and their women tore at the usual turkey, the Johnsons had beautiful lamb chops in parsley and honey sauce. Their house and family seemed immune from any unreasonable intrusion, their joy and security untrammelled and all thought of the cashier was dismissed from their minds, his thin frame and soapy smell forgotten.

Mr Johnson repeated some humorous stories from his day at the hotel. He copied once again the cook's walk across the kitchen, and the waitress's habit of leaning forward and

picking stray fluff off her companion's coat as she gossiped.
Mrs Johnson, during the pauses, recalled earlier unhappier
days in London when they were getting together the pennies
that had built their present vulnerable fortress, giving her
husband that steely glare that made him feel responsible for
all the woes that had befallen them.

Then, after midnight, they heard light steps on the stairs.

"That's the bugger, Mick," laughed Mrs Johnson,
"inhospitable as ever."

"I think you are too hard on him," said the porter.

Somehow, having the clerk back above increased their
joviality. They sat on well past the hour when they would
normally have gone to bed, making extra cups of tea which
Mick laced with brandy. It was time for them to discover
old photographs, but to avoid sentimentality which got you
nowhere fast, so Mick reckoned. Whining was out for the
traveller. You just took the scaffolding down floor by floor, so
that when you had spun off the last nut and dropped the final
bar you would never dream that that very morning, you had
stood up there abreast of the chimney tops. Or it could be, Mrs
Johnson was saying, having lost the child you'd carried three
months down the toilet, you just changed your knickers and
set off for work, for what was the sense of crying, I ask you?
They moved from chair to chair telling their stories. Once,
coming in from the kitchen with more nourishment, Mrs
Johnson heard a rumpus above. The noise ended. She brought
her husband out into the hall. They listened a while and again
the noise started with an awkward rhythm that unnerved
them both with its familiarity. She pulled her husband up the
stairs, who at that moment sought refuge from what would
only demean them both. "God," she said giggling, "I'd love to
see the auld hure at it." They listened outside Franklin's door
and the soft coo of a woman's voice was unmistakable.

"Now,'" she whispered into her husband's ear, "You have
him."

"Oh Christ," he answered, drawing back.

"Under our roof," she forced his elbow forward.

Mick pulled himself together, and as his wife swung open the door, he reached for the light and the two of them fell drunkenly into the room. And there, speechlessly, they beheld their eldest son, draped in Mr Franklin's pink sheet, whispering softly into a girl's ear something that would be always a secret to them both, while, astride her, his buttocks gently rocked.

"Get out!" roared Ronnie. "Get out!"

The incident in his room was never reported to Mr Franklin, but, unwittingly, he took the blame, for Mrs Johnson treated him now to an irrevocable silence. He seemed to eat more often at Moran's sometimes the Wednesday and Friday of every week, where the manager and himself sought to know through various arguments, bolstered up with sherry, whether the current fear in Ireland of the International Monetary Fund was justified, or proper to a legendary nationalism that fears progress. They discussed whether genuine political administrators had been superseded by personalities who might not understand the proper tenets of political behaviour and therefore spend valuable time seeking revenge against their opposites, rather than considering the Western economic world which had supported them through their every crisis, and only exacted from them basic loyalty.

"The party system as practised here," said Mr Moran, "leaves a lot to be desired. We bankers who control them in the long run cost less to employ. But," and he waved that incorrigible finger, "the family must hold together."

"The loyalists are getting bad press," said Mr Franklin regarding the recent minor disturbances in the North.

"They will have forgotten about it by the time Christmas is over," the manager tapped the fire with a brass poker, "mark my words, but either way it's not us will have to pay."

"That itself," said Mr Franklin.

The cashier was enjoying the trust of the customers and come Christmas it was he gave out the small plastic calendars, saying with a smile, "They are good for peeling frost off your windscreens." The bank made a contribution to the Christmas tree which was erected in the market square, and they contributed towards the lights, which were strung across the main street like bunting, falling a little every night toward the street below. Mr Franklin bought a set of crystal glasses for the Morans, sherry and whiskey for the Johnsons, to Ronnie *The Guinness Book of Records* and a cowboy suit for the young lad. But now he could detect the barely disguised hostility in the house.

"You don't mind," Mr Johnson had at last brought himself to speak, "we would like to spend Christmas alone."

"Of course," answered Mr Franklin, "I'll take my things and move into Swann's."

"But have you no place to go, say, in Dublin for the holiday?" asked the porter, dreading any adverse criticism that might accrue from the cashier leaving their home.

Mr Franklin said nothing.

On the twenty-third he went with his two cases to the hotel where late that evening, Mr Moran, for the first time abroad in a local hostelry where he had no duty to perform, joined him at the bar. Mr Franklin, freed of the constrictions of the house and glad to be back in the privacy of the old rooms, was in a celebratory mood, and glad to have somehow found his own level. And while the two men were there, in a quiet recess inside the door under an old fatigued lampshade, surrounded by green upholstery and quiet pictures of deer and sheep, Ronnie arrived very flustered and breathless. Before Mr Moran could extract himself from what was a mortifying situation for him, and private for them, the boy blurted out, "They should not have done that."

"But Ronnie," said Mr Franklin, "I'm only staying here for the Christmas."

"I know what they are at," said Ronnie, "I know them."

"Sit down," said the manager, "and let me get you something."

Mr Franklin looked wildly after the manager, knowing that the transgressions of his predecessor were still fresh in both their minds.

Knowing no better and having received no instructions, Mr Moran returned from the bar with a glass of whiskey. Ronnie thanked him and said, "They are trying to humiliate Mr Franklin." "Indeed," said Mr Moran. "That's enough now, Ronnie," said the cashier. The lad sat there in the embarrassing silence, then lifting the whiskey he threw it all back in one mouthful. His eyes watered as he gagged. He clapped his hands, made for the bar and returned before Mr Franklin had time to explain.

"There is another round on its way," said Ronnie.

"You've got to go home now," said the cashier.

"You are doing Mr Franklin no good, you know," said the manager.

The cashier's face grew ashen, and in a high-pitched whisper he said to Ronnie, who was looking from one to the other, "Go home, home, home!" adding with a rap on the table that carried across the lounge: "Now!" A few moments passed, "Please."

Banished Misfortune

The house that Saul lived in.

While the children slept there, outside it rained. The whole night long. Though it was warm and brown among the damp shiny chestnuts, the weather had opened under the shadows of the rambling trees. Everything was falling. The thump of chestnuts on the soft floor of the night. And the insects thrived down there in the caves of leaves. Eileen slept facing east, young child limbs learning to fly and the people of Belfast looking up in wonder. The duchess hopped along the stairs, past the dusty quiet of McFarland's door where the mother turned often in her sleep down an empty and alien past, and the cat sat up beside the small steamy window with the lead stripes to catch her breath, where the magpies had chewed the new putty. Listening to the water swirling over the stones and the loose gate banging in the lower meadow. And when little Tom coaxed her down onto the bed, she put her washing away and jumped like a little deer.

"Here, puss," he said and she stretched out one long paw.

For whatever reason the house might fall, the sleeping McFarland would build again with a sense of adventure anywhere north of the lakes and in good time, son of Saul, master builder of Fermanagh country but by pneumonia put away while tended by his wife Olive, Glan woman and descendant of J. O'Reilly who danced once with flax in his trousers, and though nominally Christian died in foreign and pagan lands fighting an unjust war, but McFarland sensing the lie of the land grew away from a sense of guilt or desire for power and prayed that the haphazard world would not destroy his family so well grounded among the moralities of chance and nature, if one could remain loyal to the nature of a people and not the people themselves, for whatever reason the house might fall.

The door opened onto the fields.

All round, that silence and damp air of expectancy after the eerie rasp of the storm had blown over.

Judy, his wife, cooked over a single gas jet in the leafy half-light, for the electricity blackout was at its worst and it seemed to McFarland like one of those early mornings years ago when he had risen in the cold to feed the cattle and heard the groan of the house and Saul's asthmatic breathing overhead. Still the echo of the sessions that had gone on through the night when he was a child. The children put on two sets of jumpers and climbed into their boots under the stairs, and Eileen picked up a toy soldier knocked over by the foot of the father as he went round the back to examine the roof for missing slates. Soft Chinese music of the rain on glass and leaves, lightly touched cymbals, ducks crashing onto the waters, the primitive crane stretching her awkward wings in a lone high flight, the land below so cold and misty it looked as if a healing frost had settled.

Little Tom chased Eileen sideways through the mist to the end of the garden, among the penitent crumbling apple trees, in her new frock and washed hair and everywhere a silent promise that she might be well.

"The night it being dark in my favour," the father sang fretfully to himself in the boot of the car, unconcerned about the helicopter that flew over the house and scattered the birds that a moment before had been strolling along the hedges. Humming a reel like a dream he was trying to remember, McFarland, out of an incapacity to deal with the extravagance of small details, involved his wife and children in discovering the pattern from last year for fitting in the case, instruments and bags. He scraped the fiddle bow thoughtfully under his chin and sang it backwards and forward across his ear as he went through the mathematics. Talking in a holiday voice to nuts and screws and old newspapers, while his wife reasoned with the children, losing her patience. Will Byrne, the sentinel of the hill, his brother murdered at his door, watched their activities with benign speculation as he lay against an old railing from which he propelled himself every few seconds and took a quick low whistle, escaping from the past for a few excruciating moments.

"You get in the back with your mother," the father said and little Tom put the cat down reluctantly in the shed and dropped a chicken bone temptingly into her dish. She was sitting at a ladylike distance away, upset by the jamming of the doors and all those signs of departure. He hid another bigger bone behind the shed after whistling down the fields, watching a weasel drink water from the cup of a leaf among the chopped timber. The duchess suddenly attended to her wardrobe. The soft scuffle of leaves and harness. After they had all driven away, the dog, with pebbles hanging from his coat, came in mumbling because he had been forgotten and the cat flew up onto the rafters, while above her the rain slanted to the west.

"What'll we sing?" asked little Tom.

The father looked up to heaven, his musical children vain and happy by turns, his child wife looking steadfastly silently ahead as she always did when they journeyed together, always heading off into some fitful future, living off the excitement of leaving something intangible behind and the wheels on the road had a life of their own. Edging down the lane, the dark purple of the sloes, sour grapes, the blackberries tidily hung between the bronze leaves and yellow roots of the hedge. Lakes, a darker purple than the sloes away below the chestnut trees. A soldier's jeep was parked on the crossroads, guns cocked. "You can learn to live with anyone," Saul had said, "it's imperial to me!" And McFarland, reared amongst a series of foreign and local escapades, took everywhere his copies of the Arctic and Antarctic voyages. "Irish musicians are a crowd of drunken children," Judy said to him once as they drank Guinness from a bedroom sill in a boarding-house. "I suppose it wasn't what the Lord wanted," he said eventually, away from her down to the Roscommon men strolling through the riotous, melancholy music. Still, tucked under his elbow as he sauntered through the dark deserted streets of Belfast where the men drank gin and the women drank whiskey, he always had his copy of Scott's final trip up the frozen Pole, a book he had read many many times and still felt the same harsh ecstasy the explorers must have experienced when, worn to the bone of humanity, they discovered that the Norwegians had been there before them. And the other explorers held down by the winter, frozen and breathless and singing songs under the snow.

The family drove through the clouds and Friday, the dog, chased round the farm for the scents that were fast fading.

Eileen lit the matches for her father's cigarettes, cupping her awkward hands like the men do in the yard to save the light from the wind. Like she was reading the future from the palms of her hands, stained with the juices of the early-morning leaves where so many faces were hidden. And all round strange wet farmhouses, the finely-cropped trees of the north, cut like mushrooms or birds settling with wings tucked, fine cars in the driveways along the wide fields, the distinctive roadway signs, the extinct lorries. Behind the sheds like railway carriages and over the hills the grim Norse-like churches. Going over the bridges there was a great empty feeling beneath your heart as the car rose. Like a roof lifting off a house. Her mother's agitated face when their uncle threatened. If time could wait. Once Eileen's stomach turned sick, mesmerized by the sudden looseness of her limbs, her head swaying. McFarland walked her up and down a laneway off the main road with his tolerant musical strides, while overhead the trees joined branches in the mist that was blinding the islanders as they rowed ashore on the flooded Erne, adjusting to the repeated deaths beside the blue-frosted lakes, at night the cool drinks, hands dextrous at cards. She hated these moments that she had no control over. But it was better to be sick and let her eyes film over with tears for a moment than arrive bleary-eyed and fatigued after dosing herself with the heavy languorous pills she took as a child that made her memory falter. Her hair was cut so short for her face that she showed pain too easily. And she was irked by Tom's cheerfulness behind her in the car, her instincts left in him.

"A big girl like you won't find the time passing," his voice above her, afraid of any weakness that might handicap their security, humming and smoking in the mist with his hand on her shoulder, we'll be there in no time. "We'll be there in no time," he said.

And that's how little Tom, anxious to laugh, attracting laughter, succeeded in getting into the front seat beside his father to pull the window down and trail his hands near the low trees that flew by like the wind, too quick even for his eyes to catch, and wave at the Customs man as they crossed the last ramp and headed down the bad easy roads, the Leitrim-Cavan border where traditions had survived even the Famine itself, a roofless countryside without trees or soldiers or gunfire at night but the road through the frost-shattered mountains and stray rain-filled clouds, the bilberry bushes and cotton grass. And Sandy Byrne and Friday were leaping through hedges and streams on their way to the village after Old Byrne had cursed the skyline and chased them from his house with a broom. McFarland's eyes were fading, he grieved sometimes for them in the early morning when his vision was hazy like that shortness of breath, and now he was aware of Tom watching him squeeze his eyes, concentrate, slow down and take the centre of the road. After the humours of Ballyconnell they crossed the dry streams where the railway lines had been lifted and sold to the Congo by order of an ecumenical government, here several of his mother's people had flagged down a train and never been seen again, going away with a wisp of smoke and single words in the old Irish. Among the Chinese and gunpowder, among poets and moneygrabbers his grandfather had been there for the driving of the last spike on the Great Pacific Railway till he fell down a frozen thirty-foot falls, his dogs screaming in terror below him and all over the snowswept Canadian valley.

"Tisin' no wonder this is the wee county that Sean Maguire sprang from," the father said, remembering, and thought of the boy in the gap and the lady's top dress and the day he had climbed here with Saul and had a nose-bleed on the mountain.

They left behind the pagan air of Glan, grey damp farms surrounded by cluttered rusty galvanized sheds, washing blowing in the garden, a pump on the road that nobody used, cottages with the thatch sunk in the middle. A huge aerial. The mother slept lazily, hearing Bach's Fantasy and Fugue on her husband's tape and she longed to lean out and draw someone close to her for a while, for someone, she said, tapped her on the shoulder naming various schoolchildren she had taught in Belfast, tall mousy-haired children who hardly ever talked or did in a rush and called to her house whispering angrily, and as her head bobbed against the rear seat she never saw her husband smile boyishly at her in the mirror. And Eileen copied her mother going to sleep, glancing through half-closed eyes at the blue-aproned women, sweeping, washing down their steps and the men crossing the streets with a multitude of different steps, their breath flying behind them. After the trip to Athlone the fiddle quietened, the bodhrán settled, trees were down everywhere after the big wind. At various times they came across groups of men standing round with saws under their arms and greatcoats hung up on the side of a ditch. The mist was lifting like the curtain in the Town Hall. They saw the first house in Connaught. They heard the musical priest. And while the sky cleared the family ate next to a stone wall, sharing the air with an odd horse that had been looking at the same spot in a gorse haggard for days. Thousands of sewage pipes were piled on the footpaths, a gate opened into a new lake. "The bit of food," Saul had said, "it's like the man begging, it will take you to the next door." And the Shannon had turned the streams into wild dancing streams, sheughs filled with wild water that stranded the cows who wandered about ankle-deep in the muck searching for grass.

At last, when they entered the city, a Friesian calf with a white star on his forehead and white back legs stopped the car in the middle of the road and peered in with large blinking enquiring eyes. "A white-headed calf is very hard on the beast," he'd said, "turn him if you can, I'm the queer quack myself."

Peace is not necessary here, she heard that and ... these people would rather endure. Who was it? Was it him? And again, I think it was St Patrick started this campaign. Was it drunk together on the boat to Belfast, collecting stolen timber from his brother on the docks, his fat belligerent brother who could kill, or was it on another day not in a boat but crossing the road in hot weather when traffic was heavy? My young saintly maidenly unmarried sister sleeping with a Quaker in that deserted bullet-peppered block of flats, oh my sister how sometimes I miss your crusade for there's nothing left for me but to become a victim who at the end of all resources admits nothing.

"Where are we now?" the mother said, wakening.

"Timbuktu," the boy said.

"You so and so," the mother said, ruffling his hair.

"I just combed that out a wee minute ago," said Eileen and she flicked out her own short hair, the holiday at last for real, trying to create some dancing curls, and patted down her fresh autumn dress and knocked the mud of the fields from her shoes, spread out her toes to release the sweet stiffness of the journey from her body, the stifling impression of having gone nowhere till she smelt the roots of the sea, the girl in her gliding down as Ennis slowed the pipes.

Her father closing his eyes gratefully as he stopped the car.

Slates littered the streets of Galway.

Shopkeepers picked their way through the debris, gesticulating and looking up at the sky like sleepwalkers. The scene was obscenely familiar to the family from the north who felt for a moment slightly superior in their ability to deal with chaos, death, laughter at death. The family booked into a boarding house that looked out on a river that ran floundering under heavy stone bridges into the salmon sea, and the nervous landlady was filled with small talk about the storm, as a man held a ladder against the side of the building and his apprentice fought off cramp as he took a perilous path across the roof. The family listened with hidden humour to the stray southern accents, as men shouted encouragement to the climber from the street below. Little Tom mimicking. The boarding house began with a big room, advancing in smaller rooms till it ended in a tiny toilet perched over the river. They spoke self-consciously of the weather and Judy glared at the son of the house who watched Eileen with cold mischievous lust as the girl stood downstairs at the discordant piano fingering the keys in time to the waves of the sea, that same rhythm in her hands as was in her eyes when they had sat in the deserted concert halls in Belfast and she was husbandless, to listen to the orchestra practising the songs of Fauré and the tiny early piano pieces of Mozart such a long time ago.

And Friday had found the bone at the back of the shed and took it down to the edge of the stream, where he drank out of his questioning reflection in the damp mossy shadows where the hesitant rain and leaves still fell.

The slow earth.

"I'll be back early," said McFarland when everything was settled and kisses had been handed round.

"God, oh God man, foolish promises," she answered him and he smilingly pursed his lips and shook his shoulders and with his fiddle case went down to a pub where the barman was a retired monk and sung songs of Napoleon and Aquinas, tapping and patting his companions down.

When first in Portaferry they crossed hands Eileen was a small delighted baby, who had to travel each day by car with her mother to school and the child never cried but lay listless for hours in the nursery, with its high windows that were not for looking through. And when he and Judy married, the child tottered quietly into the small church in autumn and laughed away brown-eyed at her mother looking so serious.

For those first few weeks Judy tired easily of the endless sessions and retired early, leaving him alone among a bunch of new emptied musicianors. And as the constant assault of songs and music wore away with his first advances, and they learned each other's ways and the way of the child, she was no longer like a false note in a slow air returning and returning. She showed none of his cunning reticence, was eager to slip into a thousand excitable abstractions. Yet how many towns had they got so drunk in the world might end, playing squash in the early morning handball alleys to soothe a hangover, her fine excited accent a mixture of cynicism and distance. Because the city restrained people, or so he believed, it would have been customary for her sophistication to endure some rural cynicism but in this instance it was his nature gave way, slipping away into a thousand nearly familiar impressions. The complexity attracted him, the adventure of a perfume alien to his sheets, the lane to the door.

Cupping his man-root in her hand, old and awkward gamblings, and she saying slow and he for all his mock heroics learning for the first time the body's music, lightly touched cymbals that rocked them both away.

Red berries next the house, and the sycamore releasing a thousand revolving wings.

Judy brought the children for a long walk on the pier till evening caught them in an early long blue light like the sheen from a silk curtain and they strolled and ran back restlessly to the house. Not that Salthill was beautiful but ugly and plain and yet it was a necessary outing for them all although she was uncertain that any of them might feel release, know the difference in such a short time for they had burrowed down so deep in anxiety that happiness was nearly hysterical. Little Tom's cheeks were warm and Eileen's hair had blown and blown in the wind and they were tired as kings now one day had ended. Judy had grown used to being on her own. In Belfast they had worked apart, she driving out of the city each morning to Lisburn to teach and he heading off in a blue van to some new disaster area. And after the sudden move to the old house and the death of the old man they were suddenly thrown into each other's company most of the day, like young lovers, finding themselves grown strange to each other as if their previous work had sustained some missing link. But one could not but feel relieved yet cowardly after being released from the rows of terraced houses. Back in their room with the wasting wallpaper and plastic flowers, the landlady's family downstairs watching the Saturday film on television, Tom turned bad-tempered and started to argue, pulling Eileen away from the ukulele she was playing. The invisible stars that blind each other. The boy started to hammer the bed with his fists and the girl squeezed her hands against her face screaming, while below the television was lowered.

"Stop. Stop," she screamed.

"Ya wanna see a wee bitch," he shouted.

"Leave me alone."

"Stop. Both of ye," yelled Judy.

I can hardly survive any more, thought Judy. Oh nature, nature who left out my instinct for self-survival and gave me this grudging betrayal of selfishness instead. When she finally quietened them down, they sulked but with the confidence of children who know for what they are crying. "Tomorrow is Sunday," she said, "and in the morning we'll all travel out to Spiddal and you'll play your whistle, Tom, for Furaisti and Pete with the bent nose will be there." Tom was the easiest to bring back, to forgive in a slow mechanical way the world that threatened to overwhelm him. "It will be more wonderful than any Fleadh. Yes. And you have no more school for a fortnight, maybe more." "Will the flute player be there from England," Tom proffered slowly, "the one who wears the bicycle clips?" "Yes. Aye. All your father's friends."

"Sleep now ye pair."

And Friday was sitting quietly in the shed beside the duchess who occasionally looked up at him and the night was there too except there was no sound, only the sharp cries of the nightbirds from down the fields.

"That's a lovely daughter you've got there," the landlady said when Judy opened the door to see who was tiptoeing annoyingly across the landing. Then to silk she washed herself, her first warm bath for months under the watchful eye of the awful blue staring fish and afterwards she draped herself luxuriously before a small electric fire. The glow from her flesh pleased her as did the silence and the small breaths of the sleeping. When she had left Belfast she had sworn she would never live in a city again, not for a day, but Galway she never really accepted as a city, it was more like a big drifting market town. She and her husband were changing, she knew. In Belfast they were satisfied politically, in that their bodies, like anyone else's, could stop a bullet, but living so close to the south was a totally new beginning, a loveplay, something they had forgotten as she had forgotten that in the south what appeared trivial, negative to her was a natural way of life for a people unaffected by war. But her spirit had once enlarged, as her sister's now had. Still she worried about their farmhouse in Fermanagh constantly, even when she went to the village with the kids she always searched the now familiar trees for smoke, as if in a way she needed a ritual, a gradual dismemberment.

Eileen turned in her sleep.

The wind in the wires outside reminded Judy of home, like the sound of distant geese; she rubbed her body in front of the fire as the evening drew on.

"Politics is the last thing in the world I want to hear about," said McFarland in a pub where he was the centre of attraction as he laid his fiddle down. "The very last thing."

"Give us a slow air," someone interrupted in Salthill as they went from "Toss the Feathers" to "The Flowers of Spring." And the bank manager danced to the tune.

"Everybody in the north wants to get on TV or into politics," a fisherman just in off the trawlers joked in The Largeys where an Irish soldier was playing the pipes in the backroom.

"Galway never changes."

"*Ni bhíonn ac súil amháin ag na nGael anois,*"* said Furaisti softly as they sat ruminating under Conaire in the square and watched a peculiar crowd spreading out from the railway station after arriving on the last train from Dublin. McFarland was restless, spending money recklessly. Saul had said, "If I died tonight wouldn't you heel up the clothes and the money, and say didn't he hold on to it tight." And he had left nothing but the view from the hill. McFarland remembered his own youth as warmth under a slated roof from the heavy rain, a vague wish on the side of a lake, and now returning years later to the house built like a church with its arched porch and stained-glass windows taken by bicycle from Donegal, he was learning the names for sounds he was born into, a tern fleeing from the rushes, milk churns rattling over the evening echo of the lake, a pheasant remembering the balls in her tail running over the mossy earth and perching on a fence to allow her scent bubble over the dogs, a perch bent in the scale-wet hands of his son. Oh history is a great time-saver, a repellent against honest thought. There was no release, not like the falling release of a larch breaking at last under the swing of a steady axe, the shivers showering the earth.

"You know, Furaisti, you could hardly make ceiling laths from the trees in these parts," he said.

"Have you put down any vegetables this year?" asked Furaisti.

"No. Next year for certain," he answered.

The dog slept by the cat in the shed and once he awoke and chased some shots off into the dark and the duchess stirred and smiled when he returned and sank beside her in the straw.

The radiators had filled the room with heavy cumbersome heat when Eileen heard the bomb open the sky in her sleep. A god filling in his time that she darted from on the verge of frightened dreams. She sank beneath the bedclothes when she awoke, silent awhile till, as her panic grew more terrible, she called to her mother in the expressionless dark. Judy

---

* "The Irish see through only one eye now."

came in naked from the other room and wiped the blood from her bewildered daughter's face. In this strange house, even for a day, we have to start out all over again, relearning those familiar parts of ourselves that resist even the gentlest analysis and praying for a timely scepticism. As if as a child one had walked into a wet crumbling house and felt the tang of decay, emptiness, drab sky. The scar on her own white body ran like the shadow of a man's arm from beneath her child-fallen breasts to the small warmth of her loins. I'd look fine, she thought as she comforted the child, on the inside pages of *Playboy* with my arms thrown open in tensed surprise like the cormorants we saw shading the waves from the island today. She threw open the window and pulled a deep orange robe over herself to get a drink downstairs for Eileen. The house was quiet. The boy in jeans and shirt was washing dishes in the kitchen and as he looked at her casually under his dark eyelids, she thought I'll take his mop of hair and squeeze his face between my legs so that he might scarcely breathe.

"I want to go home," said Eileen.

"Sleep now," the mother said and brushed Eileen's hair with her fingertips.

Judy walked through the sparse crowds, perhaps less euphoric now as they came into winter, their stale stomachs excruciated after the happy outrage of the long summer drinking, the headlights of a car brushing against the Virginia creeper that nestled against the old university walls. She had hoped they might have driven out tonight to watch the wind spend itself on the drawn-grey stones of Connemara. Oh the myths the northerners love, the places where the troops will lie down! The chagrin burning on men's faces who expect answers that will confirm their own existence. In a small hostelry, up the dishevelled stairs among loud demurring students who flaunted an adopted Gaelic and what little knowledge of alcoholism they had, she drank pints of Guinness in the early flamboyant style of a girl celebrating new values and wisdom, eager for a person to steal a promise from the ennui of the drinkers. She interrupted conversations readily, her accent tending to be either American or from a corner of Kerry, unaware or scared of the laughter.

"Do you know that Will Byrne is a real 'old fountainhead'?" she said, mimicking McFarland's accent.

"Belfast is the spiritual centre of Europe," she told a doctor.

"Fuck ye away from that house, ye bastards," old Byrne was shouting out of his lighted window and the dogs were barking, the duchess breaking away with raised hair through the long wet grass from the circling flames.

Meanwhile Furaisti and McFarland were rolling a stolen barrel of beer into a nurse's flat. The older man was out of breath and they had broken some strings on the fiddle. Four Connemara men in hats and coats stood drinking in the corridor with them, talking indifferently and happily among the endless traffic of people. They had a thirst like a chimney with a good draw. It took a while for McFarland to see confirmed in him and among the others a sense of other realities than being Irish, drink should let the mind wander to the present even foregoing the recent if not altogether past. And leaving in the dead of night, his arm round a friend, Saul spoke again. "Be like a fox boy, piss on your trail and scatter the drops to puzzle the scent." So McFarland to the air of the flogging reel took various routes home. And in the hotel the sound of his footsteps still came up the stairs to him, going from door to door searching for his room. Her clothes were scattered in a line to the bed. "I have never known a woman like her," he said as he lifted the sheets to Judy's chin and tucked her in next to Eileen. He sat on the bed looking at them. In a word, Bach. Lord it is enough when it please Thee bring my life to a close, and he placed the fiddle and bow on the chair. He read a few pages of Scott's travels, but his mind wandered to the time they alighted on Portaferry Strand among the sunning ladies from the seagulls' clamour all night and all day, with a single seal dipping and spreading a long straight line on the ocean and how he thought that day his eyes might never focus again.

My trouble. In a word. Never lie on the left side, boy, you'll squeeze the heart out of yourself. Tom awoke and saw the match flare up in the dark and light up his father's face who had climbed awkwardly into bed beside him.

McFarland smoked in the darkness.

"Judy, Judy," he whispered across.

"Are you awake, Judy?"

"I heard tonight a story when Furaisti played 'Banish Misfortune'. It happened back in the days when death wasn't an institution. Jimmy Cummins turned to me and said, 'Do you hear that? Well, there was a piper from Gurteen, a fine piper in his day who drank nothing but French wine and oddly enough just played once in a fine house. He'd mind that night if he were alive today. For there the gentry's daughter came away with him, a lightsome girl and the parents naturally enough with acres of turnips and cabbages for setting disowned her. There was no hue or cry and the Gurteen man took her on his short travels for money and baby clothes. For the girl was expecting a piper's baby and not long after she and the baby died in this town. The coffin was put up on a cart drawn by a dray horse and no one following from the cobbles of the Spanish Arch. And the piper began a lament, not too slow or too quick on account of his losses, and the men in the fever hospital sweating from their labours counted four thousand mourners as they crossed Lough Atalia for Forthill graveyard. That's banished misfortune for you,' said Jimmy Cummins."

"Do you hear me Judy?"

She heard him in a drunken vulgar way, accessible still for all his various frailties, but she was silent for in her heart of hearts she feared he was softening, losing his sense of justice, merely protesting that erratic comedy of life. Fear was so addictive, consuming all of a body's time and she wanted so much to share this vigil with him in Fermanagh but what could you give the young if they were barricaded from the present by our lyrical, stifling past? She said nothing, knowing she shared this empty ecstasy with a thousand others who had let their laziness go on too long.

"I left home too young, that's what bothers me," he spoke again. "There must be a thousand stories and songs about my own place that I hardly know. But when we return, woman, we'll try."

In a foot of land there's a square mile of learning, Saul had said, and he had learned to build from a sense of duty to the beauty of the hilly Erne.

For in April of 1910, Saul had a bad back but nevertheless he had finished building a church in Donegal Town and now with Bimbo Flynn the whistler he set about kissing the air and erecting his own house. And it was a house where the best sessions of music would be held, where you could drive a tractor through the back windows. They gathered the red limestone rocks from the hills and fine washed stones from the Erne, the broached flagstones from Sliabh Buadh. Are you after work? he asked the grimy gypsies. God, you might swear mister, they said, and the gypsies carried cartloads of rocks up the hillside and sat under the chestnut tree smoking and drinking while it rained. His wife Olive came from the old house each day with tea and sandwiches for the men taking their time at their work on the edge of the woods that fell away to the lake. He'll fire everything to get back to America, the neighbours said, knowing the long travelling of the McFarlands, but as summer came he straightened up like a post in the good weather and the roof edged across the sky.

"Let it pass by."

"Judy."

"Piss on them, boy, piss on them."

"Where are we for today then?"

"Men of Ireland."

"Do him no good to be a fife player now."

"I'd kill a man for that."

"Look, we'll hang the door tomorrow."

"Have done with it."

When the burning was a long time off they put in two rows
of slates as a damp course and timbered each room from the
yellow larch that crashed in a fine storm, Bimbo never tiring
of the saw that sang in his hands, his feet muffled in the knee-
high sawdust and the briars in the hair of the gypsy children.
A bird nested in the bodhrán young Will Byrne, a great lad,
had left in his father's barn. Boys oh boys. And in July a stray
Dalmatian came whistling up through the grass to them of a
Friday, his spots like squashed blackberries, jumping round
himself. They adopted him for the new house. The iron shone
on the range and the whistler fenced off an orchard and set
forty apple trees and Olive took great care putting down their
first rose bush. And folks wondered about the ornamented
porch that was built out front with the stained-glass windows,
and there was talk of a church but when the last stones dried
and you could hear the knock-knock of a thrush breaking a
snail in his new garden Saul was a proud man. Always before
daylight a man thinks of his destiny, as Saul did that last
morning talking with the travellers in the half-light of the
chestnut hill and he was glad to see that the cream-coloured
mare of the gypsies was loath to leave the fine grass now that
her time had come.

Occasional Stories

The Caretaker (1972)

He doused his face in ice-cold water, then took up the towel from beside the enamel basin and sat back onto the edge of the bed. The slanted light from the small roof-window fell at his feet. He rose and opened the catch lightly. Fresh air filled the room and for a while he stood barefooted to watch the armfuls of trees – limes and chestnuts – shake the wet night out of their leaves. He gave his socks a couple of belts against the sideboard, and bits of hay, small thorns and scatterings of grass fell out on the linoleum. Brushing them under the mat he straightened the quilts across the tick old Lavell had given him years ago. Then he put on his boots, and when he came down she had the range lit and the kettle chugging away.

"Anyone bin up at Lavell's as yet," he asked her first thing.

She looked at him, amused by his anxiety. "Not a one," she said. "Wouldn't they be early at it, sure it's not quite nine o'clock."

"You never can tell, some of these foreigners is early birds," he replied, glad of a woman like her. She smiled and went on cooking. He picked out *The Anglo-Celt* from behind the wireless, and tried a couple of times to stir up his enthusiasm for the Leitrim news. But it was no good, he couldn't concentrate. He picked up a lump of timber and gingerly dropped it into the range, poking back the early embers to make room, and sat leaning toward the fire, hands cupped round his knees.

The dog, tail-berserk, was peering round the corner of the door with his usual pleading eyes. "Away with you! Shou!" she said, clapping her hands. She took her husband his breakfast, the plate held firmly through her apron.

"The stummick's not up to more nor a cup of tea," he told her.

"That might be true for another man but not for you, Willie

Heaslip," she teased him in the old manner, and so he ate the little, drawing the hot tea down like a tonic. He ate in silence now, his ear cocked. At the first sound of a car he was on his feet immediately and out into the yard, but the car drove by up towards Ballinamore. He expected to see many cars of all sorts before the morning's business was done.

"You've little to do," she said when he returned, "you'll have yourself ashamed with your worrying."

He laughed at the wife who thought little of the goings-on of other menfolk winter or summer with their impatience to see things done and plans completed. For her things took years, even generations. She was that type of woman. But she'd be above at Lavell's today, just like himself, as it were to give a final salute or a first welcoming. Herself and her mother before her had done service above in the old house, when it was at its best and money was plentiful. There was many a man too in the townland had kept body and soul together with a handy day's work above on the estate in years gone by, and they had never gone short of firewood either.

He finished his tea right down to the leaves. The dog was back at the door again, so he took him a saucepan with water and milk mixed. Then he opened the gate and tied it against the pier, and walked up as far as the bridge and leaned over.

He'd made this same journey every morning for the best part of fifty years. Even in Lavell's time when he was a young man and admired the ladies there was no better place to do your courting than here at the bridge where you could look along the river to where it curled off to the left in a ragged sweep of brambles and thorns and silent waterlilies, and to where further on it straightened out and slowed up under the tall ordered spruces, with their branches thrown out in greeting, and the snow-colour at the crown of their leaves. Beyond that was the bathing place and above that again the high chimneys of the old house. Both places had their equal share of memories. He always felt a little simple here at this very spot where on a clear day he could see right through to Fermanagh and

beyond that too if his imagination was up to it. Many's the
lady still thought Sligo was only a stone's throw from where
he was standing.

A wood pigeon dashed out from O'Brien's meadow
and climbed high over the river till he watched it turn and
disappear into the loft of the stables at the back of the house.

Things had changed.

The birds and the rabbits had made a permanent home of
the house, and they'd be loth to leave when the time came.
Recently they'd as soon stop up and bid you the time of
day. Nests big as hawthorns hung round the front entrance
and there were burrows long as your arm dug in around the
courtyard. The ivy too was eating the heart out of the walls and
slowly strangling the trees, fine trees that Lavell had brought
here from the four corners of the world. But it was the water
tank up near the valley of the roof was causing all the damage;
it had been leaking the best part of three years now and the
ceiling underneath had begun to sag and grow green from the
damp. Not since the time of Lavell had a hand's turn been
made to improve or repair. If that go-boy Carny had never
been let near the place none of this would have happened.
That man wouldn't take a chance on work and according as
one room stank and grew filthy, he'd up and move to another
till he'd been through the whole thirteen with his gas ring, his
lady, his medical books and his sour puss.

"For a gay man you're at the deep end of the world this
morning, Willie," said O'Brien to him as he passed by on his
way to the creamery, the milk cans sitting like twins up front
beside him on the cart.

"The heart's not in it this morning," Willie answered.

"I suppose it'd take some five thousand pounds for your
thoughts now," O'Brien laughed. "But wouldn't you be all
right if a couple of fine ladies were to move in! Wouldn't you
be set for life." O'Brien drew his arms together under his chest
and threw your man a glad look. "Aye," he said, "it would
make me load a lot lighter."

At ten o'clock he put on his good blue suit and the long grey coat and shaved, and taking his time, he took the path through the fields. He had the big cod of a key in his top pocket. The wind was heavy with rain, and it looked like soon a shower would break with the dark swollen clouds being blown in from the Fermanagh mountains. The trees were being driven wildly against the galvanised roof of the stables. As he got close, rabbits with goats' ears watched him from a clump in the meadow. He felt suddenly better, and whistled the first verse of "Kate from Ballinamore," and crossed the fence easily onto the avenue.

The auctioneer had his white Jensen pulled up near the house. When he saw the caretaker he became all business and opened the door and ushered him in.

"Well, Carney's is about to have its day, Mr Heaslip," he said.

"Round these parts we like to forget that Carney ever owned the place," said Willie. "To us, it's always been Lavell's and will remain so till a better man takes it."

"Yes, yes indeed. I believe you've had a fair amount of visitors above looking around?"

"It's been a full time job, I'd say that."

The auctioneer shifted his arse slightly. "The land commission should have the few bob for you out of it," he said then.

"It's well known that the same crowd are good at getting their foot in every door in the country, but not so hot when it comes to handouts."

There was silence for a few minutes while the auctioneer felt round in his head for the proper thing to say. He brightened up.

"Will you smoke, Mr Heaslip," he asked.

"No," said Willie, "I gave that up when times got bad, and they haven't improved since." That was that.

A grey haze had built up on the meadow, and Willie could imagine the visitors and potential buyers hopping on their toes in the rain and the muck when the bidding would start. Men and women of all shades of opinion and dress had been to see him and the house these last six months. They were mostly foreigners or educated people who would be driven to despair at the thought of the work to be done. Education can kill or cure, the father used to say when Charlie Dickens would get too much for him. One Irish couple had stuck in Willie's mind – they'd arrived complete with shamrocks on St Patrick's Day. Willie had taken to the young man immediately. He had a good pair of hands on him and an eye for beauty; what's more, a love for trees – and that was what the house needed.

"Bad weather," the auctioneer said behind a cloud of smoke.

"It was always fond of the wet in Leitrim, but I believe they're sharing it around the rest of the country this year."

"True enough, Mr Heaslip. Tell me what price do you think . . . eh . . . Lavell's will fetch?"

Willie pondered the question. He drew his arms in under his chest. "Well, last night in McCabe's, old Jimmy Burns, who reslated the valley of the house some forty years ago, bet a pound that the bidding might top six thousand. I'd say his pound is steady at that."

The auctioneer thought it impossible but he didn't say so.

The rain had begun to fall quick and heavy when the first few cars came up the avenue. Behind them, the water filled up the wheel tracks in the mud. The rabbits, alarmed by all the commotion, tucked their tails into the air and skirted the meadow, doubling up and backtracking themselves till they disappeared into the White Wood. More and more cars screeched up through the mud and pulled in as it neared eleven o'clock, but none of the passengers budged, just sat there biding their time while the hard rain pelted down and blew holes in the puddles.

Across the fields now the locals were coming in their new-style green wellingtons to see how the old place would go. Willie, relieved at last, got out of the car and watched them arrive. These were the ancients of Leitrim like himself, old and benevolent and slightly mad, who carried their years like a war hero might his set of medals and who mourned not their own youth but the youth gone from the land, from their own country.

Even old Jimmy Burns was out, picking his way like a water diviner across O'Brien's meadow and dragging his bad foot behind him. Willie's wife, too, with a mackintosh thrown over her head, was coming up the path with a group of other women speaking softly to each other.

Willie helped old Jim through the fence. "There's a strength of wealth and foreigners out today for Lavell's," Jim said, getting his breath.

"Well," said Willie, "there was a thing I read once in the schoolbooks, and I thought it was a gay statement – ill fares the land when wealth accumulates and men decay."

"True for you, a tidy saying," Jim assured him.

The caretaker, feeling suddenly the weight of his seventy years, looked the length of the cars humped up on the grass margin like hostile cattle, and their impassive owners hemmed in behind the closed windows. "We might have a chance to put a few pounds on the place ourselves if none of them brave the weather," Willie at last said. Old Jim rocked with the laughter and sat himself down on the armchair roots of an elm, hopped his pipe on the bark and started spitting and puffing like a Trojan. Willie stood in against the tree himself and felt round him the fullness of the rain falling down to the east and west of him. Some small birds were fidgeting in the ditch. Willie knew the warm secrets of the hedge, the places where you touch new eggs, yellow flowers at your fingertips and deeper down, bluebells and red ferns in the moss. That was another world altogether.

On the hour the auctioneer took an egg-box out of the boot of the white Jensen and mounted the box under a chestnut tree. He was wearing a red dickey bow. The visitors got out of their cars, picking their steps across the muck like at any minute the whole avenue might give way. They looked a disgruntled lot. Beside him Willie heard a crisp English accent remark that "The whole thing was bloody orthodox or bloody Irish or both!" Old Jim chuckled and Willie drew his arms up under his chest, ducked his head and laughed into the ground.

The auctioneer went through all the paraphernalia of land rights and limits and the responsibilities of the new owners, and the responsibilities of the Land Commission, and had his bit said in a matter of seconds, but it was a good ten minutes of rain and small talk and persuasion and more rain before the bidding was opened by a German at £2,000. They were nervous, the lot of them, at the beginning, but a steady momentum set in and what with fingers raised and stroked chins and the nodding heads, the bidding topped the £4,000 mark before another lull occurred – a time for consideration, a time to take stock.

Just then, out of the blue, a Consul came tearing up the avenue, and Willie recognised the Irish couple immediately. He advanced to meet them, hands outstretched. Everyone had turned to watch the new combatants, and Willie's wife informed the locals that this was the pair her husband was keen to see get the house.

"Jesus, Mr Heaslip, have we made it in time?" the young man asked anxiously.

"You have hours to spare now, Keegan," Willie said. "Come up to them and get your hand in."

He took them up through the crowd, and no sooner were they installed when the young lady lifted her hand and the auction started rolling again. "She's already got the curtains ordered," Keegan whispered to Willie. An English woman with steel grey hair whose husband had done most of the bidding up to now threw the young couple a hostile look but they were oblivious to her. Angrily her finger stabbed the air like a drawn sword, while the other hand held up an umbrella as if it were a musket.

At £4,500 there were only four left in the bidding from almost a dozen starters – the Keegans, the English couple and two Germans. At this stage the auctioneer could hardly get a word in edgeways, but there was a breathing space at £6,000 when the two Germans dropped out, shrugging their shoulders in mild amazement, and retiring from the rain under Jim's elm. Willie knew the bidding was taking everything the couple had, but he was proud of them. He'd help them. The locals were becoming restless each time the grey-haired lady tugged her husband's sleeve to answer a bid, and they'd turn to the Keegans, silently urging them on. When the young couple had made what seemed a final desperate bid at £6,600, on the second strike of the auctioneer's hammer, old Jim, tormented out of his mind, stumbled up through the crowd, and with his good foot drove a kick at the auctioneer's egg-box. "For Jasus' sake, give it to them," he shouted, brandishing his stick. "They deserve it."

There was silence for a few seconds as everyone's gaze was riveted on the English woman and her husband. No move was made. The auctioneer brought the hammer down, glad himself that the job was done.

Willie, proud as Punch, walked over and shook hands with the Keegans, who were standing out in the open and soaked to the skin, relieved and nervous at the same time. "You did well," he said. "You held on well, no doubt about that." Old Jim came up to them too, his two blue eyes sparkling and his hand thrown out like a shovel to pump their grip, to welcome them home. "That's the style," he said, "you'll be good here a thousand years." Then at Willie's invitation the locals came round to shake the wife's hand and clap the young fellow on the back. Willie saw at the end of the avenue the husband of the grey-haired lady gesticulating and remonstrating with her. Some marries them, he thought, they're as well out of it.

Afterwards they had tea and brown bread in Willie's cottage, and then, followed by the dog, the caretaker took the couple up to see the house for a second time. The sun had come out and they had to screw up their eyes when they came of a sudden into the light. The rabbits were back at the clump. The July rain had washed the roof a slatey-grey, and water gushed from the gutters in mad torrents.

Back of the courtyard Willie stopped and said, "Let me show you the deepest well in the whole of Ireland." He pulled back the galvanised lid that covered the entrance to the well, beating the dog away with his hand at the same time. "This was built a hundred years ago and took over a month with men tearing through solid rock for the best part of eighty feet." He dropped a stone. Seconds passed. At last from somewhere deep, deep down, as if light years off, the hollow sound of stone on stone happened twice. Then there was a faraway splash and the stone took water on its way through.

"It's all yours now," Willie said.

This Side of Summer (1974)

The wind was tossing the cherry blossom onto the hair and shoulders of a girl walking towards ———.

He sat by his window watching. Today, he looked more sickly than usual and the dirty white shirt only furthered the feel of decay and thinness as it opened loosely onto his chest. The grey room had an air of pathological dampness, its high walls shadowed by great grim furniture out of whose drawers hung a sock, a vest, a severed arm. He felt sad and tired, even afraid. In front of his face, on the window ledge, a glass jar of faded flowers now filled the room with promise as the breeze stirred them, leaning together to the north of the city until the wind stopped and time slowed the flowers down through the leafy water, the green stems kicking up sand.

The plaster collar round his neck and the brace strapped below his chin gave him the appearance of a man concentrating on a matter of grave purpose, absorbed in a private world that could only be sustained by silence and the smallest of words. Sometimes a sharp pain darted across his features like a startled bird. To be truthful, he was not absorbed but servile, though he sat mostly upright and stiff in his chair, opening and closing his eyes with resigned love and the ache of memories, though he could neither love nor remember, thinking something else as the sun set.

The light made the darkness darker.

A bird hovered for a moment before the window, noisily clipping the air with the white blades of its tail as her yellow breast hummed with health, and she peered in and gave the man held by pain from falling to pieces a ghost of a smile. Then she dropped away in a trance of wings, like a fish. He described her to himself like this for accuracy, that he might never forget the external world in all its particulars.

He put on his coat with great care and walked down

the two dusty flights of stairs, past the erratic cracks in the walls and below the angels of stained plaster that flew dizzily across the distant ceiling. Very slowly he descended, reaching forward for the lower step with deliberation, for his head was unconscious of the business of his feet. When he got to the bottom he recalled it was April 2nd, 19———. He pondered a moment and shook his head, turned back and slowly again climbed to his room, closing the door quietly behind him lest anyone might have heard his eccentric descent and his embarrassed ascent.

Before he sat down again by the window, he wiped his forehead and chin with a handkerchief that smelled of sperm and shook his shoulders to relax the vice-grip of the collar on his head, the permanent gesture of unconcern and finality his chin made.

Through the quiet road at ——— where he lived the late traffic poured out from the city, hurtling below his window across definite distances, and the seagulls climbed onto each other's backs and shrieked and flipped across a hundred years of sky, lights went on in the tree-lined houses and there was sudden laughter and lights went out, doors closed behind every minute that passed and he awoke uneasily to the smells and folk music and disturbed air of people returning. Above his head familiar footsteps mixed with the sounds from the street, a dog chased and barked at a passing car. The arrival of the hardware man in his blue overalls carrying his bag of groceries marked the end of the latecomers to his street. The dog lay down on a step and slept.

The watcher sat there erect and stiff and still by the window till even the cherry tree shuffled away with its leaves into the shadowy darkness, a dark figure like a man looking over a wall . . . .

The person had been knocking for some moments on the door before – like awakening from sleep – he could recognise the sounds as real and intended for him. He could not wonder but rose slowly and let the sound carry on as if he might interpret some sign. At last he opened the door.

—I'm afraid I can't see you, a girl said as she peered into the room and then she disappeared into darkness like himself when the time switch clicked off with a soft pop on the landing. He stood there startled, trying to focus on where she had been for a few bewildering seconds, as if he could resurrect her from the darkness, then he turned and stumbled through the room searching for his own switch. He thought he heard her breathe in sharply behind him. He felt walls and tables and upturned cups and her breast with his hand and the long curve of iron bedstead that had been shaped into black roses. Something was knocked over by his feet. He found the switch of the bedside lamp he used since the bulb had blown in the gaudy cheap chandelier that hung like a thurible from the ceiling.

The light flickered, blacked out for a second and then held as she stepped into the room tentatively.

—Oh, she said, her eyes widening as she looked round the room, the books scattered about the floor, the tins of food on the table and him gazing with embarrassment towards her from the bed, his chin at such an angle it seemed he was about to shout out loud, the pile of newspapers thrown into the corner and on the window ledge the stray leaves of the flowers rustling against the window pane. He had seen her cross once below his window carrying a kitten on her shoulder that nibbled her ear as she walked, or heard at other times her laugh in the middle of the night, the patter of her feet as she walked barefooted down the corridor. Her scant eyes came back and settled on him.

—We are having a party in my room tonight, she said flatly. I wanted to ask you for the loan of some glasses and whether you'd like to come.

He was stunned by the matter-of-fact tone of her voice. He had expected some great horror to befall him but instead this woman was talking to him as if she had known him all the days of his life.

—Why, yes, of course, he said.

—You stay where you are, she answered him, I'll get the glasses. She started a search round the room picking up both cups and glasses and even started tidying up his scattered effects.

He looked at her thankfully.

—I don't have really many glasses, but you can take the cups as well.

—OK, she said.

He sat on the bed and silently watched her. She was wearing a man's striped cotton shirt with the front ends lifted and drawn tight below the exhausting swell of her breasts, the nipples springing out like young shrubs through the cloth. The shirt left her brown waist open to the touch of hands. The faded jeans opened in a wide V onto her full dark belly-button and then reached down widely to cover nearly entirely her naked feet. A fish with orange fins and white embroidered eyes had been knitted onto her right thigh, diving down into a cluster of bright stars.

—Will we see you tonight, she said when she had finished.

—I think not tonight, he answered gravely. I ... He stopped speaking, and the cold of the moon was in the breeze that bundled through the flowers and blew against the hollow of his back. He understood his awareness of himself then as the greatest fabrication of truth he had ever known.

—Thanks then, she said after a moment. I'll bring them back tomorrow. She left, leaving behind her a scent of oranges and fresh wine. He sat for a long time after, among the thousand vibrations, and sometimes he heard a loud cheer from the street, the grunt of a drunk as he steadied himself against a car, a cat in heat. The five notes of the pigeon. Much later the mixed hilarity of people and raised voices on the corridor, her door opening and music bursting into the hall filling the house with New York, the door closing and all was mumbling silence again.

The young face in the mirror of his mind smiled out at

him and he leaped up from the chair terrified.

For a moment he thought his head might tumble off from the rest of his body and come away in his hands.

He slept early that night in the manner to which he had become accustomed, his head resting on three pillows piled one on top of the other and his eyes fixed on a faraway tear in the ceiling paper. As a child when his hair fell out he used to pick up the light shreds and try to pat them back in on his head, and because he felt dead now, only the slight movement of the hours on his eyes betrayed any trace of life travelling in his waxen limbs, the body of a starved woman. He prayed there, mentally rehearsing the words beforehand that he lip-read from the face of a child, himself, stunned by the great climax of the freewheeling world and the fear of that earlier huge room hidden from all other rooms, where moths disintegrated and burnt out on the shades of the light bulb. When he awoke in the middle of the night he heard the five notes of the pigeon and when he reached out his arm to touch the salt of the warm woman lying there, from his neck came the long shock of pain.

He was here alone.

Six months later she was talking to her friends in a new flat in Rathfarnham they had rented. Out of the kitchen window you could see the huge roll of the green-and-yellow mountains as they relaxed in the pale sunlight and frost of centuries. This was the first time her friends had come to see her since Joe and herself had rented their new home, and their presence made her conscious of how time and circumstance had eroded whatever friendship she'd shared with them, but still unwilling to admit to this lack of intimacy she was trying harder and harder to excite or cajole them while they remained on the whole embarrassed, speaking only with a slight touch of cynicism.

She was speaking in a breathless and excited manner, even enjoying her role as the misguided lady, her eyes widening with mock modesty as she threw up her hands and hovered in mid-air and mid-sentence with the coffee pot a few inches above a watchful young banker's head, her lips fluttering with s-sounds as she described a particularly intriguing incident. Why she was trying so hard to amuse them she could not tell, it was like something insistent in her nature that propelled one meaningless word after another, something beyond her control. Had she been more at ease she would have been amused at their gravity as they chewed distastefully on the garlic bread she had cooked for Joe till it was nearly black. She would have enjoyed their obvious dislike for Joe and treated their remarks with irony, indifference.

— He had no teeth either, not a tooth in his head when I met him first, Kate was saying.

— That must have been interesting for you, the banker's girlfriend intoned with a mischievous smile.

— He doesn't seem to like us too much, the banker said.

— Oh no, it's just that he is off working somewhere or other. He's a gardener by trade – he works with some rich families in Wicklow and earns – oh – a small fortune. I mean, I needn't be working at all, Kate added, flushing slightly.

— If you are satisfied I suppose that's what counts, Esther said, who was wearing a long dress she had taken home from the boutique she worked in.

— Oh yes, I am, said Kate feeling exhausted and empty.

She felt relieved when they left. She made up the bed and set out the dinner dishes on the table, humming to herself as she swept out the room and shook the crumbled biscuits into the cat's dish. Joe had been right to clear out of the house before they came. He seems to talk so little to people except herself and anyway he is inclined to shout in company, he must get nervous or something. Sometimes she felt they were the only two people living in the whole world and when she was on her own while he was walking the mountains, she felt incredibly lonely. She would sit by the window, staring out despondently towards the mountains as if she could have picked out the small speck of himself climbing through the blues and the greens of the horizon.

When Joe came in he smelt of the pub. They kissed in a rush at the door and into the hall and into their own room. Her kisses running all over his eyes, his forehead, his cheeks. It was awful, awful, she said. I began making all kinds of excuses for you ... and for me, never again, they sat there just ... oh Joe ... and I said you were making piles of money and oh Jesus Christ ....

He laughed at her.

—I mean how could they do that to me? She tightened her fists and shook them and screwed up her eyes. I mean it looked as if I was an old whore or something. They were so ....

Not to worry, he said.

He kissed the brown curve of her forehead.

—Perhaps you were too sensitive.

—I should not have invited them at all.

—You need to see people now and then.

—I need to see no one. No one.

Joe rolled off his scarf and sat down by the table and told her he had worked up the biggest appetite that he ever had in his whole life. She looked at him a few moments with a half-smiling, half-exasperated look on her face, hands on her hips, and then having done with her outburst she went into the kitchen shaking her head.

—How do you feel? she shouted in from the kitchen.

—Oh great, he said.

As he sat there an overwhelming feeling of goodwill towards her, of happiness, enveloped him, as happened nearly every day now as his head cleared and as he broke down the insurmountable conventions that had held his real self back for so many years. Into his mind rushed so much tremendous energy, oh he need never look back again. He stood up at the kitchen door about to tell her.

—Christ, you know, he said and then lapsed into silence.

Perhaps his very nature had stifled her gaiety. He tried to reach out and assemble all the ideas that formed that rich moment, the peak of his day, and her helpful eyes pleaded with him though disturbed by his sudden wretchedness. His own silence, immobility, hurt him. Nothing answers. He went back in and sat by the table and there it came to him, as if a butterfly had just darted into the room spinning her light for one short moment, that he saw moments of happiness as moments that can never be retrieved and unhappiness as reaching out and trying to stay that moment. We live in so many small crude worlds and you say to yourself I was happy a moment ago.

—You looked so happy a moment ago, she said bitterly.

He closed his eyes and the centre passed into his imagination. I have committed suicide such a long time ago and I feed from her breast that sits round and small and hung like an unceasing eddy in a river, he said to himself, or listened to the unreal horror of the words in his head like it was a child's nursery rhyme. What would I do if she left me, he asked himself. He sat silently a moment, thinking, seeing her as a person apart that he might not interfere with the truth. What would I do? Why, I would stay as I am. Where I am. Eventually I must accept the dark corners of the mind.

—Here's the grub, she said.

Kate came in laughing from the kitchen with her hair covered in flour, and placed on the table the steaming vegetables and the roasted potatoes and the fresh brown trout her brother caught in the Dodder that dawn. I'm sure you did, she said, when he told her he had walked far. They drank from the wine in silence, for something about their relationship was inevitable. He felt like a dead man. Across the road a palm tree drifted up into the grey clouds, the branches lifting till at the height of the evening the last two arms cupped round the mouth of the sky, and sang.

Moments were too short. He sat and watched stiff and upright from his chair, the skin drawn tightly across the broken veins in his cheeks. Moments are far too short, he thought, and soon you and I must learn some new industry to bring us again into the world. He laughed a little. She brought in the dark steaming coffee, and never said a word, for it was easy to see that something was troubling him and he was always stubborn when it came to explaining, even frightened.

The Workman (1975)

Mari was the darling daughter of a teacher, and she was educated in fine style and reared by an honest philosophic household. Summers came and went and she grew into a good-looking girl surrounded by friendship and long games of tennis with the respectable lads in town. Everyone said she would go places. She worked for a while in Dublin in an insurance office and her parents often drove to the city to visit her, bringing small gifts of fresh food from the country and afterwards the family would visit the cinema, an item her father would look forward to for months ahead. Her status improved when she moved to work for a famous solicitor in the city, telling her family on her weekends in Portlaoise the inside stories of the politics of the time and the crude hair-raising stories of crime and hardship among the people. She had a spacious flat on the North Side, in a terraced row of houses in Phibsborough that she filled with potted plants of her own choice and some her mother brought her, painting the rooms herself, cooking Italian dishes that gave the air of the flat an oily European flourish.

"I don't know how you can eat that stuff girl!" the father would say.

"That's what they want these days," the mother often remarked.

The years passed and still there was no sign of the suitor everyone expected, one that seemed destined for an intelligent and unobtrusive girl from whom no item of education or specific of character had been withheld. The visits to the city continued but now the mother was growing peevish and inquisitive, asking the girl repeatedly how she spent her time and who her friends were and then the father through embarrassment eventually just dropped his spouse to the flat and went off to the pictures alone. He said it was not for him to judge his only daughter, that she had all the time in the world. For he had learned to appropriate each concept to its category, reading the old philosophers when the light was right or taking delight when Mari read his stars. But the mother was impatient for that big day in town when confetti might fly and for the time she might wrap the first child in the baptismal frock that had nursed like snow all of three generations of Cauldwells into the world.

Once it seemed that romance was in the air.

"Who's that driving up the avenue," the mother asked the father one Sunday morning as a Volkswagen entered the gates.

"I don't know," the teacher said leaving down his newspaper and stretching his chin.

It was Mari and her man. They stayed of course for dinner and the stranger talked with an unassuming nonchalance, perhaps he was not all the mother expected and she never quite extracted what he worked at but it was a relief to see Mari so happy, so talkative. Months passed without another of these visits, even though every Sunday an extra-large leg of lamb was bought on the chance that her daughter and her man might be arriving and always Tom Cauldwell took a walk after Mass down the avenue and up a stretch of the Dublin Road, where the walls of the asylum looked across the walls of the prison, for the first time in his life troubled by a neighbour's gaze. In his younger days Tom had believed himself a committed empiricist, but less and less these days did he respond to outer trivia, more and more he looked at the facts of life from a non-compromising position. Yet now again he was a victim. At last one weekend the parents drove to Dublin, an exciting enough trip in that they ran into the back of a parked car where Mari lived, and Tom had to leave a penitent note on the windscreen of the injured vehicle with his name and address.

It was one of those warm days of summer and the Dubliners were strolling in their shirtsleeves along the streets. Young couples walked along carrying their haversacks like babies. Mari seemed happy enough, yet they noticed a reticence, a shyness while they walked in the Phoenix Park where a band was practising its airs.

"I am returning to Portlaoise," she told them, avoiding a panting runner that swept by them on the footpath. "I've got a good job there."

"Why that's grand," said her father.

The drive back to Portlaoise that day was fraught with bewilderment and sadness for Mrs Cauldwell but in a way, she felt relieved, for Mari had grown so strange to them of late that at least now the distance between them should be less. For Tom Cauldwell, he looked forward to having his daughter home and, in another way, he would miss the frequent trips to Dublin, the atmosphere of the streets, the odd memories. Mari arrived a week later and took up her secretarial job with an architect and she made different succulent meals for the father at night, walking with him to the library, making photostat copies of maps and articles he was writing in his ambiguous way of the district. She took the bus into town in the mornings, being driven home each evening by the architect. She was twenty-six now and still as good-looking as that beautiful girl of sixteen, but she remained inaccessible to the men of the town, nearly transparent.

For two years things remained so in the family.

Then Mari began dating a bachelor farmer who lived a few miles out of town. He had come into her office one day to settle some plans with the architect for the erection of a new farmhouse for himself. It was so unexpected that Mrs Cauldwell ran busily round the house for days, doing things that had fallen to Mari as she herself had grown distraught and withdrawn what with the tension of living with a stranger; her supernumerary thoughts, now extra as a sudden sanity, beyond recall, but each following each in perfect name and place, her dwindling home a fortress again. The first time Mari brought Finbar to the house her mother was disturbed by the fact that

he looked so old, his hairline was receding and his manners at
the table cumbersome, but she grew to like him as his visits
became more frequent and he was rich, thoughtful.

"It's great that you can spend so much time away from the
farm," Mrs Cauldwell often remarked.

"Well I have a workman, you see. He does everything
about the farm, even more than myself," Finbar would answer.

Mari married Finbar when she was twenty-eight. On the
day she had dignity as he had pride. The wedding was small
for he had no folks in the district, his mother and father were
long dead and his brother was in America and as for Mari she
invited only the architect and his wife, and the Derry girl who
had lived next door to her in Dublin. Mrs Cauldwell became
mistress of her house again and Tom took to gardening in the
evenings, setting plants from the few tips Finbar had given
him and often Mari took them small gifts of fresh eggs or a
multi-coloured cock pheasant as they once brought her little
odds and ends in Dublin. Mari never seemed to age, her hair
was full and dark and she wore all the incoming fashions, took
riding lessons and bought a horse which she rode breathlessly
over the husband's lands, sometimes gathering wild bunches
of flowers which she placed in pots everywhere in their great
rolling house.

When Finbar drove to town on Friday and Saturday nights
for his drink she accompanied him in her finery and his friends
admired her, often making passes when Finbar got up to sing
with the local céilí band, their romantic efforts childish to her
eyes. Finbar was proud of her. The workman always came with
them to town, a young stalwart lad that made her his queen,
his mistress, attending to her every wish, bringing her cups of
tea when she lay in bed late, shifting furniture about the house
for he had a great attention to design, making the evening
meals for Finbar and himself if she had driven to Dublin to
buy some new clothes. And because Finbar had befriended
the boy since he was a labourer's son, because he loved him as
a brother he found this servile, almost loving attention to his

wife a form of gratitude, laughable, till one evening a few years after they were married, when primroses hung in the ditch like real promises, he went about the farm everywhere looking for the workman, going around the various outhouses.

"I can't find Frank anywhere," he told Mari who was preparing a nearly festive supper.

"You won't either," she said.

"Why," he asked.

"Because I've sacked him," she said.

"For what in Jesus's name," he asked astonished.

"Because you are blind, man. You're blind. I can't have him round here anymore."

"We'll see about that," he answered her, leaving the house.

The next day Frank was back working on the farm. Mari drove away to Dublin and at last Finbar had to go away for her by train to get her back. And the Cauldwells heard and the mother grew frightened for her child but after a few days Mari and Finbar returned. And then the parties began in the house. First they invited people up of a Friday night, and sometimes crowds stopped the whole weekend. The neighbours could hear the shouts and cheers from the house on the silent winter nights and perhaps when he had seen the uselessness of this compromise, Finbar would sit spitefully up in the Cauldwells' house till another false dawn drinking, while Mrs Cauldwell waited anxiously on the stairs till she might hear the front door close and Finbar drive drunkenly home. One evening her father drove up to see Mari and they had a long talk and when she gave him a short answer he said, "To my mind girl, irony is negative, it's time to meditate, reflect." And later she read astrology, and knew that moonstone and white onyx were her valuable stones, dark brown, indigo and black her colours, and for some time afterwards Mari began visiting the patients in the mental hospital, bringing them gifts of fresh apples from Finbar's orchard as she read to them from soiled religious books.

And the workman stayed away out in the fields sharing the harvest with Finbar.

Evenings would find her cycling back to the farm, meeting
blatantly the gaze of the young men cutting the hedges with
their briar knives and billhooks.

And often when the feminine smell of winter was in the air
she stood under the strangled trees to watch the happy faces of
the young children cheering as they tumbled out of the gates
of the convent.

In February the workman and Mari left Ireland and they were
never seen again. For a while the neighbours gave Finbar a
hand with the farm and often the Cauldwells drove out of a
Sunday to bring him in for his dinner but through time he
stopped work altogether and drank continuously. His plight
was mooted often among the neighbours, not that he was short
of money, but ten, maybe twenty years passed and he sold the
farm, all but an acre of land and the shack where Frank the
workman had lived, and here he set up house, drawing a huge
load of turf into the haybarn, a last act of survival. He refused
any help for there was nothing further to celebrate, except
perhaps to watch the shot roach turning onto their silver
backs in the muddy stream that ran by the door. He paid all
his debts off and sat there drinking all the nights, wakening
with the nauseating taste of old food and drink in his mouth,
maybe perhaps not drinking the following day but suffering
the consequence of his dreams and the loneliness. A few times
he dressed up spruce as ever and went into town and drank
with the younger lads and older men in the dusky afternoons,
for all their drunken commentaries upon the world.

Only the grey reflection flying up of a white bird flying down
in the stream.

When he died her family buried him for he had exhausted
his property to the final hour and it was a haunting black
day in March when the rooks shuffled overhead like a pack
of cards but life somehow keeps a promise, as if all our lives
are worthy of loves elsewhere, for a month later a single letter

arrived to the then elderly Cauldwells and first the bearded Tom checked the postmark and saw it was Australian and he looked at the envelope a long time before opening it. The scuffle of sparrows overhead. In a way it was proper that this should be Mari's last communication with them, unattended to by her but by some unknown official in Melbourne and the death certificate was so final, so much an ending that old Cauldwell when he came to himself never shed a tear but burnt it before his wife had come down the stairs, before they set off to catch the bus to Dublin for a day at the cinema.

The time had long gone when he could elicit anything further from experience, but often he thought of that inviolate moment and the strange sheet of paper making its way across that long distance, the work of the spirit of reality was here, attended to by airport officials and custom men and all kinds of unconscious hands, through the tension of human existence, that in the end told him so little after coming so far.

Jude and his Mother (1977)

I dreamed that life-energy itself could be siphoned off at the moment before death. There is nothing unusual in that dreamlike speculation, a refusal to harden the arteries, you might think, common or garden science fiction. But in the dream this life is then contained with the maximum of pleasure on the shiny surface of a penny piece, and eternalized by the coin spinning on the head of a fragile matchstick. These matchsticks (for there were other lives there spinning around besides my evidently doubtful one) moved pleasantly backwards and forwards on a thin plank in a small bedroom, the plank balanced on I know not what, but sustaining this planetary motion, these shiny, commercial, spinning surfaces.

If you wanted to put the picture into a frame, on a penny, analyse this dream in the deterministic fashion of our contemporary analysts, you might say it was caused by a mild reading of our Marxist masters, or being a Jungian, care to think that this was the way all life was planned, at least for me. You could speak of my debts and my guilt. And the aesthetic mortification of man being so reduced, but, then, can I afford to have you in my dreams?

I don't live in a relaxed regime, I'm afraid.

Not that I am dissatisfied or under pressure, I too have had my moments of joy, when the bar was cleared for the rasp of the fiddle and the songs of Marcus Sommerville, my mother's songster. But order, though I might desire it, became the great tragedy. Nor do I mean the vacuum that instinct might fill. I did not want to fill my life with decadence and indolent learning, the pastiche of Europe. Nor make a hero of my neurotic, cockless self. I preferred the political truth at this time to the musical traditional proverbs of my mother. Not the German psyche, the Andalusian colour, and yet all of these. Perhaps it was merely justifying and activating my presence in life at a given moment, by searching for a further consciousness than that which is called subconscious, and that which is called conscious. I began to plan my dreams, decide when to wake from them.

What remained after I had completed these exercises, sometimes with success but more often with fear, was that my evaluation of life did not comply with what I had hoped for. I believed I was lying, or had merely believed I was planning my dreams. This doubt became the real subconscious, the third event of my mind, which I could not control or dismiss, but only continue to gather evidences, both positive and negative and doubtful, doubtful being the category that supplied my impetus and love.

It was I, then, who put my Imperial head on the coin, I who woke spontaneously in my bedroom, and I who must discharge my duties.

But the rushing in to help someone has a strange history. To be effective it must be over in seconds, and to remain integral it must never be mentioned. I gathered that political evangelists are a bore in the intellectual sphere, yet still intellectuals are desirous of freedom of content. The status No. On the other hand, those who take an active interest in our political life and do not forego aesthetics, find the combination hard to maintain, or so tradition has it. But often upset at night, when sleep was not imparted to me readily due to an imaginary illness or a heavy cold ... like a brick lodged in the centre of my chest, its cold edges resting on my lungs ... I would lift up a translation of Marx and feel restored by that sense of colossal empty strength in the world.

The long day's drink was a cultural hardship, it happened so often.

My feet unhinged, and my mind too.

Decadence: *decline of art due to a pronounced depletion of vital energies, resulting in the rejection of practical life in favour of the composure of contemplation; an aesthetic fear or glorification of* *action; an unnecessary martyrdom; a lack of will to live without contradictions; pessimism.*

Anyway, for romantic reasons, I chose to work with my body because of its liberating effect, but this therapy only lasts for a while, becomes an excuse for boasting (craftsmen are the energy cycle for capitalists and socialists), no matter how often you conjecture or explain its necessities to others.

Beating the ends of rubber mats wears you down. The supervisor follows me around like a pal, because of my education; we stand on the floor looking up at the spacious offices, debating our future. He makes sure I receive slight jobs, brings my cup of tea with his to a separate table in the canteen, jousts, prowls, is mischievous. The factory is near Woodgreen, opposite the bookies, a grey half mile from the Underground. I stand by my own furnace, clamp down the shape of the toilet bowl, the rubber recoils under the heavy heat, my great gloves hold the flame. Keep the clamp in position, lean on it, the machine shivers, and then I withdraw the design. The burnt rubber is doused with water. The ends cut off with a knife. The threads inspected. Sometimes they hang askew, as when the strings of a harp are held aside to permit the passage of a sweeter note. Pop music is played all day, the supervisor remembers the happier tunes of Music While You Work. The walls and galvanised roofs burn, and the ladies love to daunder in the cooler air of the finishing evening, hesitate within the gates a minute longer than necessary to facilitate a more blissful entrance into the humid streets.

Scorched clothes leave behind welts of the appearance of bed sores, as if today we turned and turned and walked the factory floor but could not find solace.

The girls have forgotten the callisthenic optimism of their past, eye makeup and diesel darken their lids, they are exuberant, sexual, joking, tired-flesh makes a problem for the future. But unlike Wagner, they cannot stroke satin till the mood comes. His roughish gramarye. They expel their ghosts with lavish foreplay, as Li Ho has written:

> If Heaven too had passions
> Even Heaven would grow old.

I will never really enter their lives unless I marry one of the girls or join their union. Either way, it will be something to do with joining, but not dedication. Take Josu now, how more and more he desired privacy, changed groups, attacked from a different angle our youth. So that for us, growing older, maturing, will never come as a surprise. But after our first wholehearted hatred mellowed, it was not his desire that broke down, not his desire for companionship, it was more the strain that we, those closest to him, exerted. We suspected some falsehood, it was at our fingertips, but then it became apparent that life itself directs the course of error and truth. We, as individuals, were not so privileged. "Jude," said my abstemious mother, "You waste your time diluting truth with words." She is big and fat in the manner of many women from our district, and lords over her cattle, eternally soured by the society in town, which thrives because of its elitist momentum. The great social endeavours there sustain the lonely and the ambitious by their collaboration. It is of no use to mention to her such clichés as Urban Renewal or Machinery of Man. The despair of wanting to go someplace to be taken in. Political excesses. "Today," she says, "a country lad knows more about machinery, electricity, plumbing, and animals than his city counterpart. His awkward stance is technically sure." All deteriorations and crookedness are commonplace, and to speak of them with Puritan disdain, to her, is to speak of the obvious, things have changed, such observations have lost their original critical vitality, they just add to the nervous gestures of my mother's chin. January 31st found me back in the village arguing with her. We called on her brother, the shopkeeper. Business was failing, his sweet-jars were half empty, musty sugar filled the glass. The wooden till was full of coins only, the rashers on the counter weeping.

"I always associate such business with terror," she remarked to him, "The fear of being unable to deal with the public."

"If you hadn't the money you might be off to the Home," he said, seeking sympathy.

"Unless your marbles are unsettled, anyone that would burn you for a fool would have wise ashes."

"As long as I had millions," he answered, knocking his hand off his fist.

"The poor auld fuck," she said as we strolled home, though she felt sad for him, and taunted him wisely. In the morning I went into the field to perform my ablutions. Cold human shits in the back garden, dotted along the tangled hedge, the yellow frozen toilet paper sparkling with frost. A bird flew out from an empty place left by a missing slate in the roof. The kitchen windows were lit by winter flower patterns; sharp edges of transparent leaves lasted till midday. Reflections fossilized. Crude radio plays she turned up high, written with frantic characterizations that border on embarrassment.

The tips of the fingers disappeared from walking abroad.

Oh, my mother was not secured by a religious sanction against outrage! She had been flattened at the crossroads. Everyone at first supported the stone throwing because of her tongue and later extended it by extremism and constancy or redeemed it by prayer and power. The Passion of Christ was the local impotence. The bearded man who had demeaned her and loved her, was fattened by and exasperated by the cold, undignified clay. "Humbleness is not good enough" was one of her generalizations. She so cherished the spring, in this, her little island of thought. We rocked to the laughter of my dead father's funny stories repeated in the kitchen, the two of us, after tea. How they'd, his friends and him, tied an ass to the door on Halloween night, and twice, the knocker had sounded, she answered and saw no one; the third time, pulling hard at the door she drew the curious donkey into the hall. A bird-scuffle over her head, while kneeling she beats cloth on stone. The distant and sudden argument of nature, but "Jude," she says, "one has to learn not to grieve over futile arguments." Knowing that my fantasies cannot screen off nor add to the appearance of the future. For dialogue but satisfies my urge to communicate mostly in retrospect. Belligerent in public, working in secret, that the critic in me might choose or invent realities that the fatalist in me absolves. Rain dropping on the hot sands of the White City dog track. In the village the smell of burning feathers. Yeats sign.

Lorries and water go everywhere.

Being there or here, holidays or arguments never seem to end for me. A passage of time here, there, or hereafter, repeats itself either venomously or joyously. So I remarked to Anna as we passed by a drunk on the Underground, deliriously intimating some secret in his inside pocket. We were carrying a fluorescent tube and a bag of torn material which we'd found in cardboard boxes outside a city design centre. Anna had tried their various colours and shapes in the train, each oddment is a decoration eventually. The drunk is black-faced, vulnerable bags under his brown eyes, wearing a red and blue light-woollen scarf. An Indian scapular hangs from his pock-marked throat. He took out a photograph from his untidy wallet and looked longingly at it. Then he struck his head off a pillar a number of times.

Quickly sand was poured over his vomit and two cops carried him out of the Underground, laughing to each other, intimates, his feet dragging, roar of the train. "He's okay," I said to Anna but she threw me a spiteful look which I returned. Each drunk in a cell is a world onto a world.

At the meeting, the sound of the speaker's voice was drowned out by engine after engine, only his hands carried the momentum of his heart. He uses a mixture of wit, criticism and bravery, his thoughts strain under the skin of his temple. I mean his face exaggerates the quality of his mind. We are there, complete with fluorescent tube, to interrupt the meeting and disparage his reasoning. Anna has a formidable weapon which issues a sound like a foghorn. Jim, from the Industrial North, is urgent and versatile with his declamations. An egotist, he lacks pity and judgement, but with a spiritual flourish of his country boots he stands some seven inches above any other man in the room. He gains equilibrium from the cottage he lives in, in Sussex, with his tumultuous family. But Josu, the speaker, is unruffled. Aesthetics and adolescence were laws he had long ago dispensed with, though the young Spaniards mock him, he indulges in high-minded caprices.

"It's the man on the street, they fear," he remarked.

"Whose rhyme shall we use tonight? What word will break into a thousand recognizable pieces to suit their etymological backgrounds, the need of purity? Do you even know what I mean?"

After leaving the ill-attended meeting, we went onto the streets singing our hoarse European songs.

Though later, discouraged, when Anna and I sat talking in the darkness, she said "We may be twice as romantic as we think; when there was no politics to suit us well we went out and invented a form of our own." "That's optimism," I said, and we laughed. But could tell the distance from danger and practicality. We were just middle-class would-be intellectuals down on our luck. This led to further discussion and cruelty between us. The raucous throb of cars and machines communicated in the planks of the shanty, buildings were coming down, staccato explosions from the industrial estate filled the night, and later the swearing of the street dancers. From the other rooms, the most humane and compassionate case against revolution . . . the passionate longing for solitude and silence.

And, as always, Anna watches me as I read (perhaps as Josu once watched her), looking up difficult words with patient, annoying care, interrogating the dictionary, and sometimes arriving at the same word time and time again, as if it could not rest on my palate, its strangeness a world I could not enter with my senses or experience, needing Beckett's brisk nihilism, by its history a novel built round an attitude till the dictionary becomes The Book of Revelation. For truly no other fiction could capture my mind so.

Revelation? Fiction? Yea, sweet God, for no word would ever settle on a meaning, unless an arbitrary one. Here then, among the rich verbs and frugal nouns, the workers of the tongue, my first course in Dialectics. The Historical Imagination gives us something vital and lethal, I once read. Till Nothingness is hostile and treacherous. And terminology is not an exact science for Anna either, she too favours my mother's generalizations and their attended ultimatums and contradictions.

Of terminology: "Anything so generous with meaning, with actual principles, with indisputable laws, can provide you with a platform, a stand, whenever you so desire," she says ironically, betraying no sympathy towards man's weakness for equality or authority.

We had everything at our fingertips, but could not find the truth.

So when Mary, Queen of Scots, died, she endured two strokes of the executioner's axe "making very smale nayse or none at all." This I read in the British Museum one summer's day. Her little dog had crept under her clothes, emerged after the execution and could not be gotten forth by force, would not depart from the dismembered corpse but lay between her head and shoulders. So Anna's head lies between my heart and soul. Her art has the capacity to look at itself and society at the same time. The shift to modernity, I mean her passage across the earth, has wrenched her eyes from inwardness, harsh tempers occupy the vacuum created, and her body is as alive as the heart, both joyful and sorrowful, of that Royal dog. She does not recognize me either upon wakening or going to sleep. She is not an exile from, but champions Conscience, the effort of will.

The owning of Knowledge and nothing more.

I longed for the warmth between us to return, but too long has been spent in interpretation without the satisfaction of creation.

How human that our plot should entertain!

On the island we fought because of my jealousy. Perhaps, too, I was aware that it was her gift bringing me there. She flirted with the barboy who was chewing the seal of a wine bottle, his motorcycle helmet gleaming at the end of the bar. His age was indeterminable, about thirty-eight or thirty-nine, grey-haired, blue-bearded, with humorous eyes. I had lost her earlier and now found her coaxing him towards intimacy. In one hand she held a cold jug of wine, in the other, his. Somewhere a mouth organ was playing on the summer evening. The gratuitous life where caution stops. The argument continued out into the warm air where soon it would be suddenly cold. We beat each other fervently. Later, he came on his bike behind us, pulled up and picked her out of the warm dust. Goats bleated from the trees above our heads, upset by the performance. He took both of our reluctant hands and joined them, he spoke fluently in Spanish till we reached our wooden chalet perched among the hot blue mountains. He followed our car with outlandish gesticulations. Every violence is a restitution, then, consummated often among friends. He drank with us, we had wine from the French Quarter. This man's slight figure hung over the shady-brown valley through the unaccustomed windows till dawn. For nowhere in that land did windows open outward, but inward onto the fountains. His predicament? He only stood in for washing bottles very seldom. He had been looking for light work ever since the war. To protest without being named is useless. How you, Anna, sat on your bed questioning. Our total happiness there as we watched the lights twinkle on the mainland. Crude is my shape, her scalpel sharp. And any reality is only appraised by its followers and each ideal demolished by self-justification. The giver, then, and the receiver are equal. The female blackbirds twittered and whistled across the fields. Impulsive actions do not lead to a man of strong will. And when I return from Anna to my mother and use her house as a battle-ground for my frustrations, to accelerate her nervous devotion to truth, is this not again my Infancy? How will it be, say, in twenty years' time, when I return home some January to sit by her kitchen windows, where the coltsfoot is bracing itself and the slender spur of the wood-violet is hardening, and know I have failed. Because I will be either powerful or humane. When tottering back from her brother, the shopkeeper's shop, I told my mother of this conceit; she dropped her hands in dismay and turned to me exasperated. "What will you do for that side of the house," she asked, "You speak with the self-analysis of an author for whom all things are planned." For her, clerks, authors, are the guardians of the permanent, corrupted human nature. She would never leave her statements in the hands, in the gesture of an artist. What could I do? We don't all feel our lives are a loss, she was hinting, turning round, affectionate for a moment.

"Begin again, my sweet, begin again," she said, matron of virility, not some sweetness introduced into the masculine but beauty with strength, its existence previously in the world and now in harmony with it, favoured by unfrightened youth. The reverse of the coin.

Before the Off (1999)

From early morning beasts and men were trekking in from the mountains. The townsfolk came out their gates like they were going to a wedding party. The bank girls went to work with a change of clothes for the half-day. Ladies pinned extraordinary hats to their scalps and stood back from the mirror a moment. Stalls went up in the market yard, Eliza Satins were spread, work boots travelled out to the course in Hiace vans. Tarpaulins shot across pressed, second-hand suits, camouflage jackets were pegged to washing lines, wellingtons were arranged in neat lines.

Gamblers, who had missed breakfast below, woke in a room where a poker game had ended only hours before. The three-card trick man sat in his B&B doodling on the menu. An assistant trainer walked a lone horse along the strand. From the island the barnacle geese rose as one and flew to the mainland. Chattering madly they landed on the goose meadow by the bay.

Extra newspapers were dumped into the entrance of Cullen's shop. Matt Sheridan came out the back door of the Irish House Hotel, went up the town, selected an *Irish Independent* and tossed a pound coin on the pile of newspapers. He stopped in the middle of the street and turned to the racing pages. Phew! he said to himself. This dog came up the town and lay down by the monument. A loudspeaker shrieked to itself on the racecourse. The cattle milled into the mart that would end at one in time for everyone to be at the races by two. Testing, said a voice.

Testing, it said as Aggie Lang opened the back door of the pub to Murphy. He shook the dew off his coat and went to the toilet. Tim Pat came in.

It's a pet day, he said, for the ponies.

It is.

Is Murphy here?

He'd be out the back.

Fuck him.

Are ye arguing again? asked Aggie.

He is. He thinks I told the guards that he was carting stones off the beach.

And did ya?

I did not.

Well then, said Aggie, your conscience is clear, isn't it.

I suppose, he said. But then Mrs, is it ever?

He went behind the bar and changed a barrel of Guinness. He swept up after the night before. Then Tim Pat went back onto the street to watch the horse boxes arriving. He strolled over to the vendors and tried on a straw hat. He looked into a wellington boot. He studied Lang's. Aggie was lighting the fire when Murphy returned with a bucket of turf from the yard. There you are M'am, he said, then sat on a high stool waiting while she made herself tea within.

They're going to build a ring road round the town, he shouted.

They'd never, called Aggie.

It's in the paper, he said.

I'm sure.

Tim Pat came across the street again. He stood against the gable of the pub. Fuck him, he said again, and pushed in the back door. Murphy coughed ironically. The two men looked at each other with dismay.

Have you anything for today? asked Murphy.

No.

I'll bet you you have.

Nothing. Nothing at all.

They sat in silence at the bar for a while till Aggie appeared. They took a whiskey each.

Do you ever think about life? asked Murphy.

No.

Never.

No, why should I.

He searched his pocket for change while Murphy watched his every move.

And if there is a reason to life well it's long forgotten, he continued, so don't be bothering me.

I'm only saying.

I don't want to hear about it.

Your voice would give me a pain, snapped Murphy.

What is it but the same old story, said Tim Pat.

You owe me one pound twelve and six, said Aggie.

Good on you, Aggie, said Murphy, I love to hear the sound of old money.

Outside on the street a van door closed with a slap.

The gypsies alighted near the new forge where a young man in a crew cut was melting a rusted gate. They watched him without comment. Nodded, nodded. They moved through a herd of cattle without heeding the beasts. The father, a tall man with a blunt chin, was steered along the footpath by his two red-haired sons. He stopped, went on, stopped again. He lit an Afton to study a horse. He put the spent match back in its box and feeling his forehead with his free hand paused to think. He took stock of his surroundings.

Listen, he said.

The sons gathered round. He put his arms over their two shoulders. They huddled a moment. Then they went on. The dog got up from under the monument and followed them down the street. They walked direct to a man setting up a stall of car accessories and the father bought a black waterproof torch. The seller put a battery in. The father opened his coat and lifted it out from him till it formed a tent, then he shone the torch into the dark under his armpit. Next he shone it into the face of his son. He nodded and pocketed it. They moved on to the shirts. Past the cabbages. Then to the radios. Lastly the jams. They bought three pots of blackberry and two of goose-berry. She'll like that, said the father. One of the lads carried them very daintily. Farmers stood aside to let them past. Then they went down Lang's entry.

Murphy and Tim Pat were sitting in silence studying form. The Mangan gypsies came in the back door and moved towards the other end of the bar and collected in the dark by a low table. They sat head-to-head a moment.

You told the guards, said Murphy rising his head from the paper.

I did not, said Tim Pat reading on.

Look into my eyes and say it.

Tim Pat looked into his eyes.

You did, said Murphy.

I'd be beholding to you, said Tim Pat, if you'd leave me alone.

Those stones were for my mother's grave.

Murphy slapped the seat opposite him.

Look, said Tim Pat, leave me be.

You'll deal with me yet.

The Mangan gypsies heard the disturbance without showing any concern. In the half-light they looked mournful. It was nine in the morning. A horse across the road whinnied in terror. The gypsy father clapped his coat pockets, searched around, pulled out a single twenty-pound note and studied it.

Who is this man here, he asked and he showed the note to his son.

He could be anybody, said Jaimie.

He could. But would you deal with him?

I might.

You might is right.

He studied the note, then put it away. In a low hum hooves and tractors rattled by. A kettle whistled.

You're a bloody liar, shouted Murphy.

It's shameful, Tim Pat said, to have to listen to this.

Waa! muttered Murphy.

Mangan took out the note again, handed it to his son and
nodded. The lad approached the bar, leaned over and waited
till Aggie came back from the inner room. She buttoned her
blouse and beat her skirt.

Yes son?

A whiskey M'am, he said, and two pints a' Heineken.

Whiskey, she repeated uncertainly.

And two pints of Heineken, he said louder.

You know, she said, that if I serve you it's illegal. Opening
time is half-past ten.

The lad nodded and looked at the drinks in front of the other
two men.

Those men are employed by me, she said. They are my
handymen.

He seemed to fret and looked back at his father and then at
her.

Alright then, she said, just this once.

Thank you Mrs.

She lifted a glass to the light.

I didn't know where I was. Did you ever get that?

I did, said Tim Pat.

All that abuse over the radio, she continued. And it never
stops.

There was a time you'd hear music.

There was.

And I never slept a wink last night.

Tim Pat took a draw of his pint.

Good luck, he said to the gypsy lad.

That it may sicken you, came Murphy's voice behind him.

Dear God.

I don't think he likes you, said the lad.

So it appears.

It was you, shouted Murphy. It was you!

Not me, said Tim Pat, not me, my good man.

Don't my good man me!

Keep it down, said Aggie.

Murphy got up and stood by the gypsy with his hands grasping the bar-rail and his arms out-stretched.

Do you see that man there, he asked the lad and he hauled himself onto his toes.

I see him, young Mangan said without looking.

That man there is well in with the guards, he sneered, then dropped down to normal size.

You'll get that, said Jaimie.

You'd wanta watch him.

No problem, Mister, he said.

I was just warning you.

I hear you.

We're dealing with evil here.

God-in-heaven, said Tim Pat.

It's not our business, boss, said the lad.

I know that, Murphy said with a leer.

It's not our business, the gypsy stated again in a flat calm voice.

When he heard the menace, Murphy changed tack.

Are you for the races? asked Murphy genially.

No.

No?

I'll tell you what my business is. This is since you want to know.

His thumb wandered over the bar.

We have to be in Tuam be twelve. The uncle died.

I'm sorry for your troubles, said Tim Pat.

Ah now, said Murphy.

So it's not our business.

No.

Do you see now what I'm saying, asked Jaimie.

I do, said Murphy backing off.

It's not our business. Not ours. He turned to Tim Pat.

My father lost a brother this morning. We're for Tuam.

Take care, said Tim Pat.

Meself and the brother, he said, will drive. That what we'll do.

I'm only saying, said Murphy and he went back to his chair.

And I'm listening, said Aggie.

She sliced the top froth of a high pint of lager with a knife.

Two pints and a whiskey.

Does your father want water?

No M'am.

Neat. He likes it neat.

That's right M'am.

That's right, she said. Your people like it neat.

She smiled abruptly. Young Mangan took his change and drink.

See you boss, he said to Tim Pat, and ducked away.

What were they saying to you, asked the father.

Nothing, said young Mangan.

The less said the better.

His son put the change on the table and the father separated it into two lots, then lit a fag.

There's a pony running today has my fancy. I want that on him.

Right.

Good man, that's settled then.

He shook the fag in front of his face and brought his head forward. They followed him with their heads.

Listen, he said.

I can't sleep for the life of me, said Aggie.

I get nights like that, said Tim Pat.

You must have something on your conscience, interrupted Murphy.

I have indeed.

What is it?

You.

I don't like that, said Murphy.

I don't like that at all. You're at it again.

He got up and stood stock still with his face in Tim Pat Banks's face.

I heard what you said about me.

I just said you keep me awake.

Well I never lost a night's sleep over you, said Murphy. And I don't intend to.

Well don't.

I won't.

The two neighbours stood face-to-face, one man in a cap, the other capless, Murphy's hair askew and Banks's hat tilted back, both touched like rare things.

The pair of you, said Aggie, make a pretty picture.

Go on, Banks.

Go where.

Go on, try it.

My sporting days are long past, Peadar.

Sport my arse.

I was in the 100 yards once, said Banks, and I was disqualified.

Why, asked Aggie.

Because my nose was running, and he broke into a fit of laughter.

Jesus Christ help me, complained Murphy. He's trying to steal inside my head.

I am not, for fuck sake.

You damn well are.

Jesus Christ, Peadar.

I know you!

Mr Murphy, said Aggie.

Yes Aggie.

Will you have sense, my good man.

La-de-da, said Murphy, la-de-da.

Ya clam ya, she said.

Get out of my light, said Murphy, and he headed off to the gypsies' table.

Maisie Sheridan looked into the cold room in the Irish House Hotel and took out the prawns she had defrosted the night before. She cut parsley with Gertie. Then the French chef peppered the legs of lamb with mint and garlic. He parboiled the potatoes and scored each to make a bed for cheese and spring onions. He placed them in a tray.

Will there be lobster? he asked.

That's up to Bernie, she said.

Did you see Mattie?

No.

Where is he, she said, where is he?

To go and disappear on race day.

He'll be here.

Freddie, she screamed.

Her son came down the stairs.

See can you find your father.

Alright, he said.

Do you mind if I join you? asked Murphy.

Mangan gave him a keen eye.

Am I interrupting? Murphy asked.

You're not interrupting, said Hughie, the other son.

Just tell me now and I'll go away.

You're alright, said Hughie.

I'm sorry for your troubles, said Murphy to the father.

Mangan said nothing.

I still have my dignity, said Murphy to none in particular, which is not my own fault.

Do you have a tip for today?

I do not.

Are you not working, boss, asked the father.

I spent the morning in the graveyard, talking to them.

Ah.

And I laid a bed of stones on my mother's grave.

God rest the dead, said Mangan.

I know them best of all, said Murphy.

The dead?

That's right.

They're gone, said Mangan.

Murphy strode to the window, pulled back the curtain and looked out on the town.

Did you ever notice that drunkenness, he said, makes us all look like each other?

I did and I didn't.

Do you mind if I sit?

Sit if you will.

If you don't want me to I won't.

If you sit there you have your reasons.

I mean no harm.

There was a silence.

You were out early.

I was, said Murphy. I was.

You'd be sick.

I'm scourged, he said.

He sat down and put his head in his hands.

I'm sick, I think.

He looked at one of the younger Mangans – Hughie. The tall thirty-year-old son was wearing a boy's face. Murphy lifted his head and grinned. He stared into a safe place but the grin continued on. He put his hand to his head.

My neighbour has me cap, he said.

The father has a cold in his chest, said Jaimie.

I caught it in Clones, the father agreed.

There's nothing worse than a cold in the chest. Then he changed his legs.

On the dot of opening time Tim Pat pulled back the locks on the front door and undone the gate outside. He closed the door behind him and headed down the town to the bakers to get pastries for Aggie.

He saluted those he knew, stopped off for *The Independent* newspaper and changed his mind and bought *The Sun*. Then he changed his mind again and bought a rhubarb tart instead of pastries because it looked so fresh and wholesome. Passing the church at the top of Bridge Street he blessed himself. Kitty Shore wished him a good day.

At Lang's all was as he left it. Aggie cut the tart in slices and Tim Pat brought four to the gypsies' table where the father thanked him profusely, then he took one himself. Aggie sat down under the window to watch the street. She had a cup of tea in one hand and a slice of tart balanced on a beermat in the other. She laid down the cup and beat crumbs into her lap.

Lovely, Tim Pat, she said.

Would you care to buy an eagle? asked Mangan.

No thanks, said Murphy.

They are the best of eagles.

I don't doubt it.

We could make a deal.

For an eagle?

An eagle surely.

Mangan curled his hand. Murphy shook his head. Mangan spat.

Name your price, he said.

I can't.

She has her claws.

I don't doubt it.

Suit yourself, boss, said Mangan dismissively.

But I have nowhere to put it.

Wouldn't the pier of the gate do, boss.

The pier of the gate? asked Murphy astonished.

Aye. It's the best of plaster. Very weather proof.

And there's some have claws and some that don't, but mine do.

No thank you, said Murphy.

He knitted his brows and looked to the left where the virgin, slightly tilted, sat like a goldfish in her glass vase in the plush part of the lounge. She is cursing us, he thought, and telling us things we can't hear. Testing, said the voice again.

Testing, testing, called a distorted voice from another world.
Testing, one two three. Another silence that was filled with
urgent waiting. Testing! Then it began. For a sudden it
sounded like the call to prayer at first light. The loudspeaker
shrieked. The echo raced across the market square, down past
the second-hand clothes man with his Fiat van stacked with
yellow rain gear, donkey jackets with leather shoulder pads,
combat trousers and wellingtons; up the aisle of the open
church where a woman in a beret was watching a single candle
flutter in the dark; it hurried the steps of two farmers that had
to park on the outskirts of the overcrowded town; it was only
an echo in the Fawlty Towers bar; it was splitting the ears of
a man buying young fir trees by the monument; it frightened
the calves who heard its manic prayer somewhere back in
their genes; round the ring the men's faces never twitched as
the pitch sharpened into a whine of fine gibberish; the speaker
spoke to someone down out of sight below him in his cubicle;
he shook his head, he was not having it, he was having none of
it; a heel came down on a cigar, Excuse me, asked a neighbour
of a neighbour, is this your lot?; below the speaker a lad dusted
the sold lambs with splashes of yellow and blue from a can of
coloured aerosol; on went his master up and down the scales,
halting only now and then at the nod of a head or a finger raised;
it stopped, the hammer went down, the harangue started
again: a man raised his cap on the highest step of the enclosure,
steam rose from the cattle in one of the steel pens; horse boxes
trundled down to the race course; some ewes with teeth, and
some with none, called the auctioneer, what am I bid?

It's started, said Mangan.
Murphy listened with genuine sorrow.
    You're moving too fast for me, said Murphy.
    Is there something wrong boss?
    The world is not what I thought, so I suppose I changed
the expression on my face.
    He's crying, said Jaimie.
    I'm not. I have a weeping eye.

I've heard of that.

I often woke to find the pillow soaked.

You'll get that from the batteries, said Hughie, if they spill.

You will, said the father.

The other day, Jaimie explained, we shifted a thousand and forty.

There's an art in numbers, said Murphy.

Is there, he asked.

There is.

Daddy.

Yes?

What number are we at now?

We have not reached a figure as yet, said Mangan.

Well can we take the number eight? asked Murphy.

Eight will do, said Mangan, I can manage eight.

Well there were eight persons in the Ark.

Do you tell me.

I do.

Eight persons in the ark, the father said and shook his head and whistled.

That's a fact.

Including the boss?

Including Noah.

Now. He whistled again to himself. He must have done away with a good few to get it down to eight.

And God so loved the world he gave his only son, said Murphy.

That he did, said Mangan.

He did.

And Mary had two right feet, added Mangan.

And the Christ child had two left feet, agreed Jaimie.

Same as myself, said Hughie, and he laughed.

Don't blaspheme, ordered his father, you'll bring us bad luck.

They sat in silence with Murphy going from face to face and meeting no-one.

Bernie Buckley left his house and travelled along the beach to the town. The billows were smoking. He pushed out the boat and checked his pots. He got four lobsters. He sat on the pier a while. A helicopter flew over his head. He stood to watch it. In the market yard the dealers stood to watch it. It swooped low over the town and echoed like thunder through the open door of the Town Hall where the morning court was in session. A guard on duty at the door shaded his eyes with his police cap to see her go. Aggie heard it. Murphy missed it. A man with a banjo stepped down off the ten o'clock bus from Dublin and stood at the cross to hitch to the races. Then another helicopter with its nose set towards the racecourse shot by. The musician waved at it and gave her the thumb. Bernie Buckley arrived on Main Street and went into the Irish House for tea and a ham sandwich. He stirred a spoonful of mustard between the slices of bread.

Charlie Swan flew over, he said to his neighbour.

Was that him?

It was, I'd warrant you.

He wiped his mouth with a tissue.

He'd be in the two o'clock hurdle, you see, he said.

He went into Maisie Sheridan with the lobsters. In the backroom Kitty her sister was preparing smoked salmon with prawns and potato salad with chives. The plates were wrapped in cellophane and taken out to the van because the Irish House had the restaurant contract for the day. When the van was full Mattie Sheridan appeared at the back door with his son.

So there you are, Maisie said.

I was only up the street.

I need you here.

He sat into the van.

I'll be back at one, he said.

On the dot?

On the dot.

Don't get caught up now.

No. No I tell you.

Maisie exchanged money for the lobsters.

Tell me this Bernie, she says.

Aye.

If you see my man out there send him home.

I will.

Just tell him to come home.

I will.

Bernie stopped off at Lang's.

Tim Pat, he says.

Bernie.

Peadar.

Bernie.

Good-day men, he said to the gypsies.

I had a swan break her leg on the lough, he said to Aggie. And you want to hear her mate. He's stricken. And there she is roosting in a pool of blood. I could do nothing.

You could not.

It shows you how little you can do, said Bernie.

He finished his pint. A man from Cloone came up the town on a Connemara pony. He was wearing a bright red baseball cap. He sat well back surveying all. He waved at Bernie and Bernie waved back, then Bernie hailed the man from Barry's Tea who gave him a lift in his van. They stopped for the musician and went on.

I saw blood this morning, Murphy announced.

Not a good thing, boss. Best kept to yourself.

I know.

But you won't be the first to see blood and you won't be the last.

I thought I was looking at my own blood, he said miserably.

So it was another man's.

It was.

You were lucky.

Was I?

It could have been yours.

True.

Better it be his than yours.

I suppose so.

Well never mind, said Mangan smiling, one day it will be your own.

That's right, said Jaimie and he clapped his knee.

That's right, said Hugh winking. How many families are there in Heaven?

In Heaven? asked Murphy.

The very place.

I don't know.

Nine, boss. Nine families. Isn't that right Daddy.

That's correct.

So if there is nine in heaven there should have been nine on the Ark, Hugh continued.

There was only eight on the Ark, said Murphy solidly. I stand by that.

And where did the other tribe come from?

I don't know.

Well I'll tell you!

Do.

Granard, he said, and he broke out into a low keen of merriment. Granard town.

A great town for weddings, nodded his father happily.

See that man at the bar, asked Murphy, pointing.

I see him.

Would you believe me, asked Murphy earnestly, if I said that the power for good or evil resides in the eye?

Simple as that sir, said Mangan, simple as that.

Can you see any evil in mine?

I can not.

You didn't look.

I don't want to look.

But you'll agree that some men have it in the eye.

They might have.

Yes, they have.

Hi, said Mangan, will you stop yapping.

I'm not yapping.

If you don't stop yapping – and he looked away from him – I'll break your face.

Murphy rose.

I thank you, he said.

He approached the bar cautiously.

I'm not alone in what I think, he said.

I'm glad for you, said Tim Pat.

There's others see what I see.

Good for you.

We're talking here of sleepless nights, Mr Murphy, said Aggie.

I never had them.

You're the lucky man. There I am all night, tossing and turning, continued Aggie. And then at last you get one good beautiful thought and you think you're away, this is it now, I'm for bye-byes, at last, at long last oh God in heaven, it's lovely just losing yourself, not a care in the world and you think it's gone on for ages but when you look at the clock only a minute has passed. It's terrible. Terrible.

A pint of Smithwicks, said Murphy.

Right so, said Aggie.

He propped himself by Banks.

You were seen, he whispered confidentially.

Be who?

What fucking business is it of yours?

The gas heater popped. Murphy sat himself back on his chair and shook his shoulders.

La-de-da, he said.

McDonald came straight in and went to the bar for cigars. The lapel of his jacket was decorated with the membership tags of various racecourses. He dropped his binoculars on the counter.

Cigars, Mr McDonald?

The very thing Aggie.

So have you anything?

I heard a whisper about Ivanhoe.

Ivanhoe, said Murphy, is class.

A decent animal, said McDonald. He clipped the cigars into his top pocket and took out a handkerchief and polished his shoe, straightened up and nodded at Murphy.

You want to come with me Peadar.

Not today, Mr McDonald, said Murphy.

Are you sure?

I don't think so.

Well you're welcome.

Not today, I don't think. Later maybe.

McDonald strode over to the Gypsies.

Mister Mangan, he said.

Mister McDonald.

He strode over to Murphy and put his mouth to his ear.

You'd be better off out of the pub, he whispered.

I know that, whispered Murphy.

Good luck so, said McDonald and he left.

A grand man, said Murphy.

And why don't you go with him, asked Tim Pat.

Not today, said Murphy.

Go on, said Aggie.

Do you think I should, he asked.

I do.

He jumped to his feet and out the door.

Peace now for a while, said Aggie.

She hit the TV and the Alps came on. She hit another button and it was rock. She hit another button and it was darkness again. Then the door opened and Murphy returned.

Not today, he said.

Why is that?

I don't know.

McDonald stopped the car on the bridge. He got out and looked down at the river. He lit a cigar. At first he couldn't be sure. So he took out the binoculars and trained them down water. Then he saw a young trout in the shallows. He kept coming and going from splashes of dark sky, out into the brightness and gone.

McDonald tied his laces again.

He looked at his watch – three minutes to go. He walked the bridge from East to West then back again. He sat on the passenger seat with the door of the car open and read the deaths under the letter M in the *Independent*. Then he turned to the horses. A fine drizzle fell.

He closed all doors and sat a while with the steering wheel in his hands. He viewed the wet windscreen. Some memory made him tremble. He blew his nose into a tissue and listened to the rain on the roof of the car. It came down with a crack then went suddenly quiet. The car grew warm and lonely. He pressed the butt of the cigar into the ashtray and snapped it shut.

That's it, he said.

He turned the ignition key.

Right, he said and he drove off at last towards whatever was ahead.

Three strangers entered Lang's and lay their rucksacks, an accordion and a bodhrán down on the forum by the low window. They left the door open behind them. The sound of horses and tractors echoed in.

Dún an doras, said Murphy.

I am sorry, said the girl, my English is not so good.

Neither is his Irish, said Tim Pat. He's saying You left the door open.

I'm saying Close the door, said Murphy, to be exact.

Balls.

She tried turning the latch but couldn't.

I'll get the blasted door, said Tim Pat. The latch I'm afraid catches the foreigner.

Oh.

He resumed his place.

The girl called three pints of Guinness please, then began counting her money. Murphy rose with a scandalous eye.

Are you Germans or what? he asked.

I am East Germany, said one tousled lad and he extended his hand.

Murphy dropped a soft paw onto the palm.

So they let youse out from behind the wall.

My friends are from the Vest.

What?

Ve have problem I think.

You might swear, said Tim Pat.

Don't talk to him, said Murphy, don't even register his presence.

You speak Irish, no?

Not in his nanny, said Tim Pat.

The door flew open again. In stepped two young farmers from the locality.

He's not here, said one.

He's not, said the other.

Was Mattie Sheridan in?

No, said Aggie.

Your woman is going wild looking for him.

Well he's not here.

He's not here. He looked to his friend. Will we stop for one?

No. We'll go on.

We will. Thanks a lot.

The pub went quiet. The strangers counted money onto the bar and the girl asked for crisps.

You have crisps? she asked as she put a camera onto the bar.

No, said Aggie, but I have rhubarb tart.

Do you mind, said the girl and she trained the camera on Murphy. He gasped, then shook his head.

In the Irish House a card game in a bedroom ended and the poker players came downstairs.

Wondrous, quoted Murphy, is the robin there singing to us and the cat escaped from us.

Please? asked the girl.

Pass no heed on him, said Tim Pat.

Mr Banks? said Murphy in a plaintive voice.

Yes?

Mr Banks, he said again.

Yes! shouted Tim Pat.

Every morning I step in here you're over there, laughed Murphy.

Well if you weren't here you wouldn't see me.

I would see you – and Murphy drew a finger to his forehead and saluted – even if you weren't there.

Jesus.

That's how it is.

How can you see someone that's not there.

That's no problem, said Murphy.

The French chef came in for a gin. When he heard German spoken he piped in. The conversation continued on in French and German.

What are ye saying, asked Aggie.

We're talking about Ireland, said the chef.

Speaking of Ireland, said Murphy and he rose a finger.

Do you know the wonders of the world?

I do not think so, said the lad from East Germany.

Well this is them, he said. He got up and posed by the bar.

Right. Are you with me?

The chef nodded.

Now. Murphy laughed to himself. Right. Number one. The foal of a ginnet. Yes?

The lad looked to chef. The chef rose his shoulders, opened his hands outwards and sniffed.

You can never get a foal from a ginnet, explained Murphy, don't you know.

Oh, said the chef and he translated something into German.

Two. Number two. Right. The tops of the rushes green.

Ah.

They looked at each other in bewilderment.

The tops of the rushes green, right?

Right, said the chef.

Number three. A shoe to fit the foot of the mountain.

Yes indeed, a shoe to fit the foot of the mountain. Do you understand that?

No, I'm sorry, said the chef.

Never mind. Number Four. A blanket to cover the bed of the ocean.

He shook his head with merriment. The Germans smiled. Tim Pat looked into the far distance. Aggie rested.

Number Five, said Murphy, and he burst out laughing.

Number Five, he repeated.

Go on, said Aggie.

A square arsehole, said Murphy and he sat content.

I understand the last one, said the chef and he said slán and headed back to the Irish House. The market stalls were coming down. The poker players got into a taxi. The banks closed. A solicitor and his client stood on the steps of the courthouse arguing.

The man from the shirt stall tipped in quietly into Lang's and went to the bar.

Mattie Sheridan, he said, has done a runner again.

No, said Aggie.

He has.

The dirty bastard.

I'll have a hot whiskey, he said.

Right, said Aggie.

And I'll have a cold one while I'm waiting.

He drank the Powers whiskey straight down, shook himself and bowed his head. He arrived back to where he was the night before – then he watched the kettle boil. He watched it for a long long time and was going to say No, he didn't want a hot whiskey. I'm fine thank you. Then it arrived. A lookey hung from his nose. He wiped his face with a handkerchief. He put the lemon aside. He smelt the cloves.

Bold Robert Emmet, he said to himself.

Jaimie on his way back from the toilet shyly stood by the Germans.

Do you play the music, he asked.

We are learning.

It's a lovely yoke. He lifted the bodhrán.

Hit it for me, he said.

He handed it to one of the men who handed it to the woman. She crouched over the drum and scattered a roll.

Lovely, said Jaimie.

You play?

No, he said grinning, no.

Come back here, Jaimie, said his father. His son flew across, head-down. You know where we are going today?

I do, said Jaimie.

Do I have to tell you?

No.

Say that again.

Ya!

So you don't own your houses at home in Germany.

Nine.

I want you to say it loud and clear for that man there. You do not own your houses.

No. We lease them.

There, you see, I told you. Are you listening?

I'm listening, said Tim Pat. They said they lease them.

There you have it – we lost our language and they lost their homes. The German is homeless.

And he laughed.

Sit down, said Aggie, you're getting high.

We have everything under the sun here, daughter, said Murphy, shaking his shoulders and just at that moment the girl from Bavaria turned and snapped him. Blinded from the flash he shaded his eyes. The Mangans rose as one and left without a word. They looked in passing at the German's jeep that was parked near the gate to the mart then continued on.

A Japanese job, said Hughie.

Four-wheel, said Jaimie.

A new car in an old town makes an old town look bad, said the father.

He climbed into the back of the van and sat into an armchair. A woman drew the door shut behind him.

The Germans left. The Germans were gone. The gypsies were gone. The stallholder ordered another hot whiskey. In came a couple for a glass of Baileys and a vodka and ice. He got on his mobile immediately and began a long conversation with George. It was George this and George that as he strolled to and fro along the counter while she sat thinking of something grave, that later became lighthearted.

Then young Sheridan came in and looked around.

How-is-your-father, asked Tim Pat.

He's fine, he said.

He's tough, he said.

He is.

He is surely.

The lad left.

The phone calls continued. When one ended her boyfriend rang another number but they were not at home. It was important. That they were not there made him listless. He wanted word. I'm too late, he said to her. Never mind, she said. I had to ring to get a tip, he explained to Tim Pat. He rang back again getting more and more anxious. He could not let go of whoever was not at home. She said they should be going.

I told you, he lamented, I told you.

Don't, she said.

If we had—

But she was gone. He went reluctantly leaving his glass unfinished. Very troubled in himself he stopped again on the street to ring but they were not at home. They were gone whoever they were.

Stay just where you are, said Murphy.

Why?

I want to admire myself in you.

That does it, said Tim Pat.

Easy man.

Easy my arse.

As you get older life gets trickier.

In other words?

Don't do anything too hasty.

So tell me this, said Tim Pat.

Yes.

You mentioned a ginnet earlier.

I did.

So what is a ginnet?

You know too fucking well.

Just tell me once again.

The ginnet is the offspring of a horse and an ass.

True. But which is the mare and which the stallion.

Which is the mare?

Aye.

Murphy hesitated.

You asked me this before.

I did.

And did I get it right then?

No.

Do you know, he asked the stallholder.

No.

Right. Right Mister Banks. He stretched the fingers of his two hands round his sunken crown.

Don't tell me now.

I won't.

The ginnet – he said looking up – is the offspring of the ass mare and the horse stallion.

No.

No?

No. That's the mule.

It is not.

Is he the mule by God, said the stallholder.

It's the ginnet, Aggie, am I right, said Murphy. Am I right?

It would make a dog think, she said.

And the planning officer was down the field testing for drainage. Wasn't he.

He was. Yes.

Couldn't a fucking septic tank go anywhere in that field, dab and sand, that's what I say. Enough drainage to soak the shit of the county. He should be fucked in over the cliff. And the worst thing is the fucker is not from here.

He's not.

Drainage!

He has a job to do, said Aggie.

So have we all.

They make plans.

Haven't we been making plans for centuries.

That's right, said the stallholder and he stood. That's what I should be doing right now.

Making plans.

Do Ivanhoe, said Tim Pat.

Do you think?

I do.

Well thank you kindly. If the last horse I did had not been beaten mine would have won.

Is that so.

It's so.

Young Sheridan looked into the bookies.

Is my father here? he asked.

No, said Mister Shields.

Was he in at all?

No son. I reckon he's stopped out at the course.

Oh.

He went across to Waters', looked in, searched the toilet, the yard, then he went across to The Fluter's, all the same, no-one.

Are you going, asked Murphy.

I am, said Tim Pat. I'm off to do Ivanhoe.

Don't go.

I have to.

Why?

I can't take it any longer.

Suit yourself.

I will.

Look.

Look what!

Look at me.

I'm looking.

Did you do it?

I did not.

If you did just shake my hand. I won't hold it against you.

I won't shake your hand.

So you didn't do it.

No.

Right, said Murphy. Well shake my hand anyway.

No.

Why?

Because I didn't do it.

Ah Jazus Christ of Almighty!

I'll be seeing you Peadar.

He pulled the door behind him. Murphy stood and watched

him go through the window. The town was closing down. He
sat back in his chair.

I wonder did Mr McDonald stop on the bridge, he said.
You see, he always does.
Why, asked Aggie.
Superstition, said Murphy, that's why. And that's why I
like him. But that man who was standing just there is another
question entirely. He has deep-down problems, he has.
You're too hard on him.
Maybe.
So what's your problem with him?
He likes to be liked.
So do we all.
True. We all like to be liked.
So?
But not by the wrong people.

Aggie drew out the drawer of the till then slammed it shut.
She looked into the Harp mirror and blinked.
The sea was cracking last night, she said.
It's the frost makes the sea rise, he said, suddenly clear-
eyed.
Ah.
And the moon is on its back, God help her.
Ah.
And Jimmy's gone.
Aggie sighed with a whistle. Murphy threw a hand in the air.
She tapped the counter with her knuckles. She threw her eyes
to heaven. He let his chin fall onto his chest. Stones, he said,
fucking stones.

We left Coolaney in the van in the early evening, the lights
on dim, maybe three in front and two boys behind. We were
on our way to the horse fair after coming the night before
from Dowra mart and then I took this corner, nice and easy,
maybe two or three bottles of stout that morning with Mattie,

nothing else, slept well the night before in lodgings though what I dreamt I couldn't say and had a midlin breakfast, no pressure, just chatting away about the gypsies we'd seen that morning leaving town for the fair when the next thing was we were on a rise in the middle of a field, a stony field with the sea in the distance, lapping, flat calm, we'd gone off the road onto some sort of lane, you could say we were going up an old track, so I slid to a stop and left the handbrake on and got out to see what was going on, what's going on, Mattie Sheridan called, Are we stuck, asked another voice, I've gone wrong, I said, It would take you came the reply, and the others, all men I knew well, climbed out from the front and then from the back, and stood around laughing and looking, and there we were in a field of rock smothered in lichen and gorse blooming on the incline, so what could you say, Petey lit up and I went back on foot the way we'd come to find the gate, Stop where youse are I said, and they shook their heads like, darkness falling but I could make out their shapes in the light of the van, and I headed off down the incline seeing nothing but keeping my eyes on the ground so that I'd stay on the track, and I was walking maybe ten minutes, but was there a gate? there was no gate, I struck a match but no sign of a gate at all, and I said fuck this for a lark and I roared back up to them I can't find no gate, I shouted I can't find no gate! but you guessed it no answer, not in the earthly, there was no-one behind me, and I went back as far as I could calling out every few yards, and when I'd turn this way and that way I thought I'd make them out but there wasn't a soul, I went back up but was there a van? There was no van, and as for the men, there was no men.

I called again.

No answer.

I had on I thought a suit but now I found this coldness on my chest. I looked down. I was in my birthday suit. And my legs seemed awful long. And the worst thing of all was that my two arms seemed gone. My eyes could see no arms. Maybe they were smothered. The place lit up. Then the Japanese came, about twenty soldiers, each man struggling as if in mud, and some had guns and some had not, but most had water cans and they spilled by me as if I wasn't there. Then came the Eskimos, all in fur, breathing heavy, as if they had climbed a great cold height, and they went by me. The last of the foreigners were the Spanish, going one behind the other, in old armour and pushing through to the way ahead with their arms as if they were in a jungle. They rattled off into the dark.

A long time, nothing.

And then it started.

Horses, nothing but horses, coming up the rise, whinnying and galloping, there must have been hundreds, many hands high and each one was drawing a wheel chair with no-one in it. This could have gone for hours. Like some funeral. And the horses were still there when the four grey donkeys appeared, each coming very slowly, and I saw they had baskets on their backs and in the baskets were these birds, young pheasants, polts, and the asses came to stop in front of me and they got down very gently onto their knees and the birds tipped out onto the ground with a screech. One rose and landed on the crown of my head. I could feel his claws digging into my skull. He was a great weight and I was giving in under his weight. I couldn't shake him off.

My eyes were closing with the burden of the bird when suddenly off she flew. I was on my hunkers on the ground without my arms. A small trickle of blood coursed down my forehead. I lifted my head to shake it out of my eyes. One donkey came close. He put his snout next to my forehead and breathed me in. His lips were wet. I looked into his eyes. He drew back and whispered. The birds landed back into the baskets – then the other three asses rose and whispered. All four asses began whispering. In this way they left.

Only a distant screech from a polt then nothing.

I sat on the earth.

I was sorry the beasts were gone. Even if I had made them up at least they were there. With their empty wheelchairs and their bird baskets. Now there wasn't a sound. It was like I had heard some awful news. News of the worst kind. I stayed there like that. I was not interested in anything any longer.

Yes? said Aggie.
What?
You were saying?
Nothing, said Murphy. Nothing. He rose his glass – to the ring road!
Ahoy!
And all the small towns in built-up areas.
Fair deuce, chirped Aggie.

A farmer from Northern Ireland stepped out of a BMW, tipped through the door in high boots, ordered a pint and sat where the gypsies had been.
Does he look like an owner? whispered Murphy.
How would I know, said Aggie
Murphy walked to his table.
Are you for the races?
I am.
I thought so. He tipped his skull knowingly. I knew it.
And you?
I might, and I might not. If I do I'll see you there. If I don't I won't.
Do you mind if I sit?
Sit away.
Have you anything running?
I might.
Whisper?

Corgie in the second.

Corgie?

Corgie.

Right, said Murphy. He stood. You know they're killing all the rabbits, he said and he bowed.

Are they?

They are. Certainly.

He left down his drink.

I think I'll go before the off, he said.

Then he left. The dog at the monument followed him. Aggie arrived with the stranger's drink.

Who's your man? he asked.

Murphy, she said, is his name. Then she went to the window to follow his path.

He'd be high and when he is there's no talking to him.

He had the look, agreed the stranger.

Along the Lines (2012)

He lived in an ancient place. His house of three rooms sat to the side of a fort. Stone walls ran through the fields.

His back yard was a field of whins and grey gravel. Beyond it was the railway line where a few trains a day ran over and back between Sligo and Connolly Station in Dublin.

He was always at the back door to watch them go by as he learned his lines. After the first in the morning he made the porridge. After the second he ate the pancakes. The midday train meant a shot of bourbon. The one heading the other way in the late afternoon meant climbing on the bike, and heading for Henderson's pub where the carpenters, plumbers and house painters gathered and met up with local farmers.

They talked of nothing but money and local deaths, and shouted out laughter in a nearly insane manner.

He grew to hate that laugh.

It was not humour.

He could not enter the banter. He grew to hate that talk of hard times as more drinks were ordered. His face grew grim. They thought he thought he was above them. Sometimes his face would suddenly appear in an ad on the TV, and there'd be a momentary silence as they grinned and looked at him, and then at each other, and shook their heads before re-entering the aggression of the recession while he checked the time.

Good luck men, I have to go, he said downing his glass of gin.

Goodbye Mister O'Hehir, nodded the barman.

Good luck Joe, called the plumber.

I would not like to be here after I'm gone, he thought as he stepped out the door.

Joe O'Hehir hopped on his bike and rode to The Coach Inn, which was surrounded by cars. He sipped his Sauvignon Blanc and ordered goujons of cod with chips, and then sat by himself for two to three hours watching the old folk collect for meals alongside groups of young folk. Old professors, architects and electricians sat alongside ancient nurses, doctors and secretaries. A nun and priest led a funeral party all in black to a table. In the background Frank Sinatra was singing, then along came Dean Martin as soup bubbled in spoons and prawns slipped through leaves of rocket. Joe read his books on Ghosts and Mysteries, then headed back to his script and began mouthing the lines to himself.

Over the speakers came "I Got You Babe," "I Want To Go Home," "Take A Load Off Sally."

For weeks he'd disappear, take the train to Dublin and enter rehearsals, and eventually take his place on stage. He always stayed in the same B&B, a place filled with tourists and backpackers and computer screens. Amidst the entire furore his silence grew.

He'd stand under the bridge down the street to hear the train pass over his head. He reread old scripts in McDonald's Café. The hallucinations grew.

Then on the opening night of the play towards the end he dried up. The others waited. He stared out at the audience. It was a sad moment in the script, and the distress the audience saw in his face they read as part of the character's inner self as he approached the bad news.

Off stage a cue was whispered.

It looked like a tear appeared in one of his eyes.

He lay his head down, and the other actors watched their mate's extreme trauma. In rehearsal the sadness lasted only a minute. Now it had reached three minutes of silence. Then suddenly he threw up his head and out of his mouth came all the mad laughs from Henderson's, the laugh at what was not a joke, out came scattered lines with always the Ha-Ha, Jesus there's not a penny to be had, Ha! Ha! Bastards, give me a half one, Ha! Ha! He bobbed to and fro tossing imaginary glasses into his mouth, read imaginary papers for a second, Look at what's going on down there, he said, prodding the non-existent article, Ha! Ha! They know nothing, nothing, do you hear me, nothing! Win a stroll in Christ! and he roared laughing as the curtain came slowly down and the lights went off, ten minutes before they should have.

I have inherited the gene, he said to himself as he ran down to his room, undressed and prepared to go.

Joe, stay there please, shouted the director. We need to talk. Badly.

Joe eyed him.

What happened? he asked.

Images (2013)

After Jack retired as a lecturer from the IT college we often saw him with camera in hand honing in on the black windows of deserted cottages above the beach. If the doors were open he'd step inside and haunt the ruin. I could not tell what he was after – the architecture, the stone work, the past – or maybe all of them.

He's a strange bird, said Mrs Jay.

He is.

I could understand what he was looking at when the dead whale was washed in. Jack was at his side for over a week, circling and circling. Some other days he'd head off to the forts and stand centre stage, walk the alts to reach the old man-built defences, and many times head out the rocks to catch the flower-like fossils in his curious lens. That made sense. But why haunt the abandoned? What are you after, I'd ask myself, then one morning there was a knock on my door.

My car has broken down, could you be my cabby for two days, Miss Jennifer? he asked.

Certainly Jack.

I got into the Ford and he sat in beside me, his camera on his lap, and the haversack at his feet. I turned on the engine.

Where are we for? I asked.

How about above the valley?

Fine.

And so we headed up the road below the mountain on the northern side of the lake. On the way he jumped out and helped himself to a few strands of the white flowers of wild garlic. The smell filled the car when he sat back in. We passed lines of lived-in houses, some thatched, all looking the same way onto the waters below. Above them a couple of streams scored an old path down the cliffs. Cherry blossom trees shook their wings.

And so began the procedure. Every few hundred yards or so he'd make the sharp request as he'd spy another emptiness. We'd stop suddenly and awkwardly. Then he'd step out to take shots of the ivy-covered walls of roofless ruins, the old blue and yellow doors locked by chains and the darkness floating beyond the old window ledges.

At one old ruin fresh daffodils were shooting up among the debris in the garden.

Mortality is rife, he said, as he caught an image of the flowers.

After each photograph was taken he'd study the snap, tip his chin off the back of the hand that held the camera and look closely at the place in question.

Maybe, he'd say. Maybe.

We shot up a side road where he tried the front door of another deserted house – whose tiled roof was still intact in places – but could not open it. He went round the back and was gone for maybe ten minutes.

Come here, he said, emerging from behind.

I followed him, and found he had the back door open. He led me in to the middle room. Underneath a window to the side of the front door sat an old grey wooden piano and across it the top lay a huge torn mattress and eight blue cushions. I hit the keys. There was no sound.

Can you hear the music? he said.

I can, I said.

Play another tune, he said, and he watched me stroking the silent notes.

He looked fondly at the gutted armchairs, said something to himself, and a look like aggression came over his face as he smiled.

How did they get a piano up here, back then? he said. The past is like a herd of deer.

We stepped out, he pulled the back door closed, and stood a while, wondering.

A girl in a motorized wheelchair went by with a small dog on a lead.

Off again.

We arrived at what might have been a forge, then onto a deserted post office, an old RIC barracks, a deserted farmhouse with a dog barking out of one of the top broken windows at the tulips and mayflowers sprouting below.

A big house makes you lonesome, he said. That place reminds me of my grandmother's home, he said, she lived alone with a dog, and when she was in her seventies she committed suicide.

Dear God.

I should keep my mouth shut. The past has a lot to answer for.

Next we headed to a lonely, empty, big cement block building out on the main road. It had eight glassless crucifixes on the windows looking in on the dark. That looks like an old school, said Jack. Crows waddled across the tarmac. I parked by a gate into a field across the way and this time he did not try to enter the premises but took pictures from all sides on the road, nursing the lens with steady fingers.

I have been here before a few times, he said.

As the cattle watched me I began to imagine him imagining the kids arriving for the Irish class. Maths. Religion. Sonnets. He went to his knees and strips of wet hair crossed his bald head. At last he sat in and said in a boy's voice: I have just being talking to a Miss Buckley and a Master Coyle. Oh yes! Study my dears, they said.

And be a good boy.

I will.

Off we go.

As we drove round the lake the waves stuttered as mists flew over.

This valley is renowned for rain, he said.

All of a sudden there was a rap of hailstones on the windscreen.

Ah Mother Nature can be very articulate, he said.

Then it was up a side road to another deserted cottage on the side of the mountain. He tried the door and it opened.

He disappeared inside, and was gone for some time. Up above sheep climbed up the sheer side of Ben Bulben and hung there like markers. Old paths crossed over. Down below tractors passed with piles of the first cut of grass in their trailers. When he stepped out he was shaking his head and said Look! and he showed me the photographs in the camera, all in black and white. The first shot was taken from inside a room in the house and was aimed facing a window – through the old wooden crucifix that once held glass panes – that looked down on a steep dangerous fall to the valley and the lake below.

Now look at these, he said.

In the next appeared a kitchen table, with a bottle of Jameson whiskey – quarter full – sitting mid centre; then two chairs facing each other, an old metal ashtray and finally an *Irish Independent* newspaper from years back. We walked in and looked at the scene.

What do you make of that?

He lifted the newspaper, gone wet and black at the edges, with the print slipping into the unreadable, and read out the wandering headline concerning Vietnam, and then placed it back exactly where it had been. As we headed outside to the car a farmer driving black and white sheep and newly born lambs appeared on the lane.

Hallo. Not too bad class of a day, he said.

We've just looked inside the cottage, said Jack.

Oh yeh?

Just taking photographs.

I'm sure the Bradys wouldn't mind.

I'm glad to hear it. Did you ever see that bottle of whiskey?

No, not me. I have never once stood in that house since they've gone. I couldn't. I just heard the story from neighbours. The brothers took off for America, back in the sixties. The hired car came and off they went off leaving everything behind exactly as it was. They was great in fairness to them. Aye and that house has been empty a long time since then.

Jesus Christ.

And there's no relations in the area. One day the boys might come back. So there you go, good luck folks, take care, and he headed on down with the sheepdog racing and circling at the front.

Now, said Jack, history is a password.

Off we took again through another fall of hailstones and this time headed for an organic café for a bite to eat. On the way we passed a graveyard and he stared at the tombstones. Tranquillity can be very noisy, he said, there's always a war in another land. At the car park an old lady sat on her own in the passenger side of a jeep slowly feeding light green rosary beads through two fingers. Jack got out, waved to her, and took off his wellingtons and lifted a pair of white shoes out of his bag, then off came the jacket and on came a yellow jersey.

We had fish soup and scones, and he ate his ice cream like a child, all tongue and suck. Before we left he ordered two salad sandwiches for takeaway.

When we got back to the car the white shoes and jumper came off and he went into his old gear.

Will you drive me back to the piano house? he asked.

Of course. Could you put on your belt?

Oh dear.

We took off back along the same path, past the school, and up the side road, and when we reached the grey debris he stepped out with his bag and his camera, pulled a fifty from his pocket and handed it to me.

I have a favour to ask you, he said.

Go ahead.

Will you collect me in the morning?

Sure thing.

Well, good luck!

What do you mean?

You can collect me here.

What?

Yes here.

Here? I thought you meant back at your house.

No here! I'm going to stay for the night. I will have to wait till after midnight before I sleep. You see I never go to bed on the same day I got up. And when I get up tomorrow I'll head for school, and don't you worry, I have all I need, even a sleeping bag, and he headed round the back with a wave.

Jack, are you sure? I shouted.

I am! came the distant call from someone I could not see.

I drove off filled with guilt past yellow piles of whins and forsythia. I stopped the car and thought can I really leave him there, then went on. I collected the pair of kids in Bundoran, an hour late, and on the way home I began to look at ruins I had never looked at before. My eyes wandered across the fallen walls, broken sheets of asbestos, crunched pillars, old lovers, black windows, shattered little iron gates, the tree shooting up alongside the chimney through where the roof once was.

Ma, keep an eye on the road, said David.

Sorry.

I thought of Jack all that night. In sleep I lost my way; then I dreamed I was carrying a friend's baby in my arms. I found him, or he could have been a she, when I entered a small theatre with infants on stage. Inside the front door to the left was a medical room for training in folk. They were all in long grey gowns. It was here I found the babe. I set off down the town and it was near my destination that I got the first bite on the edge of my palm. The babe held it tight with his teeth for nearly half a minute.

Then a few minutes later came the bites on two of my fingers.

I handed the child over to the mother, and then an old business man took my arm. He'd take my elbow again and again as we started walking round the strange town, and as we did so his head began to droop forward dangerously, and suddenly sometimes he'd go face down from the waist forward.

And no passers-by would help.

At last he straightened up and went on. I woke and wondered, and next morning drove off at nine o'clock to the

piano house, lost my way, and started going round in circles.
At last I found the correct route.

I knocked on the front door.

Hallo! I called. There was no reply.

I knocked on the back.

Jack!

Again no answer. I pushed the back door in and it swung
open on a single hinge. The two rooms were empty and there
was not a trace of his gear. Not a sign of anyone. A pile of
dust sat in a corner by an old sweeping brush. He had been
cleaning up. Jack! I screamed. I began to get that ghostly
feeling. The piano sat silent again. Panic set in. I listened to
him say he was going to stay in the piano house. Now what
had happened? I heard him say *And get up for school.* I leaped
into the car and drove down to the old ruins, pulled in at the
gate and stepped out opposite the huge dark inside the eight
windows.

Jack! I called.

An ass in a field behind me roared. All of a sudden out
of one of the black windows of the old primary school came
the haversack thrown like a schoolbag, then with the camera
round his neck Jack appeared at another window and waved,
disappeared, then reappeared out through a door in the side
of the building.

You're early, he said.

Good morning.

Sorry about that, missus, I was about to head back above
to meet you.

Okay Jack.

We climbed into the car.

I'm afraid Miss Buckley and Master Coyle were not present
there this morning, he said.

No?

No. Reality is more complex than the imagination. Look!

And he rolled a few photos for me to look at. First came
the sole of a boot stuck in mud. Next came the interior – a

long room behind the windows that contained lines of cages made of rusted tin bars.

What are those?

Cages for holding pigs. There were no old desks. There was no school. A farmer informed me this morning that it was a blooming creamery and after it closed, the new owner brought in the pigs.

Oh.

I was wrong, he said, forgive me.

No problem.

He took his camera to his eye to read the images.

So where are we for today? I asked him.

That's a good question, he answered.

I turned the key. We sat there for a few moments with the engine running.

Smile, he said.

He turned the camera on me.

Pretend I'm not here, he said.

Okay.

In the flash I disappeared into the dark.

A second later we took off.

Maybe, he said.

Appendices

First Snow of the Year (original 1973 version)*

It was Jim Philips' first day of retirement. He realized he was no longer a postman when he awoke, and looked at the stained boards that ran the length of his ceiling. Jim spent the entire morning retrieving his habits as a young man, stayed in bed till late and took his ease about the house, looked up the chimney to check for crows, remembering that time of perpetual youth and céilí music before life had propped him up on a bicycle till the end of his days, a messenger in three townlands. But it was a fine thing, he thought, to outlive your job that you could die in a time of your own making. He left his woman-less bed with a light heart and laid out his drinking clothes before the fire, that he might be warm this day itself in Grady's.

Elsewhere in northwest Roscommon, it was a winter's day.

The ground was rock hard, and the frost had frozen the colours about the bog. Jim had to break the ice on the surface water of the well, his reflection shattering into a thousand pieces, face and hands sliding away on tiny flat sheets of ice as he dipped with his bucket. It was bitter cold. Down towards the valley the clownish trees and thick green moss peat crowded close to each other in family groups, the roads of wind swerved backwards and forwards across the yellow reeds and whins, the earth was on its side. A great rainbow had spun across the sky joining the two mountains, and out of the gaps in the thunderclouds sunlight slanted down like searchlights probing the glass-blue waters of Lough Gara.

The postman's clothes were warm and dry when young Phildy called.

Phildy waited about impatiently till they were ready to go. He was known locally as 'the bag of weasels' because he was given to argument at the best of times, and a hard upbringing

---

* Dermot Healy, "First Snow of the Year" ["New Irish Writing" page, ed. David Marcus], *Irish Press* (11 August 1973): 7. This original version, which is reprinted here for the first time, is substantially different to the extant version first published in *Banished Misfortune and Other Stories* (1982).

in a land lacking the touch of women had not softened his temperament. Nor would it ever, Jim reckoned, till there was some settlement of a kind, perhaps a few French ladies installed down in an open house might ease the situation. The young ones that stayed here had to learn the industry of hardship and silence; that was the way it was.

"Worst cold I've seen," said Phildy as they set off down the valley.

"Sure as '47," said Jim nodding, "the snow will be here afore the day is out."

"What do you think," said Phildy slowly, "of Mrs Owens dying like that, not wanting anyone at the funeral."

"Well, that was always her way, the poor woman."

"I don't know about that!"

"It's a bad day for the burying, that's sure."

"There are those who know how to keep warm," replied Phildy, with a hint of anger, was it, in his voice.

"You'd be better leaving that alone now. It's better leaving that alone."

"No harm in what I said," said Phildy half to himself, as he tested his steps gingerly on the frozen main road.

The postman realized that nothing could thaw out the hate in the young man's heart – it was the endless struggle and sin of their small society, the civil war between friend and friend, Phildy's mind was being eaten alive by the loss of a woman to another man, he could not explain or forgive, it was part of the weather of life that relaxes and freezes the pain in the soil.

"It would be better if you spoke to Pedey," the postman said. "He could do with a friend now."

Phildy did not answer.

They started the afternoon cheerfully enough with hot whiskies in Corcoran's. There was Sean Devine in the pub with his brass box of secondhand watches, a lifetime's collection that he took the length and breadth of the country buying and selling. He had let his farm go to wrack and ruin, he once explained to the postman, in order to take up a job in commerce. The truth was he didn't take to working too easy, and he had a great thirst for conversation and wandering. He had a watch on each wrist, his prize pieces, and a story to go with each, and a price befitting the story. He put his watches away nightly at eleven o'clock. There was O'Grady himself behind the bar who was obliged to blow the first round in honour of the postman's retirement, an act which exceedingly pleased Mr Devine who on the spot saluted each member of the company. The kettle was set up on a crate behind the counter and plugged in, a measure of cloves and sugar dropped into each glass and the evening began.

"You'll be making plenty of personal calls now that your hands are free," said O'Grady with a smile.

"Oh wherever he sees the glimmer of a dress," said Phildy, trying with difficulty to be funny toward the man who befriended him always.

"A glimmer of a dress surely," and the postman laughed hysterically into his drink, laughing and spluttering. He had a soft spot for women.

"You're hittin' the high spots now," the watch-man put in, and patted Jim on the back affectionately.

"I'll have a woman above in the house in no time, true as God."

"She'll need be quick on her feet to keep up with ya, that's certain."

The drinks were lifted up to the light, and shook and drunk. O'Grady leaned over the bar confidentially.

"I saw them go by this morning," he said.

"Did you now?" the postman asked.

"I did. Dowds did the burying."

"Was it now."

"Dowds it was."

"Is that so."

"Driving like a ginnet, he was."

"That man's a hard driver," said the watch-man, shaking his head, "no matter what the function."

"O'Dowd's the man to put steam up under the dead," Phildy added in his reckless way, knocking back the dregs of his drink.

Jim Philips then bought his first round of the evening, the first of many.

Somewhere in the dark and cold of Monasteraden among the appealing shapes of stone and marble, the flowers under glass, the shape of things to come, Pedey Owens was burying his mother and his past and Drumacoo pressed down on his heart like a great weight and his woman stood away from him like a stranger, her belly full with his child, the lust of his blood running in her veins like a sean-nós falling and rising over the years that led to this moment. He despised her now, his dependence on her, her head turned to the open spot in the fresh clay shedding tears over a dead woman who would not have her as nurse nor daughter, nor even would bid her the time of day. Would it always be like this? Do women ever let go? He was silent and emptied of everything. The snow had begun to scatter without sound down onto the coffin and the spades wheeled in the air and —

"Here's health!" the postman said.

"The best in the world," the watch-man said.

"Aye."

"She knew she was dying too," O'Grady continued. " She left the door unlatched and lay out in the bed in her clothes, clean and fresh out of the wash, and Eli-Jane trying as best she could was chased out of the house, and hid in the barn in dread of her eternal life from the moans and the crying. They say the mother cursed her with her dying breath."

"Of course Pedey was nowhere to be seen," said Phildy.

"A sad time for Monasteraden and the dead being carted away by the day," the watch-man said, "and it'll be hard time on Pedey and the woman now surely."

"No more than they should expect," Phildy said angrily. "It's between those two the evil lies."

"Those are bitter words," Jim Philips said. "When you're young you'll have little percentage for life if it's bitterness you have at the back of your head."

"Well, what of Eli-Jane then?"

"She'll stand by her man. It's her place."

"Will he stop by *her*, now that the farm is his. He's made for life. That's the point. Can't you see what's—"

"He will," said the postman. "We've said our bit, now leave it alone."

"Youse are too high and friggin' mighty," said Phildy rising off his stool.

"Now Phildy," said O'Grady, "take it easy like a good man."

"Wasn't it you kept it up," said Phildy hopelessly in a shrill voice, banging his fist off the counter. The situation was relieved somewhat when the door opened into the pub to admit one, Mr O'Dowd, undertaker, grocery-shop owner, dressed complete in black suit, his head and shoulders piled with snow that he shook from his coat when he entered the pub. The postman nodded his head slowly when he saw the snow.

"It came after all," he said. "The snow, I mean."

And Pedey had eventually left her to find her way home herself. She had stood there, so delicate a being, trussed up in the snow beside the grave, yet he had no heart for words. O'Dowd could bring her. It mattered little to him what she did. He felt cold and heavy, drained of all energy, a little time and the feeling would pass, it wasn't the cold of the weather that was on him but the cold inside him, something that refused to allow him think, a hollow feeling that made his limbs heavy, the big ugly body of him swollen with work, hands that refused to feel what was around him and gave him no hope. He thought he might have cried. He heard, as he walked along the side of the hill away from the graveyard, the sound of the Penny streams glancing down from the mountain, hanging onto the secret of their quiet vocabulary, as they went blindly feeling their way into the valley. He must get to a pub soon. He'd have a few to settle himself in Monasteraden, and then go to Grady's maybe if he was . . . back to himself, if he could face them . . . Jim would know what was best . . . Jim would know, he'd retired today.

"God, that's a shocking day," O'Dowd said in a blustery manner.

"'Tis. 'Tis indeed. Sit yourself down by the fire and warm yourself. A shocking day indeed," the postman replied, indicating a chair.

"Quite frightful, I can tell you, I decided to stop here before going on to the supermarket."

"You were quite right on a day like that."

"The worst I've seen. I've just driven a young lady down—"

"A shocking day," the postman went on, "as bad as '47. Now sit yourself down by the fire there and what will you have."

"Well if it's hot whiskies, that'll be fine."

Jim ordered another round, taking his time with O'Grady, and then ordered four stouts along with the whiskies.

"The roads will be impassable before the night's out," the undertaker said. "And only today—"

"You know," said the postman, "I remember the whole eleven mile of me round and the snow piled head-high that man nor beast couldn't get through. Sure even for days beforehand there was hailstones hopping the size of your fist that if they hit a man would strike him dead."

"In '47?" said Sean Devine, taking it up.

"In '47 surely."

"I remember," said the watch-man, "being able to stand up on a snowdrift and damid if I couldn't touch the electric wires with a stick." He shook his head. "There never was the like."

"Well yes, gentlemen, but—"

"I don't think I handed out a letter for ages. The first day of the snow I was lucky to make it home. I had to make my way up to the house with a grape. Yes, and I didn't leave the house for over a week."

"Well I wasn't in Ireland in those days," O'Dowd said. "But I can tell you chaps that it's a shocking day. A terrible

day for burying a human being." Here the postman lowered
his head. "When driving that young lady back to the Owens'
place after the funeral, we skidded left and right across the
bog road, why – I thought I'd never see myself home and dry."

Phildy got to his feet and stood staring at the undertaker a
long time. He looked along the company in general, his eyes
sharp with anger.

"So Eli-Jane went to the funeral after all, and he didn't
think fit to take her home himself. Didn't I tell ya —"

"Not interruptin' ya there," said Devine the watch-man, as
he looked away into the distance, "but that '47 blizzard wasn't
so bad in the morning but by evening it 'id smother a body.
For I lay in me bed that night without an ounce of sleep, and
the following morning I lay on and on thinking it was dark,
and then got up I did eventually and pushed open the door
after a long harangue and lo and behold ya it was bright . . . ."

All during the watch-man's attempt at talking, Phildy
was standing there running his fingers over and back across
the edge of the bar, a nerve twitched under his eye, and he
slammed down his glass with a wallop on the counter.

"What does it matter," he shouted, "forty bloody seven or
any year for that matter. For frig sake, do you think I can sit
here like a bloody fool listening to your load of tripe! Good
Jazes, can't you see, can't you see – I'm going to settle Pedey
once and for all."

He got up and started to put on his coat. Jim Philips put
his hand on Phildy's shoulder and with his eyes tried to reason
with him, but Phildy looked away into his own hurt.

"I'll break his friggin' neck," said Phildy before he slammed
the door behind him, the snow sweeping in with a rush and
the blast of cold air upsetting the drinkers.

"My God," said O'Dowd with feigned distress.

Pedey sat in a snug, bowed like a woman in the back of a
church, delivered into his own acute silence which the spirits
of the dead make their own, turning a man's head inward
against himself till all his senses become a riotous crowd of

evil, demanding evil, and he fought for his sanity and layers
of himself peeled away like autumn does to the trees, sparing
no fear or leaf, but the drink didn't spare him nor the images
that tumbled into his head, and drunkenly he babbled to
Eli-Jane and his mother explaining and explaining, but they
stood with drawn faces away from him, strangers, till his mind
struck rock-bottom and he was gone . . . .

"Certainly," said O'Dowd, "I said nothing to offend him."

"Divil a thing," said the postman. "It's just that he can ill-
accept turning out a bachelor like meself and Mr Boylan here.
It'll pass."

"Like it did for us all," said Sean Devine, "but I might add
that it wasn't from want of trying in your case."

"Not from want of trying surely," said the postman
laughing into his drink, and he clapped his knee in time to
the good of it all.

"Well, I hope he intends that young Owens chap no harm,
especially on this particular occasion!" O'Dowd said.

"You can rest easy," the postman replied, "it's nearly all talk
with young Phildy."

"Still, I must admit I fail to understand."

"Rest easy, it'll sort itself out in the end."

"Well, you gentlemen know best."

The watch-man nodded and indicated his empty glass in
an offhand manner, synchronising his watches as if time was
getting on.

"And er . . . Mr O'Grady," the undertaker continued, "two
hot whiskies for the gentlemen, and a small brandy for meself."

Sean Devine pulled his sleeve down over the watches with
satisfaction, a glint in his eye like a mirror in the distance
suddenly caught by the sun.

Out in the night, the white snowfall had made new horizons,
stark trees begging on the sides of the mountains or bowed in
their poverty, men of the earth, the whole place crisp as a child's

brain and slow too the falling snow like the happiness of an old man's head. And Pedey was riding a bike crazily down the hill from Monasteraden, bending and swerving in the torrents of snow that took the wheels on their own mad journey. He freewheeled on not caring at all now where the bike took him, it relieved him of everything, it was childhood again and went on forever, that he might never stop feeling the wild rush of the snow in his face and the soft kick of the trees that blinded his eyes. On now. At Edmondstown Cross he went right for a ditch, headlong. As the wheels hit the high grass margin deep down, he was flung off the bike and carried on his back a few yards up the road. Phildy on his way from O'Grady's had seen the final impact, he stood silently watching from the far side of the road, not moving, blindfolded. A snowdrift had nearly covered the fallen man, he surrendered gladly to the shock of the fall, lying quiet, swallowed blood from a cut on his lip. He lay facing the earth, gathering the feeling of pain back into his bones. He rose himself up on his elbows, moaning, onto his knees, and stayed there in that position a while till he focused on a dark figure silhouetted against the ditch, standing away from him. He called across. The man standing did not answer, he bled inward, the job was done for him, he took himself up forcefully toward Monasteraden, his anger anaesthetized by nature for a time, and the fallen man gathered himself up and took the bog road, away from O'Grady's, into the great empty silence.

"Well, here's luck to your good company," said O'Dowd.

"The same to yourself," said the postman, as he still felt a postman, and a king too from the warm feeling in his stomach.

"The very best," said Devine the watch-man. "And to go on now about what I was saying about '47 ... I opened the door and looked out and lo and behold ya it was bright ... so bright that it 'id dazzle your eyes ... and I stood up at the door and I called, and I went up to the low hill from the door and I called and called .... And I thought all me beasts were dead, taken from me during the night . . . . When Lord save me, out of the drifts by the galvanise shed they came, one by one, struggling up toward me like the newborn . . . . And I fed them like a man whose wits had got the better of him . . . nudging and poking at me chest . . . Lord wasn't I the happy man, when they came up striking outa the snow and took the hay without a word." The watch-man was looking away into the distance, winding one of his watches over and over.

"You were blessed, Sean Devine, blessed."

"Aye and that same afternoon I took the gun and the dog down to Lough Gara, and I shot some wild ducks, 'cause there wasn't a bit a food in the house, not a bit . . . . Sure there was no eating in them . . . . The dog rose the poor things and up they got fightin' their cause, and they as poor and thin as you'd see and dyin' on the wing . . . . Sure hunger 'id drive a man to anything."

"Well, damid, Sean Devine, but I never knew you'd taken a gun in your hand."

"There you are now! There's a side of me you don't know!"

O'Dowd the undertaker got to his feet and buttoned up his coat tightly about him, hammered his heels on the floor and tipped his hat forward across his face. He looked round the company, and rubbed his hands together breezily.

"Well gentlemen, I don't want to interrupt your reminiscences but I'll be off or the family won't know where I've got to."

"Give my regards to the Mrs and all," the postman said.

"I will do that," said O'Dowd as he left, closing the door quickly behind him.

There was silence for a few moments, till O'Dowd's car revved up and after a couple of false starts pulled away.

"I wouldn't be surprised if that man drove here in the hearse," said O'Grady, who inwardly was cursing the weather that kept his customers away, and funerals that had no mourners, and old men that a few drinks could keep happy.

The two old men pulled their chairs up closer to the fire.

"Poor Pedey," the postman said, his toe tracing a zigzag line through the ashes that had fallen from the grate.

"It's rough enough," the watch-man said, nodding.

"He had promised to come here tonight, but sure what can a fellow do."

"It's hard times for a man to have his dying mother and his best friend turn agin him over a woman."

"Well Eli-Jane is the salt of the earth, many's a time I told him. And he'll see her alright in the end, when this has blown over, and that's a fact."

"True for you. There's people in this part of the country 'id begrudge you the use of your right arm."

"He'll marry her now, and what matter when they've a roof over their heads."

"Son of God, if it's drunk he is going back to the home place, he'll have a hard time making it there on this very night."

"A hard time, surely, but he'll make it back to Eli-Jane," said the postman, and he topped up his glass and blew away the froth with pressed lips.

Pedey Owens was in the thick of the strong silent snow. He had been lost for hours. His feet dragged through the silence like many people walking. He passed the river but heard nothing but the horror in his head. Hadn't he built a raft that went the length of the river and across the five lakes of Lough Gara, hadn't he strung together palings and posts with bull-wire and tied on the petrol drums with his very hands, and the raft so sound they could have made it to the sea in Sligo itself. Hadn't he cut turf when his arms were like polished bronze with the sun, cut enough for two villages. He told himself these things as he got lost in the snow, turning his mind inside out till he could find the way home, he ran madly this way and that, frightened of the long drop into the bogholes, but his senses failed him, he could make nothing of this great white silence. He cursed the weakness in him, he had never known this blind panic before, and he stood for a long time trying to get his bearings but the light was the same everywhere. He called out to Eli-Jane, trying desperately to understand, to focus on her that he might never lose sight of her . . . .

"Do you know what 'id be great value now," said the postman, his eyes misting over.

"What's that," asked Devine, the watch-man.

"The kali, the auld colcannon, that 'id warm a cauld woman's heart."

"Now you're talking," said the watch-man. "It's the weather for it."

"A skillet full of kali, with the onions and the homemade butter."

"That's the stuff!"

"And the boxty."

"The boxty. Ah man dear."

"And the potato cake."

"Will ya stop."

"But damid, if I haven't set a spud in years."

"Christ sure, sure you could be settin' the potatoes now in a barrel or an auld box, and when they'd be anyway started, layin' them out on the sunny side of a hedge, away from the frost, and yid be as right as rain."

"As soon as this weather is over, that's what I'll do, Sean Devine."

"All you'd need is the drop of buttermilk ye'd get from Byrne's wife, and mix that with the potatoes or oatmeal, and ye'd be set for a week."

"Sure a man would tip the highest gate in the county after a meal like that."

"Now you're talking," said the watch-man, "now you're talking."

Pedey was out of breath. His lungs were bursting to the beat of his heart. He had pitched forward so many times onto the sharp heather and thorns that his face was a mass of cuts, and round his mouth the blood had frozen solid. He was trapped in the centre of a quiet persistent storm that had begun somewhere in the depths of his own being, and he prayed. He prayed on his knees when he'd fall, or while standing as he got his breath. He prayed as he ran. He tried to find his footprints back to the Cross but they'd filled up with snow. And when he saw there was no way back, when he accepted that, he gathered himself up with a new strength, when he saw how far there was to go, it was peace inside him. He walked along slowly testing the ground ahead of him with the end of a stick. And he abandoned the stick as his surroundings became familiar, though he could see or hear nothing. He walked through the years of his whole life, and voices out of his childhood spoke to him. Not in words. Something he heard. The dead forgave him. He saw Eli-Jane, he couldn't tell, he'd try, Jesus God how he'd try. He heard her and she was warm and alive, and her breasts were full, awaiting him. Pedey froze up under the pain of his vision and cried, laughed. He recognized the gravel track on the far side of the bog as in a dream. He fell forward in joy, laid out in the snow there, the body of his young woman, Eli-Jane, the salt of the earth, turning into a real person under his frozen hands, hands into which some feeling was now returning.

"You know what I'll be doing now, Sean Devine? I'll be giving you my watch for damn the use I'll be making of it now," the postman said.

"Bless my soul," said the watch-man astounded.

"Well, there'll be no more getting up at the crack of dawn for me."

"It's a grand watch, I've had me eye on her for many a day."

"Well, you're welcome to it now," said Jim Philips as he unstrapped the watch, and handed it over, following the second hand with his eye.

Legal Times (1980)*

"The surgeon has suggested Gradenigo's syndrome," the doctor said as he leaned closer to detect the cause of Señor Alarcón's declining sight. In the front lounge some of the villagers sat awaiting the outcome. Each day they normally came so that the old policeman might go over their paperwork, prepare references for their young sons, write out suitable memorial cards for their dead. "Mastoid, I think," the doctor added. "You see the fifth nerve and the third nerve cross each other at the petrous bone and there is the danger." He tapped the policeman's skull, focused closer to the alarmed pupil, holding the hot lightbulb in his left hand. This was the same overworked doctor that had slept the night with Señor Alarcón's wife, delivering José in the early hours. Now sixteen years later José, standing by the window, became acutely aware of the inflamed honeycomb of cells behind his father's ear. His sisters busied themselves in the kitchen, hurriedly aware that the lights of the old scholar were going astray.

The doctor lifted Señor Alarcón's dropped eyelid. He stared an incalculable time towards the point of light which withdrew continually from his gaze. The doctor packed his things, and went into the street where the sunset was growing long in mid-February, with cottage windows sparkling on the hills.

The paperwork continued, though Señor Alarcón developed a number of spasms throughout the spring which appeared like premeditated contortions, and in the same manner the jump of the nerve under his left eye was seen as a distinguished feature by the villagers, rather than a tic of inward pain. No theory would satisfy his craving for freedom, yet he had not yet consigned his will to fate. José confessed to great love for his father, and the inarticulation of that

* Dermot Healy, "Legal Times," *Icarus*, no. 75 (1980), ed. Gerry McDonnell: 35-41. This was originally subtitled "An Excerpt from 'Sciamachy' – A Novel in Progress". Of all the Sciamachy extracts published in various periodicals and anthologies, this piece seems sufficiently self-contained to stand as a story in its own right.

youthful confession was due to the intensity of the age rather than embarrassment. His father's hand on his shoulder, they walked by the sea. "My soul's bliss kills my body but will not satisfy itself," Señor Alarcón said. They walked into the little village and met first an old soldier talking earnestly to a curly-haired chap with three gold earrings in each ear.

Opposite the figurative Revolutionary Memorial, a humorous pale statue with an arm raised, was the bookshop.

In the field behind the bookshop, sheep were lazing on the harsh irregular ground, contented; in the next field, they were cavorting about wide awake.

Lawyer Smith, in an anxious manner, ushered father and son into his car. Files and sketches of accidents and houses filled the backseat. Señor Alarcón, as befits a depressed spirit, commenced a long conversation about exports and imports. The lawyer replied that a horse will eat twice the amount of a cow. He had two accents, one local, one neutral, and veered between both depending on whether the issue was one of compromise or authority. The journey to the hotel was friendly. José in the back tried to detect among the various documents statements that might have been taken from a murderer's lips, while the men leaned towards each other, talked, gestured and eventually silenced each other as the morning began to drift cloudily over the twisting roads. Someone had torn strips out of a cinema poster. Someone hit their son across the face. The lawyer coughed angrily and spat onto the gaily-decorated path to the hotel. A country family swayed through the murky caverns, women all tissue, men wringing out their frosted collars. Out from the hotel, three things. A black dog among rocks, a magpie perched on an orange cow's back, and rhubarb bristling from the earth.

The necessary papers were placed before Señor Alarcón on the bar table. "You will sign away your interest in the farm and outbuildings," the lawyer advised, "and leave the sale in my hands."

It was like this. Señor Alarcón's house was to be surrendered, though admittedly as a former policeman he was not without a sense of pride and corruption. His wife's relations would now be his whole life, their small businesses his sustenance. He was not surprised to find that the matriarchal life attracted him, yet there was no happiness in being totally bereft of responsibility.

José's father drew in his breath and looked hazily toward the out-of-season carpets which were rolled up in the breakfast room. Through the window there came the smell of meringues from the sea. The barmaid, who had wide brown pupils like the sheep in those parts, seemed to understand his misery. "These men tackle their lives with cohesive philosophies," the lawyer said with neutral intonations, as he indicated some Western-accented elderly people who were seated at the next table. The woman of this group, poised in mottled scarf and heavy coat, leaned upright and forward from her two male companions. The men discussed the markets, humorously aware of her arched inquisitive figure. "Had I the strength I would carry it through," José overheard her say. Her liberation had been late in coming. She was interested, anxious, homespun. "We are doing the place up," the barmaid explained tentatively to Señor Alarcón. One of the sheep farmers arched his fingers in the peace sign as he tickled his scalp, his other hand cupped loosely under his chin. His friend had his arms tucked to his chest, the better to concentrate on critical speech. "There's an awful lot to be said for being stupid," the sheep farmer went on in aggressive tone, "at least, you keep your balance."

"My eyesight is leaving me too," said Señor Alarcón.

"José, get more drinks and be a good sort," Lawyer Smith asked.

José told his order in manly terms across the counter. Now he had the barmaid's eye a minute before she turned. In the lounge opposite he also saw a girl, desirable as any he had seen. Her absorbed face was chinned by a reclining arm, caught between two talkative youths who were grinning and possibly offensive to strangers. She took over their conversation in a puzzled though confident fashion. She wore brown socks, brown boots, white woollen dress and brown Aran jumper with a long white scarf. Her man touched her cheek with one finger. She flicked off the touch and continued talking, could even look direct at José, who paused with two squat glasses pressed to his chest.

"Here, this will keep you on the road," and interrupting that affectionate moment, one of the sheep farmers pressed into his hands some seaweed, soft and salty.

"Tell us your story then," said Señor Alarcón.

"So since I was a child I have had malformed kidneys, and have been in hospital near every year," continued Lawyer Smith. He smoothed his agitated, spermy trousers. "Then I met this priest when I was working in the South. He told me of a nun. I travelled all the way to the Northern coasts to see her, and she was so beautiful when I saw her, like a spring day. She told me her story."

While speaking in such a manner, the lawyer's eyes, the white brimming with thought, sought out Señor Alarcón's attention. The elderly scholar was looking into the fire, dusting turf mould off the grate, only too aware of this beseeching intimacy. It reminded him of a drunken prisoner in a cell protesting sobriety, but who can tell. He himself was arranging his own sickness, his fate, to confound the forthcoming miracle. The lawyer continually looked to the left of Señor Alarcón's temple as he finished each sentence. In the background, "The Can of Spring Water" was being sung by Michael Joseph on the barmaid's tape.

"She was teaching in a place in America, she told me," continued Lawyer Smith. "During the night a voice says, 'you have my gift, go out and use it.' A priest and a stranger woman came and proceeded to tell her that they had been visited in their sleep and the same Word had been told them concerning her. It was an open-and-shut case of spiritual mediumship. I'll be brief. Going up the Northern coast, into your border country, I could feel this great calm. Proceeding away I knew I was cured. And I could tell something spiritual had happened to me as well. At the consecration of the mass I could feel people drawn to me, people would turn around and look into my eyes." Through the lounge window a peasant fanned out a dismembered swan's wing to protect his garden from crows.

"Isn't it sad that after six months this whole sense of love, when the Sacred Heart would smile at me, and truth, when the Host would confirm the future, no longer gave me a sense of spiritual insight? I had been given the gift but didn't use it myself. I had been cured only. That nun was the one that started the movement. I sit here turning these things over in my mind."

His pupils lifted to a point left of Señor Alarcón's head.

"I believe every word you are telling me," the old man said.

Intimacy of this kind ended immediately once they entered the car.

Señor Alarcón talked of vegetables, of everything rural, it was a holding talk, a heroic speech of the mundane that at this moment in time the charismatic lawyer did not properly admire or entertain. Outside the world was in torment. Señor Alarcón spoke of the dangers of the sea nor would his voice allow José to sleep in the freezing backseat. He was afflicted by drowned faces, that perpetual fear. Nobody was stirring about on those steep climbs. A small bird was blown from the edge of a drain across the road like a piece of twig, her small claws gathering the wind into her cupped wings. Seagulls fell away like puffins into the freezing valley below, except for one brief moment when maybe twenty of them were stationary above the bushes, on the same level of the road the car had climbed, before they dropped away. A group of sleek-feathered rooks tottered to their left in flight, lightly-feminine-limbed, they arched off.

And on the descent, those beautiful sensual daydreams returned to José, with strange hands stealing across his flesh, mouths tugging at his enlarged penis, a sudden wet kiss on his pleasant buttock, his white cheek rocking, surrounded on all sides by sundry and saving arguments from the courts of the District, Circuit and High.

He awoke completely frustrated to the laughs of the villagers in the hall of his house. Bicycle-menders, cartmen, lovers of his aunt, various unsuccessful suicide cases, women with sons abroad, a few fishermen, had matters that needed attending to. All stood a moment by the huge windows looking out through the mist, those strange rich generations, talking of nothing but the island and the city. When José stepped outside the East wind grew furious in his ears. Youths, silhouetted by the river-fog, kicked football. "I have to deal with urban lawyers," Lawyer Smith said, by the supper table, as he lifted a forkful of bacon to his thin lips. "It makes it hard on me." Señor Alarcón did not reply. "It's a pity that your family should choose this time to side with the renegades. You will get no price worth talking about since you will not return."

"The more inland you go the more patriotic and dull the people get," interrupted García.

"Yes," said Señor Alarcón. José did not know that his father missed the border country so. Apollo and Miguel longed to live there, as theirs was a tedious existence. His uncle García, the carpenter and café-owner, had been manhandled by the police there and charged in court with conspiring to blow up a police barracks. The fact that the documents were forty years old and relating to a previous revolution did not emerge till halfway through the court proceedings, and Señor García was rejuvenated that the police should think him capable of attacking a police barracks that had been much extended and fortified since those early days.

"José here will have to go to Manager Francis in the city," the lawyer said. "He owes you money and can afford the luxury of a common rebel. I have arranged for the hospital, as a liberal I prefer the term hospital to asylum, to take in your daughters as trainee nurses. They will hardly be a stone's throw from here."

Plans, plans, plans.

After supper Tessa and José walked through the seeping ditches, through the rain that was hardly rain, chewing on the stringy seaweed. All about them white stones in turf, paint splashed on dry bog. His eardrum nearest the East heard nothing. A peasant in a light blue suit and woollen hat was coming down with his coat blown open, his eyes full of tears. Tessa and José climbed onto the new trawler that had pulled into the pier, a million-and-a-quarter pounds worth. She had her own ice-making equipment, hot and cold water for the skipper, sonar equipment to give the exact position of a shoal within a quarter of a mile from the boat, their depth from the surface. García, drunk with freedom, was out on the trawler with the sailors, butchering the carcasses of two sheep he had taken out in a canoe. Over his shoulder into the sea he slung the unwanted innards. He had no tattoos from his periods in prison, but kept a strict silence, ate not at all well, for of all things he hated his own emotionalism and greed. He hated himself with a deep hate, and only the fierce slog of heavy work could obliterate his guilt.

By Christ, he fucking hated himself, and that's better said, for he worked little enough.

"I worry about him," Señora Alarcón often said.

"Ah worry of that kind is like jealousy," summarised Señor Alarcón.

"He's a good man, I worry over him."

And in the morning the drizzle still came down, sheep were out on the strand in their hundreds nibbling among the seaweed, their alert heads darting away from Señor Alarcón, his head tightly covered in a spitting sheet of cellophane, as he went along mumbling to himself awful mad, bitter prayers about people and animals. Everybody, himself, the village were sick with lethargy. There it was. It was not that he wanted to be young again but that he might endure anew the intense discipline of the spirit, not transcendence, but mutation. And irony! Irony! There were no houses where he walked but the overhanging mist and the dark brown peakless mountains, where black-faced sheep hung out of the clouds, staring down an instant.

He entered the village again, amongst the young people on crutches and women in Volkswagens. The peoples' tweed imitated the frequency and pattern of their granite, the stone wall of the school worthy of a garrison. The Marquis of Sommerville, in his frock coat, sat on the steps of a caravan in a humpy field, playing his fiddle, and around him the innocent Alarcón girls, Geraldine, Brid, Maura, listening to his romantic songs. Behind him a conglomeration of mountains, seagulls and children, and José below walking on the strand with Tessa among green and blue stones, the tide sliding in over the level of the other tides, against rock polished and perfected like plate glass, right to the gleam of light encased in a pretty almost cut-glass shade in the toilet where Señor Alarcón sat, straight and upright, tracking his life through the unfamiliar present.

The Smell of Roses (2009)*

The day we arrived in Ecuador we spoke in Irish. Through a timber worker en route to Columbia we found a room in a hotel. All we had with us was a letter of introduction to the cultural aide, the phone numbers of the Irish Consul and a Divine Word missionary. At breakfast, the waitress lit a Carroll I gave her, and threw marvelling eyes at the ceiling. We took our first walk in Quito, stepping downstairs into memory.

The street was filled with the smell of fireworks from a festival of the night before.

I dropped a dollar into the cap of a man. He was sitting, head down, on a deckchair on the street with one hand palm-upwards. He had enormous blue-veined thighs wrapped in bandages, and huge crutches.

His fingers wriggled in reply.

I met him again a few days later in a park, where we went to watch three-man-a-side netball. He was lying back, eyes closed, with his legs crossed, hidden in a copse of trees. Then we encountered him being dropped off at five in the morning onto his patch. Two helpers were wrapping the bloody bandages round his thigh, and painting the blue sores onto his skin, for the day ahead.

When he saw me he rose a finger to his lips. I dropped a dollar at his feet. He gave a grand gesture. I winked at him and he stared back outraged. The wink I later learned means that you are about to inform on someone.

We got an apartment after two days. Each morning Indians on the street below opened rubbish bags, took what

* Dermot Healy, "The Smell of Roses", *Irish Times* (6 September 2008), repr. *From the Republic of Conscience: Stories Inspired by the Universal Declaration of Human Rights*, ed. Seán Love (Dublin: Liberties Press, 2009): 45-51. A Headnote in the *Irish Times* notes: "In a new story, Dermot Healy responds to Article 3 of the Universal Declaration of Human Rights, as part of a series in association with Amnesty International to mark the 60th anniversary of the declaration." Under Article 3, "Everyone has the right to life, liberty and security of person."

they needed, and retied the bags. The poor dressed in white. McDonald's had armed personnel on the door. The Indians studied us as we set off each morning to various government buildings with the letter of introduction, but each time we arrived to the wrong door. A woman on the street felt my beard. We ate in a local café, and I led the way home. We were walking in a breathless maze for forty-five minutes.

"Are you sure you know the way?"

"Yes."

"How do you know?"

"I took down the name of the street."

"What is it?"

"Una Via," I said.

"One way," she said. I had brought us back up through all the one-way streets in Quito.

On another aimless walk, I tried a police station. I was searched and shown upstairs to see the chief. It was 4.30 of a Friday. He was sitting alone in an office laughing to himself. I gave him the letter and he offered me a rum. Two men materialised alongside the far wall.

"You seek Señor Philatao?"

"Yes."

He laughed, lifted up the phone and rang, and shook his head. "Go to the Casa Cultura," he said.

We went to the museum the next day, and for the first time got out of the modern city into the old. We began to feel more at home, as our estrangement grew, but found no cultural aide. We stood outside. The army passed, rifles cocked. I looked up at a sculpture of a boy archer on the balcony of the building.

"Do you see him," I asked. "See how he is shooting the arrow out."

"He is shooting it in."

"Out," I said.

"In," she said. "Everything I say or do, you find fault with," and she burst into tears. A small angel had started a row between us. The smell of fireworks was at its height. We climbed back to the apartment exhausted. The night grew dark. I phoned the Irish Consul. It rang out. We watched a lady cook on the TV. Her hair went into the soup.

"What's going on?"

"I don't know."

I lifted out the phone number of the Divine Word missionary that a philosopher I hardly knew had given me in the bar of the Abbey Theatre. I rang, and a voice answered in Spanish.

"Do you speak English?" I asked.

"Are you Irish?"

"Yes, and there's something wrong."

"Where are you?" he asked, and in ten minutes he climbed up the stairs, entered the living room and looked at us and said: "You have altitude sickness, you are at 11,500 feet."

A weight lifted off my head.

Through him we would visit the equator; and join a protest march in solidarity when six priests, and their housekeeper, were killed in San Salvador. The brains of the religious were cut out. Priests in shawls arrived from all the poor quarters. A nun grabbed the mike outside the university and said she was ashamed to teach among Jesuits who had let the deaths pass without protest.

At the Peruvian border, we would attend a mass for the second funeral of a woman who was dug up a year after she died because a voice told her son she was in the wrong grave. We'd visit the Village of White Fools. We tried to visit the Virgin on the heights of Quito, but the woman in the shop at the bottom of the steep ascent said, "No Señor," when I told her where we were going.

She stood in front of us on the road, looked at Helen, and drew her hand across her throat. We turned back. She had saved us from knife-wielding toughs above at the monument. We found the cultural aide, an office and a translator. With the oxygen reaching our brains, we moved into a hotel room in the old town, and planned trips to the Valley of the Volcanoes. I met an American historian who taught us how

Magic Realism came out of the forests. When the woods were cut down, like in North America, the magic was lost.

I was coming home from my first day at my desk on a bus. To my right, on the street outside, there was uproar. Suddenly a soldier fired off a round of tear gas that landed in through the door. Everyone jumped out, including the driver. Crowds ran. I ducked with a man into a courtyard. We put our heads into a fountain, lifted our mouths to breathe but the arcade had a roof, and the place was filling up with bitter smoke.

We were collapsing with coughing, and tears, when a small door opened and a prostitute ushered the two of us into two indoor toilets. We stood silently alone. She let us out when the danger had passed. We walked down the hill with handkerchiefs to our faces, and shook hands outside the hotel.

The fireworks were tear gas; the festivals confrontations between student activists and soldiers. The workers supported the students, but paid for it. Buses were banned. Each late afternoon I joined the workers trudging home. Outside the hotel, another confrontation started. A woman and her children got caught in the swirls of gas. Helen lifted one kid and ran along with the mother up a hill and hid in a church.

Inside, Christ wore a Panama hat.

When we came out, the women were waving rolled lumps of lit newspapers to clear the pepper from the air. Next morning on my way to work I arrived into a stand-off. The students, in a side alley, were facing police and soldiers out on the main street. I looked round the corner judging the run. One policeman raised his hand, a student answered in reply, all weapons were lowered, and they let me cross.

We were invited to a concert. My translator showed us into seats in a private box. At the end of the show the lover was dancing to a lament as her man played the guitar to the side. Suddenly, rose petals, in thousands, fell down onto her, and into the gods. The roses stopped, then the skies opened again, and it began to rain; and underneath, the singer stood drenched in a garden of petals.

I found a distant other sense awakening. The applause started. The rain stopped. Helen's hand came down on mine. It was as if we had stepped out into the open air, as slowly, the waft of roses, at last, reached us in the balcony.

The audience came to their feet.

It was the most powerful, yet faint, sensation of smell I have ever experienced.

We tiptoed round in circles down the winding stairs and out onto the street. A few minutes later a jeep pulled in, braked hard, and two armed policemen jumped out with batons. They grabbed two lads who were walking ahead of us, and began hauling them across the footpath.

Suddenly Helen ran up, and touched one of the policemen lightly on the shoulder and shouted "Theatre!"

He swung round.

"Señora?"

"Theatre!" She pointed back at the concert hall; and the lads, who looked like trainee clerics, began nodding. "They were at the theatre."

"Theatre?" asked the policeman.

"Sí," said Helen.

"Sí, Sí," said the lads.

We showed him our passports. The police got into the van and drove away.

"Gracias Señora, gracias," said the students.

They were shaking. One lad drew the third of a Carroll into his lungs. We walked a little way along together, then we stopped, and reluctantly they went on, but kept looking back at us, waving.

A few weeks later on Stephen's Day our boat broke down on a tributary of the Amazon miles away from everyone. The boatman handed me the rope. I pulled hard, the engine took, and then gave again; we tied up, and set off afraid into the isolated jungle in search of someone the boatman knew. He began shouting a name into the trees. "Marcos!" "Marcos!" As darkness fell, a voice answered. That night we slept in a hammock in a small wooden hut in the forest. In through the canes next morning came a faraway scent that we knew of old.

About the Editors

Neil Murphy teaches contemporary literature at NTU, Singapore. He is the author of *Irish Fiction and Postmodern Doubt* (2004) and editor of *Aidan Higgins: The Fragility of Form* (2010) and of the revised edition of Higgins's *Balcony of Europe* (2010). He co-edited (with Keith Hopper) a special Flann O'Brien centenary issue of the *Review of Contemporary Fiction* (2011) and *The Short Fiction of Flann O'Brien* (2013). He has published numerous articles and book chapters on contemporary fiction, Irish writing, and theories of reading, and is currently completing a book on John Banville.

Keith Hopper teaches Literature and Film Studies at Oxford University's Department for Continuing Education, and is a Research Fellow in the Centre for Irish Studies at St Mary's University, Twickenham. He is the author of *Flann O'Brien: A Portrait of the Artist as a Young Post-modernist* (revised edition 2009), general editor of the twelve-volume *Ireland into Film* series (2001–7), and co-editor (with Neil Murphy and Ondřej Pilný) of a special "Neglected Irish Fiction" issue of *Litteraria Pragensia* (2013). He is a regular contributor to the *Times Literary Supplement* and is currently completing a book on the writer and filmmaker Neil Jordan.

About the Author

Dermot Healy (1947-2014) was born in Finea, Co. Westmeath, but grew up in Cavan near the border with Northern Ireland. He edited the regional magazine *The Drumlin* (1978-80), and co-founded the Hacklers Theatre Group in Cavan in 1980. Following stints in London and Belfast, Healy settled in Ballyconnell, Co. Sligo, where he founded and edited *Force 10: A Journal of the Northwest*. Healy was an accomplished poet, novelist, playwright, screenwriter, and all-round literary enabler (he taught creative writing classes for prisoners as well as for local community groups). His debut collection, *Banished Misfortune and Other Stories*, first appeared in 1982, and this was followed by four novels – *Fighting with Shadows* (1984), *A Goat's Song* (1994), *Sudden Times* (1999), and *Long Time, No See* (2011) – and a memoir, *The Bend for Home* (1996). Healy wrote the screenplay for Cathal Black's *Our Boys* (1981), and played the lead role in Nichola Bruce's 1999 film, *I Could Read the Sky*. He also wrote five collections of poetry and thirteen stage plays (his *Collected Plays* will be published by Dalkey Archive Press in 2016). Elected to Aosdána in 1986, he was the recipient of two Hennessy Literary Awards, the Tom-Gallon Award, the Encore Award, and the AWB Vincent American Ireland Fund Literary Award. Dermot Healy died at his home in Sligo in June 2014.

Dermot Healy's **The Collected Short Stories** (2015) is part of a multi-volume sequence published by Dalkey Archive Press and edited by Neil Murphy & Keith Hopper. The series also includes an edited reprint of Healy's debut novel *Fighting with Shadows* (2015), Healy's *The Collected Plays* (2016), and a volume of essays about his work entitled *Dermot Healy: Writing the Sky – Critical Essays and Observations* (2016).